Isle of No'Man

Isle of No'Man

Martin J Dixon

Published by Vulpine Press in the United Kingdom in 2024

Cover illustration by Ruby Ball

ISBN: 978-1-83919-573-0

www.vulpine-press.com

To Rose, my captive audience

1

Water Water All Around and No One is Going Down on Me

I didn't even know I could be seasick. This should give you an understanding of how unfamiliar I was with boats. The sea spray spat on my face as I took heaving gulps of air and stared out at the horizon.

Ahead of us was land, gradually looming closer. Light shone through the clouds, making the island look heavenly, I hoped. Looking at the horizon helped with the nausea, but it was boring. My stomach settled. I turned to lean against the railings and scanned my fellow passengers. There was a family with young twins. The dad wore long socks with trainers, khaki shorts, a black plastic-y bumbag, and sunglasses on a chain around his neck. They were a young couple, and I wondered why this man had decided to confidently embrace the look of 'unfashionable dad' at such a young age. Perhaps I was being bitter, but, as a dad, I think I'd dress better. Although maybe I'd wear a bum bag if I had a family of my own? There was another couple who made me feel inadequate. They'd not parted lips since we left the mainland.

The only other passenger on the boat was a ridiculously handsome man who reminded me of a famous actor; I think it was his gold-rimmed Ray-Bans. I stared at him as he came aboard but had to look away for fear of being a creep. I wish we'd kissed the whole way here, but he was busy looking at his phone. And, of course, the crew, which were all men. I wished I could've kissed them all, but they were too wrapped up in being boaty. Water water, all around, and no one is going to go down on me. That's the famous quote, no?

I forced myself to turn back to the front of the boat.

No George! You've literally come to the Isle of No'Man. Emphasis on the No Men!

The island is pronounced Norman and if you didn't know I wouldn't blame you. I didn't realise until two weeks before arriving. The boat docked, and I gathered my belongings, joining the queue of people getting off the boat. I felt a tap on my shoulder and turned. It was the handsome actor man, and I was so taken aback, I'd lost the ability to hear.

No, hold on, I had headphones in.

"Sorry," I said, removing the headphones.

"I think you left this," he said with a smile, handing me a nude photograph of myself in a black frame. It had the words 'love of my life' written in glitter, and I guessed it had fallen out of my bag when I rummaged for my headphones. The photo was a gift from my friend Nat, but it might've seemed vain out of context. I wondered whether I should be embarrassed that such a typically sexy man was holding a black and white photo of my fat body rolls proudly on display as I looked coquettishly into the camera. His smile was a total betrayal. That was Jerry Hilk. He had the best sex scene I've ever seen on screen. I've touched myself thinking of this man.

"Thanks, that's really kind of you," I said, grinning.

Jerry was close enough for me to smell him, like sex and money, aftershave-y. I went to explain why I had a naked photo of myself, but Jerry just smiled and waved and then wandered off the boat. I wanted to follow, but I had much more luggage than Jerry, including my emotional baggage. Overall, I felt too weighed down to run after him. I thought it was the beginning of something wonderful, but I was wrong. And thank God! Isle of No MAN after all.

Ahead of me, the bohemian mother of the twins took the hand of a willing seaman as he helped her onto the pier. I walked the plank, looking ahead at Jerry who was getting into a car at the end of the dock. I held out my hand for the seaman, who had turned his back. I almost tumbled into the water trying to step over the lip of the boat. It was sexist that he assumed I wouldn't need help, but probably, as a man, I ought not to have been the one complaining. Perhaps I should've been grateful that the seaman thought I was a strapping young stud.

"Do you need help with those?" he asked, pointing at my group of bags.

There were three. One contained clothing and toiletries, the other was homely belongings like books, and the last was a crate filled with hard-to-find ingredients and cookware.

"I might need a hand; I don't know how far the café is?"

The seaman shook his head at me.

Arrogant.

I bloody hated him. He looked in the distance and adjusted his woollen hat.

"It's up the top of that hill. Are you taking over the café for the season?"

3

His voice was deep, as though his vocal cords hung deep down in his body, all the way to his groin, and you could tell by the way he said 'season' that he was outdoorsy.

"That's the plan." I was annoyed at myself that, no matter how quick I could be with a microphone in my hand, I couldn't muster a ruder reply in real life.

He picked up the crate. I found it gratifying watching him struggle under its weight for a split second. I followed him onto dry land passing the other tourists. I despise walking fast, so this man's speed challenged me.

"Thanks for your help…" I tailed off, expecting him to tell me his name.

"No problem."

It seemed as though he'd never had a conversation before. I caved in.

"What's your name?"

"Sam," he replied without asking my name. I thought I was on the Isle of No'Man, but now I was tempted to ask Sam if I was on the Isle of No'Manners.

He led us up a slanted cobbled path with shops and houses to my left. Over the road was the sea view and even sight of the mainland. It seemed much further away from this side of the ocean.

"Do you live on the island Sam?" I'd held my breath to ask the question, concealing how out of puff I was.

"Yeah."

Just the one-word answer. I gave up on trying to talk with him. Not everyone wanted to be my friend. I could cope with that. The road moved inland. There were buildings on both sides of the street as we walked further from the dock. The houses were mismatched with slate roofs and colourful doorways. I allowed myself a moment

4

to look back at the wooden jetty and the adjacent beach. It was picturesque, if not a little too windy to be relaxing. Tourists on the beach fought with the towels they were trying to put down. I half expected to see a house and a girl in pigtails blowing past.

The gentle incline picked up its gradient and I grew embarrassingly out of breath. You have to remember I was carrying two large bags. Sam was ahead, so I got a wiggle on to catch up. Droplets of sweat formed on the back of his maroon T-shirt. He was struggling just like me. I stared. His back seemed incredibly strong. Perhaps the T-shirt was too tight.

We arrived outside the café, Fifty Shades of Coffee (& Cake). I recognised it from the pictures I'd been sent, even without a thumb obscuring half the image. Sam dropped my precious crate on the floor and knocked on the door next to the café. I stared at his face trying to decide if I fancied him or not. Was he attractive, or did he just have a good beard? His bottom lip was big, which was a plus. His forehead was furrowed, but he didn't look old. Just rugged. Sam turned and I realised he must've felt my intense gazing.

"I thought you had some blood on your ear, but I think it was a trick of the light," I said.

Smooth.

Sam wiped his ear of phantom blood. The door clicked, clunked and swept open revealing a woman with a short, sensible haircut, wearing a denim overshirt and a practical watch. The kind of no-nonsense woman you might be frightened of disappointing.

"You must be George?"

She extended her hand, and I took it.

"I'm Eileen. Come on in. Do you want a cup of tea?"

5

Eileen moved back, and we stepped through the threshold and straight upstairs to the flat above the café. Eileen entered the kitchen, but I followed Sam, who took my box to the bedroom.

I always felt like a horny teenager following a man into a bedroom.

"Are you staying for tea?" Eileen called Sam from the kitchen.

"No thanks," he called back; his voice was deeper with the higher volume, and his Adam's apple bobbed. I think I fancied him – mainly because he was a man in my new bedroom.

"Thanks for your help with these. Stop by the café when I'm up and running for a freebie."

"Alright." Sam put out his hand, and we shook.

After Sam left, I found Eileen in the kitchenette, briskly wiping down the counter. The flat was sparsely furnished and mostly cream, but the kitchen was clean, and the grey sofa looked comfortable. There was a vintage-y looking bureau tucked into an alcove and a little table with two chairs. Eileen gestured, and we sat. I could smell the spray cleaner, masking the slight dampness in the air. Not that I was complaining, it was clean.

"So, what do you make of the flat?" Eileen crossed her arms over her front, with one hand free to sip her mug of tea. Her eyes were shiny like she was waiting on a compliment.

"It's lovely, thank you." I felt shy sitting across from my landlady and employer.

"I'll show you around downstairs in a moment. I won't hang around all day, as I'm sure you'll want to unpack."

I nodded and gratefully sipped the weak tea. We chatted about my journey and the weather. I tried to drink as quickly as possible so I could look downstairs. Despite the wind and lack of sun, it was a warm spring day, and after walking to the café, I was too hot to drink a cup of boiling liquid. I basically shotted the whole mug and made an excuse to go back to the bedroom and open the window for a view of the grey sea. I inhaled deeply, smelling the fishy salt air. I'm honestly not sure if I agree that sea air is all that pleasant.

Eileen led the way down a second set of stairs to the café. She moved fast, and I bet she'd call me a dawdler if we ever hiked together.

Please, God, don't ever make me hike with Eileen.

"You won't even have to take your dressing gown off to go to work," she laughed, "but you should."

Eileen's face lost its mirth and her eyes focussed; she was serious. I was used to being in trouble for making silly jokes, but this wasn't even my joke.

"I promise to always get dressed for work," I said with more solemnity than I felt was necessary.

I carried the crate of ingredients down with me. The stairs ended with a door that opened to the kitchen space with red tiles on the floor and halfway up the walls. There was a metal bench in the centre of the room, a deep sink on the far wall and a window with bars across it. Next to the sink was the backdoor. On the opposing wall was a set of swinging doors separating us from front of house, the stage for us theatrical types.

"So, this is the kitchen." Eileen began the tour by announcing the room's function. She then took her time pointing out the fridge, freezer, temperature gauge, log sheet and several other boring things. I felt they were boring, but Eileen seemed to perk up as she launched into a 20-minute talk about the fire extinguishers. I certainly want to be safe in a fire, but we all have our limits. There was a mixer with different attachments for bread or cake making. Her hands moved so fast that it was a struggle to see exactly where she was pointing.

"I've ordered stock for a week. I might have a cake you want to make, but we're not trying to reinvent the wheel. Milk and cheese come from the dairy on the other side of the island, and they'll deliver every day."

We moved through to the café. There were eight tables, three on the left, three on the right and two in the middle. There was a counter with a coffee machine plumbed into the wall.

"You know how to work a steamer," Eileen told me; she didn't ask.

What I didn't know I'd have to google. There was a glass case up front and a till around the side. There was also a fridge stocked with cold drinks. To my relief, everything was clean and worked. Eileen excused herself and went back up to the flat. I took a seat on one of the chairs. If all went to plan, I wouldn't often get to sit in my café. The café. My café. I felt twitchy. All my doubts repeated through my mind, but I was here; I was doing it. Eileen returned.

"Here's your keys, and can I get you to make your mark?" She placed a contract in front of me. I signed and passed it back. Then I wondered if I'd signed too quickly without reading and if Eileen would think I was an idiot. Whatever she thought, she took my hand and shook it firmly. Was she asserting her dominance? Surely there was little debate that the dominance was hers.

"The café opens from 9 am until 5.30 pm, Monday to Saturday. Sunday's we're closed, as you can see. You can travel back to the mainland or explore the island. You've never been to No'Man before?"

"Never before, until I got off that boat."

"Very daring. I'm certain you'll love it here. I'll get out of your hair." Eileen swept her contract away and went to the front door of the café to let herself out.

After I'd waved her off, I started having a proper poke around. The café part made sense. The fridge had milk, and there was a bag of coffee beans next to the grinder. The only thing empty was the glass cabinet I was supposed to fill with cakes and sandwiches.

I may have fudged my baking prowess when I applied for the job, pun intended. In fact, I absolutely did and had to. Eileen was impressed by my A* Food Technology GCSE, but I'd gotten a C. Also, I'm not afraid to admit GCSEs were a long time ago now. I continued my exploration of the kitchen. There were bread and sandwich fillings aplenty. They were a bit gross or sad looking. Supermarket savers bread and the sandwich fillings came in big mayonnaise-y jars. I'd have to make do with these for tomorrow, but eventually, I wanted to offer something more impressive.

Unpacking my essentials box, I decided to make some brownies. They were my most trusted recipe, so a good way to measure how the oven liked to cook. I weighed out the ingredients. It felt quiet, like I was in someone else's space. I wanted to ask permission before I opened any cupboards, as though some phantom mean parent would shout at me if I broke the rules. I ran up to my new lodgings and found my speakers. Back in the kitchen, I plugged in my phone and made the brownies, working my way through Beyoncé's discography.

Twelve brownies, one Victoria sponge, two chocolate cakes and a chocolate lime and mint loaf later, I heaved myself onto the counter, feet pulsing in my trainers. I had one more cake left in me, a lemon drizzle. But I needed a break before I baked anymore. I left

9

two loaves of bread to prove and decided to get acquainted with my new flat.

The window was still open from earlier, and it had been raining. The end of the bed had gotten a bit damp. It was still drizzling, so I could only open the window a crack, not wanting to get the bed rained on again. The temperature had plummeted, so I had to work out the heating, to help dry out my duvet. I unpacked the clothes in a few moments, hanging up two shirts and jacket, the rest fitted in the dresser. I took my toiletry bag to the bathroom. My wee could no longer wait, so I looked at my new commode. How many people had been on this toilet, I wondered. I wiped the seat with some loo roll and sat down in a bid to make it feel more like home. There was a shower over the bath, and the curtain looked new, although why Eileen chose a shower curtain with a kitten cuddling a duckling, I'll never know.

I took my bag packed with books, DVDs and pictures into the living room. I filled some of the shelves as best I could. I put up a poster of Beyoncé on a blank wall. It looked a little sad; the fold across her forehead made it seem like she felt sorry for me. I felt a little old for a poster, but I was afraid that a blank wall would feel miserable. I put some photos on the shelves. There was a picture of my best friend Nat and me at the Beyoncé concert where I got the poster. I put up a photo of my mum and me, even though we weren't speaking. It almost felt homely. I took a blanket from the bottom of the bag for the living room, then hid the luggage in the wardrobe. All my unpacking of everything important to me was done in 15 minutes, with a long wee break in the middle. I tried to convince myself this wasn't depressing. It was spartan.

I returned downstairs, played some more music, and knocked back my bread dough. I left them to prove again and got on with my last cake. Zesting a lime and melting chocolate were the only reasons I liked baking. It might've been the overpowering smells or something else, but they made me feel witchy. I'm not saying I believed I had powers; just that lime or chocolate made me feel something otherworldly. Zesting five limes put an ache in my hand and took the ache from my heart. God, I was bored by how miserable I was being. I finished the cake in record time, closing the oven with the bread and cake cooking together.

Back upstairs, I foraged for food. Eileen had kindly bought some bits for me as she knew I'd be arriving on Sunday when the island shop closed. I got ready for bed. The second I sat down, the oven timer went off, and my last cake was baked. I rushed back upstairs to relish a cheesy pizza and *Sex and the City*. I sometimes wondered if I were placed on an unknown planet in space, I'd probably fare quite well with access to a TV show I love and some decent chocolate. Perhaps Maltesers.

It wasn't until much later, post pizza, lying in bed, that my mind shifted into overdrive. I barely knew what time to set my alarm. I chose 6.15 am as I needed time to get sorted, but I didn't want to be so early that I'd struggle to hold up my head later in the day. I turned over and over again. At one point, I put on my lamp and read my book. Sometime around 1.30 am I decided that touching myself might calm my nerves. A fairly average time later, I was a little calmer. I still couldn't sleep; my efforts to avoid the fear were in vain. I lay in the dark, allowing the scenarios of failure to form a queue and march through my mind.

I'm not sure when I fell asleep, but when my alarm beeped, I was livid. I jumped to action to turn off my alarm before padding to the toilet. I performed my ablutions and knocked my toothbrush into the sink, clumsy from tiredness. I dressed, rushed downstairs, put on my music, and set another alarm for 8.30 am to give me the heads up for opening time. It was time to prepare. I stuffed the grinder with coffee beans, turned on the coffee machine, filled the cake display, and stuck some frozen croissants in the oven. Looking around, my work was almost done. I had forty minutes to kill. Time for a nap under the kitchen counter? There was a knock at the back door. I jogged through to answer it, and a man was standing there with a milk crate.

"Hi-hi, you're the new manager then?" he asked me.

I nodded, not realising how tired I was until I was expected to form words.

"Nice to meet you," I managed. "I'm George."

"You can call me Mr Sharp," he replied, ensuring I felt inferior, or at least that's how I felt. He passed me the crate and waited. There was a beat, and his eyebrows bobbed up in expectation. Was I supposed to pay him? I'd not managed the money side of things yet.

"Do you have any empties for me?"

I gave him an 'ah' and stood in place. I scanned the kitchen. I didn't have the foggiest. Mr Sharp checked around, kicking his leg toward a seagull pecking a few metres away. The bird didn't flinch, but Mr Sharp grunted.

"Usually under the sink," he said, angling his balding head to the sink. Lo and behold, there was a crate filled with empty milk bottles.

"Best of luck," he said with a thin grin. I don't think he wished me luck at all. I suspected he lusted after my downfall, and I'd either have to succeed or keep my downfall private.

After putting the milk away, I realised I didn't know how to work the till. I'd figured out how to make everything I might need: coffee, tea, hot chocolate, mocha, flat white, cakes, and sandwiches, but I didn't know how to make any money. My fledgling business was about to become a charity.

A knock at the café door. I wasn't ready for a customer. I thought about crouching behind the counter and waiting for them to leave, but I'd already been seen. Through the glass, I spied a woman in her late forties wearing a denim jacket. She had wavy dark hair and was smiling. I opened the door.

"Hi, I'm sorry we're not open just yet."

"I know, I'm Priya; I work here," she beamed. I scanned my mind and remembered vaguely Eileen mentioning Priya.

"Yes, come in." I stepped aside for her to pass. I felt like a cross between a butler opening the door for a guest or a head teacher about to scold a pupil. I didn't know where to look, so I focused on the door frame, squinting as if I'd found something fascinating.

"How's it going?" she asked, looking around the café, potentially for a sign that it was about to implode. I drew my attention back to her. Now she'd entered the room, I needed to be normal again.

"Not so bad. I think it's all set up. Sorry if it's a bit different; I forgot you'd be coming, actually. Otherwise, I would've waited to check."

"It all looks fine. We'll struggle through," she said, before throwing back her head and singing Gloria Gaynor's 'We Will Survive.'

Not the whole song, just those three words. I gave her a double thumbs up and moved on.

"My only concern is that I don't know how to work the till."

Priya walked over to the machine, and it came to life. I felt betrayed by the till, which was clearly homophobic or something. Why else wouldn't it work for me?

"It's working fine."

"I haven't put any money in it or anything?"

13

"Ah," Priya chuckled, "let me show you what I know."

She taught me how to open the till without making a sale and showed me where the safe was. It all made sense, and we were in business!

"You've saved my life. Do you want a coffee or anything?"

She accepted a cappuccino.

"Only this one or I'll be climbing the walls the rest of the day."

I was glad to offer her a drink, but also, I'd forgotten to test my skills on the coffee machine before she arrived. I smiled and got on with it, finding that making a cappuccino is like riding a bike. Hard to forget, but also something I hadn't missed doing.

Come opening time, and I was a little hurt when we weren't immediately swamped with customers. It never occurred to me, until just that moment, that I might fail as a barista just through a total boycott of the café. I was almost surprised when a customer did turn up.

Slowly, people trickled in; someone else would pop in as soon as one person was served. Priya was on the till, introducing the people who lived on the island she knew. My neck felt stiff from turning to say hello whilst also frothing milk. At lunchtime, we got a queue. Priya took over serving drinks and customers and I became sandwich maker extraordinaire. I've never buttered so much bread.

Nobody has.

We ran through my loaves quickly, and I felt like a cheat defrosting more baguettes to keep my customers happy. The people from the island were friendly and asked where I was from and how I was finding it, which was sweet but slowed me down. The holidaymakers were less curious. I had one family stop me, mid-buttering, to ask where they could buy more sun cream. At around 3.00 pm, the number of customers dwindled.

14

I felt oddly proud to be mistaken for a local.

"Right, all looking good here. I'll head off." Priya removed her apron.

"Thank you so much for today. Are you back tomorrow?"

"Working eight to four, Monday to Friday," she sang her response. "I think today was alright." She smiled like she was lying. Was it out of pity, or had she been enjoying my downfall?

"Are you going to be OK cashing up?"

"I think so."

"Glad to hear it, as I'm going out," she sang to Diana Ross's tune, 'I'm coming out,' before adding, "I have book club tonight."

Priya rubbed my arm with her hand, and I had to try not to cry. You know when someone you don't know shows you some unexpected kindness, and your heart might burst? It was much like that, although her fingertips tickled, and I immediately itched my arm, which I think looked like I didn't like being touched or was uncomfortable with displays of affection.

There were no customers left, so I whipped around to tidy the tables. It was five to closing, and I was almost done. The door swung open, and I beamed my brightest grin, expecting a customer. Instead, I found myself face-to-face with a sex god.

It was Jerry Hilk again.

"Hey," his mouth parted to reveal impossibly white teeth. He was wearing jeans, a long-sleeved T-shirt, and a woolly hat. The sleeves were pulled up so I could see a tattoo of his first wife's name – Isabella. I'm ashamed to admit this idiotic tattoo, in medieval alphabet font, wasn't the turn-off it should have been. Although, I questioned why such a rich person would continue having such a rank tattoo, despite their horrendously public divorce. I love gossip. So sue me.

15

"What can I get you?" I asked, as casually as I could muster, nervous I'd appear overly keen. This is why I left my job in London; celebrities are just people, why couldn't I be myself?

"Flat white, if you've got it?"

"Sure thing, I can bring it over," I said.

"Cool."

He didn't say thank you, just "cool." If I'm honest, I didn't think that was very cool. I set about making the drink. Jerry and I had met before: twice if you included the boat. He'd never remember it, but when I started my career in TV, I worked as a runner and got him a coffee then too. He did at least say thank you that time. Perhaps he left his manners on the mainland?

"Here you are." I placed the cup in front of him.

Jerry jigged his leg, and I must've been staring as he smiled again. I had this overwhelming feeling that I should touch his face. My hand twitched, and I backed away and checked the clock – closing time.

I flipped the sign on the door, half-made a hot chocolate and pretended to tidy up. I'd planned to eat two slices of cake to celebrate my first day, but I didn't want Jerry to see me eating.

"I can leave if you're closing?" Jerry called over.

"No worries, sit tight until I have to move you."

"Thanks...pal."

I opened my mouth to say something, but I wasn't sure what that would be. I turned and walked into the kitchen. I cleaned the whole thing. It wasn't until I went out to start sweeping I realised that Jerry had gone. It was a shame he didn't say goodbye. It seemed unwelcome, that a piece of my old life would float into my new one. I considered whether it was real. Maybe I was on a reality TV show without knowing? Or, more likely, my old job sent him to try and lure me back? Although, I quickly discounted that theory because I was really shit at working in TV. And I don't think they'd waste money on Jerry. I'd probably have gone back to my job for an upmarket doughnut. I distracted myself with the rest of the cleaning and cashed up the way Priya showed me.

After a quick freshen up, I made my way out into the street. I'd changed into a romper with an adorable, knitted cardigan; I looked like an evacuee from WWII. The air was cooler than I'd expected. The wind whipped the hair on my legs, and I relished freeing my calves of material. The sun was almost out of sight over the water, which I could see between buildings as I walked along my new street. I live here, I repeated to myself. The cobbles were smooth underfoot, and I felt grateful I'd managed not to slip yesterday whilst carrying my bags. I weaved around the few streets, spotting hotels, a yoga studio, an ice cream shop and finally, a restaurant. There were two on this part of the island; I remembered Eileen telling me. One was expensive, and the other was affordable. I arrived at the expensive one. I could tell before going inside because the pasta arrabbiata was £16. From the awning's cleanliness and the patio area's heaters, it looked really posh, so I guess it would be a place I would go when I wanted to celebrate. Although, that wasn't tonight. Despite a successful first day at the café, moving hadn't been cheap, and I'd taken a considerable salary cut. I was tempted by the expensive restaurant, not just because of the fanciness. My stomach growled, and I realised eating couldn't wait much longer.

Another two minutes along the road, I found the cheaper restaurant next to a little supermarket. After longingly looking at the menu, I forced myself into the shop. It was closing soon, so I couldn't peruse the shelves in a way I would've liked to. I bought some basic ingredients and, yes, quite a lot of chocolate.

17

"Hi-hi, how's it going?" the cashier asked me.

"Not too bad, thanks, you?" I offered back, desperate for a friend. She was around my age, wore her hair in a neat ponytail, and had French-manicured nails. She looked out of place behind a till and would've looked more natural on Instagram. The only break in her facade was the speed at which she scanned food items, skidding them through the till area like she was annoyed to be there.

"Pasta for dinner? The pasta next door is pretty reasonable. If you don't fancy cooking on holiday."

"I'm not on holiday. I'm the new manager of Fifty Shades of Coffee, by the beach."

"No way," the woman's jaw dropped open. She looked me up and down. Her demeanour changed instantaneously. From warm to frosty, quicker than one of those instant ice cream chopping boards. I didn't know what to say, so I smiled in reply. I dipped my head to get my card up on my phone. When I looked back, ready to say that it had been my first day, she interrupted.

"That's twelve forty-five. Thanks."

I swiped, and she immediately started scanning someone else's item. I panicked, trying to bag my things quickly as possible. I broke some bars of chocolate, for sure. I thought I'd almost made a friend.

The walk home was short but enough time for my mood to change. The same questions I'd ignored all day started to cloud over me.

Had I made a mistake coming here?

I felt moody as I finished my chores, ate, and went to bed. It was raining, but I found that it suited me. I'll admit to singing Celine Dion's acapella verse of 'All by Myself'. Annoyingly, I only knew the first verse and chorus, which I repeated for about fifteen minutes. My voice was so beautiful that a single tear rolled down my cheek.

My mind wandered, and it didn't need to look far for misery. Rob's face floated into my head yet again. I was thrilled to realise this was the first time I'd thought of him since I'd gotten on the island. In the dark, I smiled to myself. The island was doing its job. I wasn't thinking about him, except for that one time, I hoped. Although, as he was on my mind, I fell back into my familiar fantasies. The ones where I'd see Rob again and give him a piece of my mind. I felt like I'd been lying there fantasising for hours and worried I'd never sleep again. Except I must've fallen asleep because I woke up at 3.00 am, convinced the kitchen had flooded. I ran downstairs and found the floor bone dry.

I couldn't shut my mind off when I got back to bed. Rob loomed in my thoughts, and the night we broke up played on a constant loop in my head. I'd come home from seeing my mum, where we'd argued. I'd been scrolling on his iPad, refusing to turn on the lamp as a punishment to myself. I'd started looking at new jobs and stumbled onto an article about working on No'Man, and how remote the island was. It was only accessible by ferry. Imagine an ocean between me and my problems. It sounded blissful when I sat on Rob's sofa in Rob's flat. I was living there, but it always felt like Rob's flat. I heard him come in the door behind me.

"I think we need to talk," he said to the back of my head.

"What?" I asked, unsuspecting.

"Oh, what's up?" He realised I'd been crying. Maybe he was going to change his mind, but I'd caught up with the situation.

"What do we need to talk about?"

He hesitated.

"Quickly, I've got a show to go to."

As an aspiring comedian, even being deeply sad meant I couldn't afford to miss a spot. Besides, I considered at the time there was a chance I'd be much funnier than usual; perhaps this devastating news could work in my favour.

"Look, maybe this isn't the right time, but things aren't working."

I stared down at the coffee table. I'd be lying if I thought I was entirely surprised. For weeks, months even, Rob had been pulling away. He'd get out of spending time together and wasn't talking. In turn, I was becoming clingy and irritable. I'd flip out when he left plates in the sink, which he did every night. Then he'd disappear for hours, and I'd be in a silent panic awaiting his reply. Rob started drinking slimming shakes in the morning, which I took as a slap in my fat face. After many failed attempts to explain why it bothered me, I secretly poured sugar into the powder. I wasn't proud of who I was becoming.

"Right," I said.

"What do you want to do?"

I stood and walked to the bedroom.

"I'll just get some stuff together; I'll pick up the rest another day."

My voice was flat, resigned. Rob came to stand in the doorway.

"I'm sorry."

I didn't reply.

"Don't you want to talk about it?"

"Not really. I've been killing myself these past few months trying to get you to talk. I'm enjoying the fact I don't want to talk, and I don't know why you've changed so much."

"I've met someone else."

I made a choking noise. Astounded and embarrassed not to have noticed.

"I knew it," I shouted, even though I had no idea. How could I be so stupid?

"It wasn't planned, and I haven't cheated in the strictest sense. But I think we could both be happier."

"That's so kind of you to think of my happiness."

The nastiness dripped from my voice.

I threw my belongings into a bag and ran to the bathroom to collect my toothbrush and moisturiser.

"Sit down, and let's talk about this," he pleaded.

"Don't you think you've wasted enough of my time?"

This stunned him into silence.

I grabbed my bag and left.

I had to get out of that flat and away from him. If I didn't, I was going to lose control of myself, and I didn't know what it would look like. Even in the moment, I remember thinking how odd it was that I was worried about saving face. The love of my life, potentially, was breaking up with me, and I wanted to look unbothered. The moment we'd break up, I'd always imagined I would beg him to change his mind. All I could do was try and save face. The utter humiliation of being dumped was a surprise to me. Even sitting in my bed alone, remembering the dumping, made me blush.

***

I was tired when my alarm went off, and I dragged myself downstairs. The milk delivery came.

"Morning," Sam called on the other side of the open-door frame.

21

"Oh…hey." I wasn't expecting the worthy seaman at my door. "Are you a seaman and a dairy farmer?"

"A seaman?"

"Is that not the right word?"

"Sailor is more common, I suppose. I don't think of myself so much as a sailor and more of someone who works on a boat sometimes."

"Are pirates the same as sailors? What's the difference?" I asked, the first thing to come into my head.

"Are you asking if I'm a pirate?" Sam replied, smirking.

This conversation had veered further off-course than I could control. I needed to get back to some sort of point.

"Not a pirate, but why are you delivering?"

"The sea is too rough this morning, so I'm helping with the milk delivery."

"You're helpful."

"I am."

Sam's teeth shone as he smiled. Was I in a dream?

"I appreciate it. You're still owed a freebie from here. I don't have any croissants baked yet, but come back, and I'll do you a sandwich for lunch?"

"OK then."

He waved as he lumbered off toward the van.

Did I fancy Sam? I kept flip-flopping about it. I felt a bit rumbly in my groin. I put it down to tiredness and went about my work.

Priya arrived right on time. We were busy, so I waited an appropriate amount of time to tell her about Jerry.

"Priya, do any celebrities live on the island?"

I was nonchalant; I think I'd got away with it.

"The mayor is a minor celebrity. She presented a show about the low soil quality on the north of the island. She was a big hit on the science academia circuit, but that would've been a while before you were born."

Priya's answer, although factually correct, was wrong. I wanted her to start up a gossipy conversation about why I asked. Then we had a rush of customers. Lots of people arrived with their bags, seemingly annoyed.

"It's so busy."

"Happens whenever the sea is too choppy for the boat. They'll be running the ferry again soon enough, and we'll get a new lot of holidaymakers."

But the café didn't get quiet again as more and more families came and went with hot drinks. Some sat inside and came for regular refills. My lemon drizzle cake was selling fast. Just before lunch, Sam made an appearance. I called over the top of the cake container.

"You here for your free sandwich?"

His eyebrows bobbed up in acknowledgement.

"I'd take a cheese and ham to go if I could," he said, and announced to the room: "The boat is getting ready to leave. If you'd like to go down as soon as you can."

Everyone made a mass exodus whilst I buttered some white bread and filled it. I cut it into two triangles, wrapped it in paper before sealing it with a sticker and passed it over to Sam.

"Whatta man, whatta man, whatta mighty mighty-might nice boy," Priya sang, at me, I felt pointedly, "Sam I mean." Almost like she approved of me fancying him?

The lunchtime rush took over, and we barely had a chance to talk. When it was her home time, there was a short queue of new

23

people with rucksacks and suitcases. At the end of the queue was Sam. Priya stayed on for an extra ten minutes. Sam seemed to be permanently at the end of the line. I guess he wanted to let the tourists go first. Finally, everyone was served, and Sam was the last one standing at the counter.

"I'm gonna head off if you don't mind," Priya said, looking pointedly at me, then to Sam, and then back to me. It would've been a subtle gesture if Sam had been on a different island, millions of miles away. I gave him my full attention.

"What can I get you?

"I'll take a slice of the cake too. And can I get a hot chocolate?"

I agreed and went to fulfil his order. Strangely, I've found not many adult men would order a hot chocolate. Toxic masculinity, I suppose. I warmed to Sam entirely. It was as though we were friends now. But I don't know if Sam got the memo. I handed him his hot chocolate, and he looked blankly at me. He was expecting something.

"Enjoy."

"How much do I owe you?"

I laughed.

"I completely forgot."

I totalled up on the till. Sam took out a battered wallet, unzipped it and tipped a bunch of coins on the counter. He was in no rush to count them out. Did people our age still use cash?

"I hope your cakes are as good as your sandwiches," he said as he took his things and winked. He rushed out the door so fast, I might've made it up. I stared after him, unsure what had transpired between us. I saw the woman from the supermarket walk past. I almost waved at her; you know how exciting it is to recognise someone in an unfamiliar place? I served another customer, and she walked back the other way. This time I did wave as she was staring into the café. I started to wrap up the sandwich things and wind down for the day. She walked past again. I wondered if I was missing some island event. I went out in the street to see for myself.

The woman stood about two doors down, her shoulders rising and falling with each breath. Her fists were clenched, and before I could call out, she whipped around, waving two middle fingers at the café. She saw me and immediately dropped her hands to her side, smoothing her skirt.

"What are you doing?" she asked.

"Just checking to see why you kept walking past."

I couldn't come up with an excuse on the spot.

"I've not walked past a lot. I just had some errands to run. I was going to get a cake, maybe."

"Brilliant, come and get a slice. It's free."

"I'm not sure I've got time."

She looked at her wrist without a watch on it.

"I insist."

I stepped back and made a space for her to cross in front of me. With a little foot-dragging, she walked into the café.

"What slice would you like? I've got one left of the lemon drizzle cake?"

"The famous lemon drizzle cake…sure."

"Famous?"

Was I blushing? Maybe. Well, no, but I was proud. I put the last slice on a plate. The woman picked it up and sat in a seat I couldn't see. I pottered for a few seconds, working up the courage, and went to talk to her.

"Is it any good?"

"It's bloody delicious," she said. I almost didn't hear her.

25

"Huh?" I asked, fishing for a compliment.

"I said it's fine."

She frowned, seemingly annoyed. Was I in trouble? It seemed she might strike me, and I wasn't sure I didn't deserve it for some reason.

"I'm sorry. What's your name, by the way?"

"Dianne," she said, her voice rising toward the end as though the name might prompt something. Nothing came to my mind, so I continued to smile at her. Maybe I'd misread the situation, but Dianne did not want to be my friend.

"Enjoy the rest of the cake."

I straightened a chair and went back to serving. A family with three young children came in. I served them some hot chocolates and tea for the father (I told you). They left, and Dianne came to the counter. She placed her plate on the side.

"Thanks," she said, through gritted teeth and avoiding eye contact.

"You're welcome."

I picked up the plate and put it with the remainder of the dirty dishes. I turned back to make more of a conversation, but she'd left. The door slammed, cementing her exit. I was alone in the café until Jerry came in again. Today he wore a denim shirt and jogging shorts. They were short. They might have been women's.

"Can I get a flat white and a slice of lemon drizzle cake, please, mate?"

Everyone wanted a piece, but only of my lemon drizzle cake – the story of my bloody life.

"I've run out of lemon drizzle cake. Do you want a mint and lime and chocolate cake?"

He grimaced.

"No, I'll just get a brownie."

Fucking dick.

Nothing wrong with my mint, lime, and chocolate loaf. I told his highness to take a seat, and I'd bring over his stuff when it was ready. I thought about spitting in his coffee, really briefly. Then I realised I was being a bit oversensitive. I took over the mug and plate. He looked up from his phone as I set them down.

"We've met before," I said. "I used to work for Wake Up UK and you were being interviewed."

"Cool," he said and looked out the window.

I felt a bit like a massive twat but continued with my tidying and left him in the café again to finish clearing up. Everything seemed to go a lot smoother than the day before.

Back in my flat, I finished off the pasta and watched TV. Objectively, it had been a good day at work. We'd taken more than usual, and I was getting the hang of everything. Still, I couldn't banish the feeling that not everything was brilliant. As they often did, my thoughts drifted back to Rob. I practised what I would say:

It will take me years to undo the damage you've caused me.
I regret how much time I wasted on you.
You're not a bad person, but you were a bad boyfriend.

I fantasised about punching his face. I'm not violent, but I'd love to cause him pain. I'd concocted elaborate storylines where I was unwell. He'd come to my bedside, and I'd scream at him to leave. He'd have to prove his love before I let him back in my life. But I knew I'd let him back.

After I showered, I sat on my bed in my towel and stared at the wall. When I was dry, I decided to lie on the floor. As a child, I remembered lying on the floor in every part of the home, and I felt

I knew it exceptionally well. The carpet was harsh under my body, so I adjusted the towel beneath me. My mind, insistent on ruining the evening, recalled my last night on stage. The night Rob and I broke up. Heat flushed my cheeks and chest as I remembered walking into the pub. My eyes were red and puffy. I don't know why I didn't cancel my spot. I was in no state to go on. I arrived late. The floors were sticky, and the median age of the patrons was 50s. Not 'reads *The Guardian* 50s'. These were curmudgeonly *Daily Mail* subscribers. The vibe of the pub was mardy at best. I went to the bar, ordered a cola and asked where the show was. It was in the basement.

Grabbing my glass, I walked downstairs to the back of the room and arrived next to the stage. There was a comedian mid-set who made some quip; nice of me to join them. I wanted to conjure up an instant comeback: "It takes a long time to look this good; you wouldn't get it." But I was too sad. Instead, I smiled and said nothing, finding a seat. Halfway through, I introduced myself to the MC and apologised for my lateness. They agreed to put me on in the second part. I kept trying to go over a set in my head, but my bottom lip trembled each time my mind tried to go still. The lights dimmed, and the second part started. When I was called on stage, it felt brighter than usual. I couldn't see anyone and held up my hand to shield my eyes.

"I feel like one of the mole people. I can't see anyone," I said into the mic.

A murmur of laughter.

"Although I look like someone at the end of the night at a club when they bring up the lights wandering around in just their pants looking for their trousers, crying."

There was some laughter, although it was more a suggestion of a laugh, like a loud polite smile.

"I've just been dumped."

I announced this like it was the beginning of a joke, except I started to cry.

"Sorry, I'm not being funny."

A dribble of snot flew from my nose and landed on the wire mesh. My crying was about to begin in earnest.

"I suppose the joke is I thought we would die together, in each other's arms. That's not a punchline, is it?"

No one laughed. It was like one of those super public breakdowns. If I were famous, or sexy, or a woman, this disaster of a show would be front-page news. Why was I here?

"Get off," someone shouted.

"Excuse you, where do you get off, you little butthead," I called back, faux annoyed. "I'd love to get off, but I'm also hoping I'll stumble on a joke in a minute. Because we've all been laughing at you your whole life doesn't mean comedy is easy."

No one said anything. I scratched my forehead, trying to cover my face.

"Right, I was just in the middle of bearing my soul for a laugh, so I was dumped, my ex-boyfriend cheated on me…"

"Shut the fuck up," yelled another heckler. I wished more than anything I could shut him the fuck up, but I had stage time to fill.

"Is that him? Look, these nice people are desperate to hear my side of things; either take me back or let me be sad."

No laughs. I couldn't do this.

"Right, thanks for having me, gang. I'll leave with this rhyming couplet. Some of you must be wiping back to front because you're acting like shitty cunts."

29

I dropped the mic and looked defiantly into the audience. It would've saved the moment had I not kicked the mic down the steps and tripped on the wire. I walked to my seat without a single applause. I picked up my bag and rushed out. Stopping on the stairs to catch my breath, I heard the MC trying to boost the room.

"Sorry about that, folks, it's stand-up comedy, not therapy," he howled and got a laugh, mainly as a tension breaker.

I ran up to the street and was sick. Resting my head on a lamp post, I wiped my mouth with the back of my hand. I remember walking to Nat's flat and showering. Then I curled into a ball on the end of her bed and wept until I fell asleep. She stroked my back.

"And now, you're here," I said aloud to no one. The carpet was getting uncomfortable, and under the bed was just horridly dusty. I stood up, put on some PJs, and mooned around my flat. I wanted to call someone and tell them about the stupid points in my day. I picked up my phone, unlocked it, and put it down again. There was no one to call.

2

Saving a Slice for Myself

On my first Saturday, a stream of customers kept me busy. I was desperate for help. I'd prepared the night before, baking double the amount of cake and stocking the whole café, but there was a queue out the door. The pace picked up, and I wondered where Trevor had got to. Priya worked Monday to Friday and reminded me that Trevor, Eileen's son, worked Saturdays. He turned up around 20 minutes late and got to work. He didn't introduce himself; he just came behind the counter and started making drinks. He smelled very teenage. A whiff of body odour and Lynx body spray, doing their best to cover the undeniable stench of beer seeping from his pores. A hungover adult-sized child. What a treat.

"Are you Trevor?" I asked, in case he was a stranger, part of an elaborate ruse to murder me and take over the café.

"Yeah, obviously."

He simultaneously rolled his eyes and shook his head in annoyance.

"Good to meet you."

I was annoyed that I was being wet. I wanted to give him a telling-off; 'It's one thing to be late, but you're also being a dickhead.' That didn't seem very managerial. I was his boss, but his mum was my boss. It was best to try and establish a friendly rapport.

"Are you happy to make the drinks for now? Or we can swap, and you serve at the till?"

"I don't serve the till," he grumbled.

"Not to worry," I said, but I did worry.

Bloody annoying.

The afternoon wore on, and eventually, the orders died down. Trevor said something about washing up, but when I looked through the window, he was sitting on the kitchen counter, eyes closed. The front door swung open, and Sam strolled to the till.

"Hey," I was casual.

"Can I get a tea? And some cake, please."

I turned my back to fulfil the order. I could feel Sam's eyes burrowing into me, so I made an effort to drop something and bend to collect it. I checked behind me to look bashful, but Sam's eyes were drawn to something out of the front window. I got back to making the tea, regretting the burlesque performance.

"Busy day?"

His voice carried over the sound of the steam, and I half turned to face him.

"Not too bad, thanks. How're the high seas?"

"Eerily quiet."

"Did you see any mermaids?" I joked, finding myself quite funny.

"A couple," he smiled, "but they weren't the sexy ones with seashell bras."

"Good to know."

I wrapped up a slice of Victoria sponge, put the lid on the tea and passed them over. At that moment, Trevor left the kitchen, and his face lit up.

"Y'alright mate?" he asked.

"How's it going? New boss?" Sam's eyebrows bobbed up. I wanted to laugh.

"Yeah…"

The rest of the afternoon trickled on until Trevor finished. I managed solo for the final hour until Jerry came in, marking my last customer. This was becoming our thing. I was Jerry Hilk's official cake and coffee dispenser, and I loved it.

"What can I get you today?"

Jerry leant on the counter. "What would you recommend?"

Tentatively, as I didn't want to look like a loser, I leaned forward on the counter and then turned to look at the board above the drinks machine as if I were trying to see from his point of view.

"Great question, I would say…are you a hot chocolate fan?"

"Sometimes, not typically."

"Our hot chocolate is particularly good, but I am biased."

"Sold. I'll take a hot chocolate and a lemon drizzle cake if you have one today?"

"I saved you a slice," I said as a joke but then realised he thought I was serious. "I've saved three actually. We take customer satisfaction super seriously. Take a seat, and I'll bring it over."

He saluted me, which made me laugh and sat in his usual seat, leg bouncing. I delivered his order and went to the front door to turn the sign. Although, I paused in my tracks as Jerry spoke up.

"I think I do remember you from Wake Up UK," he said, dipping his spoon into the hot chocolate, "you were the runner."

Jerry lifted the spoon and licked some cream from the end. His tongue looked extra pink. I wanted to touch it with my tongue. A long time had passed, and I hadn't said anything. Oops.

"I was but…I don't want you to take this personally, but you're a big fat liar. There is no way you'd remember me."

"No, I remember; you, erm, got me a drink."

"I mean, yes, I did, but that's probably all I did back then. In fairness, it's all I do now, too."

It dawned on me for the first time that being in the café was potentially a move backwards for me, so I laughed loudly. I was OK, right?

"Don't worry. I only remember you because I was new. I've met way more famous people now."

He laughed. I was relieved, unsure if I was being too cheeky.

"I'm quite famous."

He was grinning and put his head in his hands.

"I'm embarrassed. I said I was joking, but I don't think you'll think I'm joking."

This time I laughed.

"It's funny because you are famous. But I also met Judi Dench once, so I'm also a big deal."

"I was in a film with Dame Judi."

Jerry emphasised the Dame, and I felt that I'd been very rude.

"Oh shit, you were. I completely forgot. Don't tell Ms Judi, Dame Judi, I mentioned her. There's no way she'll remember me."

"I loved working with her, but we don't hang out that often; I think she's probably too famous for me."

"One hundred per cent she is. Bloody love, Judi the Dame."

We shared another smile, and I went back to tidying. And, since I'd forgotten to turn the sign, a family came in with two teenage girls. The daughters went to find a seat. I heard one of them gasp. The other said: "Oh my god, too cool for school."

I offered them some of the last few cakes for free whilst Jerry took a selfie with the youngest. I was surprised she'd seen so much of his work, but then I remembered he'd played the dad in a trilogy about teenage witches. I remember it well because it was when I first began to use the acronym DILF.

"What are you doing here?" she asked, lowering her phone.

Jerry let out a long umm, and his leg began bobbing again.

"It's a really big secret. Can you keep a secret?" Her eyes widened with seriousness. Jerry leant in and whispered, "I'm getting ready to be in a new film."

"Shut up! Another *Bad Witches* film?"

"Unfortunately not! My next film might be a bit boring for you. It's all about a boring adult doing boring things."

"That sounds amazing."

I took some things out to the kitchen and tidied up. As I returned to the café, the family got up to leave.

"Come on now, let's leave Mr Hilk to his hot chocolate," the mum said, corralling her family into leaving. She glanced at me, rolling her eyes as if to say, 'What are they like, kids.' Which, in turn, made me feel like a fellow mum. I didn't hate the feeling.

"Good to meet you," Jerry said, high-fiving one of the daughters. And this is stupid, and I shouldn't have entertained the thought, but seeing him be so sweet to that girl made me feel warm inside. Like I was looking at the future father of my babies. It was instantaneous. I saw us in a tall house in Zone 3 in London, two daughters and one son, plus his daughter from a previous marriage; maybe a dog if he could convince me, but I wasn't sure. He'd go on location in the summer, and we'd visit him as much as we could, settling back in London in autumn. I'd write cookbooks or something Chrissy Teigan-esque. But without the modelling back-ground.

Cracks were beginning to appear.

The door closed, breaking my reverie. I carried on tidying and Jerry seemed in no rush, so I presumed we'd continue as we'd been going, where he'd leave whenever he was ready. However, he came up to the counter.

"I don't suppose I could take that off your hands?" he asked, eyeing the remaining lemon drizzle slice. He was noticeably not holding his wallet.

I frowned. I'd been planning on having it myself.

"It's just I saw you offer them to the family, and I thought they all needed to go?"

"They do all need to go, but…"

"This feels a bit like I'm being discriminated against. I can pay for them."

I laughed.

"It's just that slice has already been allocated."

It was his turn to laugh.

"I'm sorry I asked."

Jerry walked back toward the door. I felt guilty. I'd made it weird.

"No, I'm sorry." I looked down, and my cheeks glowed red. Excuses ran through my mind; I could be saving them for some needy kids, a nice nun, or a little kitty. The truth won out.

"I was just saving this slice for myself. I'm embarrassed."

Jerry covered his face and moved back to the counter, laughing.

"I thought I'd asked for a charity cake. That was mortifying."

"I didn't mean to make this tense. Here, you can have it."

I folded up a takeaway box.

"I can't take your slice. I wouldn't dream of taking that from you."

"No, it's fine, don't worry about it."

Jerry gave me serious eye contact.

"What if we shared it?" His lips bent upward into a grin. They were a great pair of lips.

"Excellent idea," I said, taking the slice out and cutting it in half. Jerry picked up his half and held it out. It seemed like he wanted to feed me. I held my cake similarly, and he bumped the slices together like we were toasting. It was adorable.

"What a pleasant end to a rather uncomfortable exchange. I hope we never speak of it again," he said between bites.

"Alright, that's a deal."

He extended his hand, and I wiped my own on my apron before taking his. Smooth. Never worked a day in his life, but also strong and warm – slightly colder fingertips. I felt a tingle shoot up my body. I didn't gasp. At least, I think I didn't. He took his hand away, and I wanted it back.

"So formal," I joked.

"I only French kiss for deals I make about chocolate cake."

He shrugged his shoulders. I looked at the cake counter.

"Do you fancy a brownie?"

I was joking but panicked that it was too forward. "I jest because I plan to eat them as well. Busy night ahead."

"I can imagine. I'll leave you to it," he said, saluting me again as he left. I waved and then locked the door. I turned around and walked straight through the kitchen's double doors and up to my flat, where I rolled up my apron and lay on the hall floor. With my eyes screwed tightly shut, I masturbated for about four minutes

until I came. Once my breathing returned to normal, I shuffled off
to the bathroom, cleared up and went back downstairs to tidy.

Later that night, despite my sexy evening, I still thought of Rob
when I climbed into bed. Although it felt different. I didn't feel
weighed down by sadness. I got into bed, and he popped into my
mind.

***

The next day I didn't want to set my alarm as a little treat to myself,
but I was annoyed when I woke up early anyway. I had my cereal
in my pants and watched TV. Eventually, I did get changed and
meandered down to the dock where I had arrived only a week ago.
I had my reusable tote bags, headphones and a book. I even saved
over a croissant from the day before, a second breakfast on the go.
I was ready. I went to the little office shed and enquired within.

The man in the hut looked up from his newspaper: the *No'Man
Daily*, featuring a seagull photo on the front page. Behind the paper
was Mr Sharp, who delivered the milk sometimes. Whenever he
came in for his tea, Priya called him grumpy guts. I didn't find him
grumpy because he smiled so often – at my misfortune. He was
mumbling about seagulls. The *No'Man Daily* was obviously crank-
ing up his outrage.

"Won't be for a while," he said, without so much as a glimmer
of recognition, as though I were a stranger. "Boat's off this morning."

"What time is the afternoon boat?"

Mr Sharp shrugged. This was no way to run a service. As a local
business manager, I felt angry. I straightened my shoulders and
crossed my brows, ready to give him a piece of my mind. Then I

caught sight of my reflection in the windows of Mr Sharp's hut, and I lost my nerve. I didn't look righteously indignant; I looked possessed. I didn't realise my nostrils could flare so widely. I settled back into myself and decided on a different tact. I leaned forward on the window, resting my croissant and palm at the edge of the window. Mr Sharp scowled at me.

"What time will you reassess?"

"Usually, we get an email when the sea has decided to calm down."

"How do you let people know when you get that email?" I asked and then realised what he'd said. "I thought you meant the coast guard or something. Obviously, the sea doesn't have Gmail."

The man laughed at his joke, and I considered setting his pathetic little shed on fire.

"Cool, thanks for all your help. I guess I'll swim there."

"Doubt you'll get far," he muttered, "without sinking."

It was one of those comments that was a fat joke, but because he didn't say *fat*, I didn't feel like I could rip his head off. I was tempted to point out I was an excellent swimmer, but even if I wasn't, he had no right to make assumptions about me. I walked off, and Mr Sharp shouted, "Don't go dropping your litter either. We've got enough pests around here, thanks."

I rolled my eyes. As if I'd litter. I walked away from the shed in a stinker and decided to stroll along the beach. The sand was wet from the rain the night before, and the wind blew me ragged. At the other end of the beach was a collection of rocks and not much else. I turned back. What a fun little adventure, I thought to myself as I headed home again. I could see Sam walking along the jetty from the tethered boat. He was rubbing his hands together and blowing into them. It was not that cold. He stopped at the shed. By the time I caught up, he had walked on.

"Hey there." I waved.

"Hi-hi." He waved back. I think his wave was making fun of my wave.

"Nice day for the beach."

"It's lovely. Nature."

"You exploring the island?"

I considered his question as we fell in step with one another.

"I'm probably going to go home. I need some ingredients from the mainland, so I don't want to travel too far from the boat."

"Oh, OK." He gave me a tight-lipped smile. It felt disapproving.

"What are you up to?"

"I was going to go up to Pal-Dominar's point."

He pointed his finger to the highest point of the island. Most internet searches about the island will mention it.

"That sounds good. Gonna take you a while, though. Is the boat not going out later?"

"It doesn't take that long. I'll pop up there, enjoy the view and be down in time for late lunch on the mainland."

He was going into so much detail. I felt like I should ask to go with him. Which was madness because I don't hike. I looked at that hill and knew it would take a day to surmount. Sorry, did I say hill? I meant mountain.

Didn't I have enough to surmount in the week?

"I'm so jealous; I think it would take me two days to get up there," I said, light-hearted, easy, breezy.

"No, it wouldn't, not the way I go."

His neutral expression gave away nothing. He sounded almost bored, but in the pit of my tummy, I felt like he was asking to elope.

"Would you like me to come with you?" I asked.

"I'm not going to force you."

What was he saying? This was such a confusing conversation. We walked along a little further and past the café.

"I'll follow for as long as I can," I said, thinking maybe I could return when it got too much.

"No, no, no, you're committed now. We're going all the way up." He was grinning. We walked up a different street than the ones I'd already visited. He led me to a house and asked if I trusted him.

"Sure, I think so," I said.

"Close enough." He grabbed my hand and ran down the side of the house into a stranger's back garden. I followed like an idiot because he was holding my hand! He made us duck behind their shed. We waited, hands still linked. Then he broke apart and leapt over the fence. I looked around, the coast was clear, so I rushed behind him.

We arrived in someone else's garden, which we ran through. Sam took my hand again. I was amazed at his casualness. If I were to have taken his hand, I would've had to text two separate friends about it first. That's a lie. Even after speaking about it, I still wouldn't have done it. We sprinted through the garden, which backed onto a field. There was a solitary shed, which he pulled me toward. Outside the door, he indicated I should wait. I crouched down whilst he disappeared inside. My thighs hurt, and I struggled to breathe, but I was having fun.

Rob used to get me in trouble like this. I shivered as a breeze blew around my exposed ankles, and I thought back to our holiday in Spain. He made us go skinny dipping in the hotel pool on the last night, and we were chased around by security. My trousers had scrunched up and pinched the inside of my knee, dragging me back to reality.

"Oi, what are you doing?" I heard behind me. I turned to see a middle-aged man in a Barbour coat and flat cap. He absolutely had a gun, I couldn't see it, but he was the type.

"I…" did not know how to answer his question. I stood up and looked in the direction of Sam.

"Think I'm lost actually," I finally said. The man kept stomping toward me. I heard an engine turn over and then a zooming sound. I moved to the shed's entrance, and the farmer started jogging toward me. Sam roared out on a quad bike.

"Get on," he shouted and passed me a helmet. I took the headgear out of his hands and jumped on the back. He twisted the throttle, so I clung to him with my free hand and managed to put the helmet on. Just. The bike propelled forward at an alarming rate. I put my arm around Sam. He was laughing, and I laughed too. The furthest edge of the field was ahead of us and entirely uphill. As we approached, I could see a gap in the fence. It led to another field, but I also recognised a muddy path from seeing the hill in the distance. It led to the top. We slowed down to move through the gap and hurtled through it.

I squeezed tighter and felt his ribs under his clothes. Was I about to get an erection? With the vibrating seat and the proximity to a man, I started worrying. Sam was still laughing, but I could hardly hear it over the din of the quad bike. I needed to think about something else. *Hang on a second. Have we really stolen this bike? Was I going to get in trouble?* Frustratingly, my fear of being in trouble made the erection situation worse. What was I thinking? Sam was still laughing. I held on tighter, praying for it to end. Sort of.

"Open your eyes," Sam shouted above the engine.

He must've been psychic or something because he was right; I had clenched my eyes tightly shut. I peeled them open and gasped. The colours of the sea made me wish I could paint. It was deep turquoise, like a Caribbean beach. The light blue gave way to deep indigo, with pure frothy crests atop the waves. It was a tremendous ombré. Beyond the ocean, the mainland seemed close enough to touch, with emerald-rounded mounds beyond the coastline. The bike thing started to slow down and I could feel the surface levelling out. We'd reached the summit. I swung my leg off and stumbled backward.

"Watch out," Sam laughed.

"We've just stolen this? Are we stupid? I've never stolen anything in my life." I was screeching. I'm not proud. I so badly wanted to be relaxed and adventurous, but I couldn't go to prison for Sam.

"Relax,"

"Do *not* tell me to relax; you've just made a criminal out of me. Is there even a prison on the island? Or do you tie people to a post in the sea and wait for the seagulls to peck them to death?"

"That was my dad. These are our bikes. I borrow them all the time. It drives him mad, but I promise we're not about to be arrested."

I placed my hands on my bent knees and bowed my head, allowing my body to catch up with the news.

"I'm sorry. I didn't mean to freak you out."

"What do you mean?" I looked at Sam with my best 'I'm cool' face. "I'm not scared."

"I'd be scared of being tied to a post in the sea."

I straightened up and walked over to a bench on the very top of the hill. There were two benches, one facing in on the island and the other looking out to the sea and the beaches, and my house. It was spectacular. The island was much bigger than I'd realised. I turned to look inland and saw a cluster of buildings on the far side with houses dotted around. There were patches of trees, maybe not big enough to be called forests. I could see cows, presumably from the farm, at the bottom of the hill.

"What do you think of the view?" Sam asked.

"Bit boring, isn't it."

I scrunched up my nose before laughing at myself.

"That was an opportunity for you to say that you loved the view whilst staring at me."

Sam shook imaginary hair from his face, placed his hands on his hips and posed. After all my debating, I could admit that he was attractive.

"The view is…none of my business. I suppose you're very typically handsome." I grinned at him, and Sam smiled.

"You fancy me so hard."

Was he flirting with me? There is no way Sam was gay, but some straight men, in my experience, do enjoy receiving compliments and attention from gay men. I guess it's a confidence boost. Sam sat down, facing me and patted the seat next to him. I sat down and leaned back, getting comfortable. We were close together. His arms were spread along the top of the bench. Our knees bumped.

"This is such a perfect spot for a first kiss," I said, trying to diffuse the situation. Or was I trying to put kissing in the forefront of our minds? Was I being flirty?

"It is, for sure."

Sam didn't say anything and I worried I'd overstepped.

"Who was your first kiss?" I asked, bumping into his knee again.

"It was Dianne Datten. I think you've met her?"

"Dianne? That's mad."

44

"It's a tiny island."

He grinned.

"Were you any good? Was she?"

"It was a first kiss. It was a dare, I think. We came up here with a group of kids from school."

"I feel bad for Dianne. Maybe she'd be nice with a bit more romance in her life."

"What about me? Don't I get some romance?"

Sam turned to face me. I looked at him. God! My whole body felt fizzy.

"I don't know. Have you had any?"

"Not with the right person, I guess."

FUCK.

Did you notice he said, *person?*

"Well, once you find the right person, you should bring them up here."

He looked down, licked his lower lip, and looked at me again.

"I did."

I'm not 100% sure I wasn't grinding my body against the bench. He leant into me. I leant into him. Our noses touched, and we paused. Was this happening? I was aware of my breath. Was I breathing in his face? Finally, his lips touched mine. I responded by moving slightly closer. Our mouths opened slightly and I felt the tip of his tongue. As easy as it started, Sam pulled back and ended the kiss with a smaller kiss. It was perfect. We both pulled away. Sam smiled and looked out at the horizon. He bent forward, rested his elbows on his knees, and bobbed there for a second before jumping up.

"I wasn't expecting that to happen," I said to his back.

"Me neither. I wasn't even sure…"

He tailed off, leaving me wondering about his uncertainty before heading back towards the bike.

"We should get back."

He smiled, and I followed him back, replacing my helmet. He climbed on and put his helmet in place. Before he fired up the engine, he peered back.

"I don't wanna be a dick, but I've never spoken to my dad about this. When we get back, do you think you could not make it obvious?"

My pride was a little hurt, but I also remembered feeling that way once.

"I don't think I could convince him I wasn't gay. I won't make it obvious we were snogging."

He thanked me, and we drove back down the mountain. It seemed less scary, so I only placed my hands on his shoulders going down. We arrived back at the shed, but Sam's dad wasn't there. This time he didn't take me by the hand. I followed as we trudged back through the fields and gardens. In the final garden, Sam stopped, but I wasn't paying attention and bumped into him.

"What are you doing?" a woman in her sixties called out, not as alarmed as I would've been in her situation. She was knelt by a patch of something green and barely looked up.

"We're just cutting through, Mrs Gardner. I'm a bit late for work. Sorry."

"Not to worry, Sam." She smiled and returned to gardening.

I followed closely behind, and we scurried out of her garden, soon finding ourselves back in the street and almost at the beach.

"She was gardening, and her name is Gardner. How fun!"

"Don't take the piss." Sam picked up his walking speed, fuelled by a wave of anger.

46

"I'm not. I just thought it was a fun coincidence. I don't know Mrs Gardner well enough to make fun of her."

"She's nice. She taught me in years four and five."

"That's cool. It was lovely of her to let us run through the garden she was named after. I feel honoured. Will you slow down?"

"I can't. I'm late. I'll meet you by the boat."

Sam stormed ahead, and I lagged behind, seeing how unwanted I was. It's always embarrassing to be left behind.

3

Am I Miss Havisham?

I was exhausted after my trip to the mainland and it was getting dark. I unpacked the few bits I'd bought and tried to settle. Trying to ignore Sam as much as he'd been ignoring me had been awkward. I was worn out. I turned my focus to baking to take my mind off the kiss. My peculiar mood manifested in charred cakes. I could raise neither my spirits nor my bread. I climbed the stairs and the burnt stench of failure followed me around the flat. That familiar Sunday night mood came over me. It was a mood I thought I'd come here to escape from.

The questions floated through my mind: 'What am I doing with my life?' 'Am I wasting my life?' 'What is the meaning of life?' I was stuck to the chair at the table, unable to garner motivation to make myself comfortable or be productive. Eventually, I pulled myself up, trying to distract myself from the questions. I sat in the shower and cried for a little while. I felt like I was in a music video, but when I caught sight of my reflection in the tap, I laughed and ruined the moment. I went to bed and in the dark, I kept thinking of that quote, 'Wherever you go, there you are'. It mocked me as the thought tumbled around my head. It was the mental equivalent of hugging one of those pillows with the word 'HAPPY' stitched on it, even though you feel like shit.

***

My personality came thudding back into my body when Priya arrived on Monday, and I could talk to another person. I wasn't alone anymore. We talked a bit about our weekends, between dealing with customers. I felt guilty for omitting my kiss, but it was great to chat. The morning plodded along and I kept looking up at the door, expecting Sam to come in and apologise. But by lunchtime, I'd forgotten to keep vigilant and was surprised when he did pop in.

"Hey, are you busy?" he asked as I furiously buttered six slices of bread.

"Not at all. Do you fancy going for a long walk in the middle of the business day?"

"Right, sorry." He picked up on my sarcasm, and I felt like a twat. "Can I see you after work?"

"Sure, I'll be here. Stop by."

He gave a curt wave and left. A minute passed as I finished the sandwiches and passed them on to a father and his two small children. I heard the door again. Sam was back.

"Can I also get a ham sandwich? Sorry I meant to get one earlier, but I was distracted."

His smile was sheepish, breaking down the emotional barrier I was struggling to maintain. He was sneaky. I'd have to watch that.

"I'll make it now."

I couldn't decide if I wanted to make a great sandwich or a bad one. I used barely any butter, so it'd be dry, but then loaded it with ham to appear kind. I wrapped it for him to go and didn't charge him – that felt exploitative, since we'd kissed.

49

"The main thing about selling cakes, sandwiches and drinks in a café is selling them," said Priya, "or you'll never make any money."

She had an excellent point. I was starting to feel like anyone, but me, would do a better job of running this café.

"Why aren't you the manager, Priya?"

"I like my life exactly as it is. Who can be arsed to cash up a till?" She laughed. It was a big sound, much like her singing voice. It was infectious enough but combined with Priya's elbow nudging me in the side, I started laughing too.

About twenty minutes before she left, I asked her to hold down the fort whilst I popped up to the shop. I told her we needed more ingredients, which was true, but I also wanted some chocolate. My need for cocoa-y goodness increased when my heart dropped, thinking I'd seen the back of Rob's head. I ducked behind a low wall. I talked myself into standing and the phantom Rob was gone.

In the safety of the shop, I scuttled around, throwing things into a basket and noticed Dianne at the till when I was paying.

"In a hurry?" Dianne said, in reference to me tapping on the conveyor belt.

"Sorry." I begrudged having to apologise to her, but I worried my tapping would look entitled. "I'm just thinking."

"Something on your mind, other than cakes for once?"

Was this an opening? For friendly conversation? I needed to share something with her, something to bond us.

"Yes, actually. I kissed someone," I said, hoping gossip would bring us together. "A man, obviously."

"Bill? From the pub. I think he's bi?"

"Not Bill. It was someone else."

"Was it Sam?"

My face froze, trying too hard not to react.

"This isn't a guessing game. Who it was is not important. I'm just not sure what to do about it now."

"You're not special just because you got off with Sam. We kissed once, nothing to write home about."

Dianne scanned my shopping through the till. It dawned on me that I shouldn't have shared my gossip. Gossip is only fun when it's about other people and won't potentially ruin your blossoming relationship. Whoopsie!

"I didn't confirm or deny it's him, but can you not mention your thoughts on this to anyone?"

"I'm not surprised. I could tell he wasn't into it when we kissed. It's a small island. As far as I know, he's not kissed anyone else."

"But it's not him, or it might not be since I've not said who..."

"Right. That's £8.55, please."

My things were all scanned, and I'd forgotten to pack my bag. I paid and also realised I'd forgotten my tote. I had to balance four bags of sugar, two enormous bags of flour and a bag of Minstrels on top of each other.

"It's 10p for a bag."

"Better for the environment. Someone's gotta care about the world." I was being stubborn but felt superior.

"You city types have a lot of guilt about all your climate change, don't you."

She glared at me, her eyes burrowing, seemingly making me responsible for global warming.

"We all need to do our bit," I said quietly, all bravado leaving my voice. I turned to go, and Dianne called after me.

"Don't be too flattered by Sam, by the way. You're probably one of the only gay people he knows. Except for Bill at the pub."

"Thanks," I said, before hurrying out the door and down the hill to the café. Dianne's conversation had left me a little bit clueless. I didn't know what to say to Sam, and I didn't know if I was asking too much of him. I hoped he didn't come back too early that evening so I'd have time to think of a plan.

I was distractedly obsessing over Sam when I heard the door go. I looked up, expecting to see Jerry, a smile plastered across my face. My mouth dropped when I took in the scene before me.

Rob holding hands with another man!

His smile fell as he noticed me behind the till. My knees felt like jelly, instinct probably telling me to hide under the counter.

"Hey, can we get two flat whites, please?" the man with Rob asked. Unable to make words, I turned and silently made their coffees. The only sound was the whirring of the fridge. In the coffee machine's reflection, I could see Rob pointing at me and the man's mouth making a perfectly shocked 'O'. I turned to give them their drinks. In the silence, I tapped on the till.

"That's £5.20, please," I announced.

"What are you doing here?" Rob asked, not going for his wallet.

"I work here. What are you doing here?" My voice was neutral. I didn't want to reveal anything about my feelings until I knew what Rob was thinking.

"First holiday together," the man answered. "I'd never heard of No'Man, but Rob kept getting adverts for it."

MI6 or whoever tapped our phones had betrayed me. When I used Rob's iPad to search No'Man, I must've triggered some algorithm malfunction. Anger rose in me toward myself, but I decided to redirect that rage toward technology. I made a solemn vow to smash my phone on purpose later, to punish the algorithm. I managed a smile, unsure of what the protocol was. I'd tried to escape Rob, yet here he was.

Inescapable.

"We're headed back on the ferry now."

Rob tapped his card on the machine, and he and the man picked up their cups.

"Take care," I said, which was peculiar as I'd never said that phrase before, even when I meant it. I'd wanted to shout, 'I hope you drown', but reined myself in at the last minute. They left, and I exhaled until it hurt. Through the window, I saw Rob walking back in.

LEAVE ME ALONE!

"Sorry, that was awkward. I don't know what to say."

"You coulda not ordered a coffee, I guess."

"I'm sorry you're here. Hopefully, you'll be back on your feet in no time."

My face changed, anger rising to the surface, but Rob closed the door and left. With that pitying statement, he's won the break-up. I snatched a cream cake from the fridge and sprinted out the door.

"Oi Rob," I shouted, although he wasn't far away yet. "Eat shit."

I was screaming and launched the cake at him. It landed square in his chest and bounced on the floor. I blinked a couple of times.

The cake remained in the fridge.

The throw hadn't happened.

Thank God because, honestly, my aim has never been that good. I slammed my fist on the counter a couple of times. I paced behind the café, needing to move, like when you hurt your finger and need to walk away from the pain. I didn't get far as Rob returned to the doorway.

"You're back," I said, resenting the hope in my voice.

"I didn't want to leave without saying if you ever want to talk to someone..." He shifted the weight from one foot to the other, figuring out what he wanted to say. "I think we can still be friends."

"You hurt me, Rob," I said plainly. It was factual. "I know that ultimately, I'll be OK, better off without you. But when things were hard with us, I chose to fix it, and you didn't. And on the way to deciding that we were irreparable, you disrespected me. I don't want to be friends with you. You should leave now."

Rob respected my wishes then, turning and closing the door. I wiped my eyes and flung a milk jug across the room.

After screaming in the kitchen for a few moments and cleaning up as though the coffee machine were to blame, I managed to calm down enough for Jerry's arrival. Jerry looked relaxed, and maybe he'd caught a little sun, which seemed impossible considering it had been cloudy and vile all weekend.

"What do you fancy?"

Jerry scanned the cake counter.

"I probably shouldn't get anything after the weekend I've had."

He patted his stomach and puffed out his cheeks. I think he wanted me to laugh, and I would have to be polite had Rob not sucked the joy from my aura. Jerry looked slim, as always, and I felt awkward because I was bigger than him.

"I don't want to be a dick, especially to one of my most loyal customers, but I feel like you're implying you need to watch what you eat. That's rooted in a fear of getting fat, and I'm fat, so it feels a bit tone-deaf on your part."

"You're not that fat," he began to stutter. I almost enjoyed seeing such a cool guy flustered.

"I am, and it's OK. It's not a slur. I have a fat and sexy body. I don't want people coming to my place of work and implying that being fat is bad."

Neither of us spoke. I wanted to take back what I'd said and make him chatty again. Was he going to stop liking me? Would I make it worse if I screamed, 'Say something?'

"I feel like I've fucked up a little bit. I apologise. May we start again?" His formal tone was light-hearted. I felt like he cared that he'd said the wrong thing.

"Of course."

"In that case, I'd like a slice of the lemon drizzle and a brownie."

He took his usual seat, and I finished clearing up. I was a dab hand at tidying now, always rushing to spend time with Jerry. I padded back to the café; I didn't want to be alone with my thoughts. In a bid to not look desperate, even if I was, I looked out the window for Sam and pretended to be distracted. Jerry cleared his throat.

"Sorry, I'm a bit unmotivated to get going. Do you need me to leave?"

"Not at all. I'm waiting for my friend to come by," I said, even though I'd have said 'a boy' in normal circumstances. Was I worried about making Jerry think I was unavailable?

"In that case, pull up a pew," he said as he kicked the seat from under the table. Following his lead, I sat down.

"So, what did you do with your weekend?"

"I went to visit some friends in the south of France."

"That explains the tan."

"Do you think I've caught the sun? I wasn't trying to sunbathe, but they did have a pool."

He finished the lemon drizzle cake, patting his stomach, making a point about enjoying the food. I smiled at his efforts.

"Oh, how the other half live."

"Do I sound like a wanker? Sorry."

"No, not at all. Well, maybe a tiny bit. I'm wildly jealous."

"I must invite you sometime."

I thanked him. It was an empty gesture. I wasn't about to get my calendar out. We sat in silence as people trickled past the café to the beach or back to their hotels. In part, I was keeping vigil. I wanted to make sure Rob wouldn't return.

"Can I ask you something?" said Jerry.

My shoulders shrugged as if to say 'go on then', nonchalantly.

"Why have you never asked me why I'm here?"

I tilted my head, demonstrating that I was thinking but also buying time to come up with a good answer.

"If I had asked, would you have told me the real reason? Don't most celebrities fib about that kind of thing?" I couldn't reveal that I thought about him so much so soon. "So go on, why are you here?"

"I'm taking a break, officially. Unofficially and strictly off the record, I'm sober."

"You don't drink? I don't drink either, never have. Isn't that funny?" I smiled. We have so much in common.

"No, what I mean is, I'm in rehab." Jerry bit the inside of his cheek and looked out the window. I didn't speak, sensing he had more to say. "I'm an alcoholic."

"I'm so dumb, sorry. That's a cool thing to be doing, though. Not struggling with alcohol use, more just being able to face it and do something about it."

Why was he telling me this? He was confiding in me, and I was ruining it. He might never speak to me again.

"Thanks. I don't think everyone in my life thinks it's cool," he said, turning his cup around.

"Is it hard, keeping it sort of secret?"

He took a moment to consider his answer, pursing his lips and shaking his head.

"It's not easy, worrying that people will find out before I'm ready. I don't think there's anything wrong with people struggling with alcohol, but I am ashamed of some of my behaviour. Does that make sense?"

"Yes, shame and acceptance sound familiar, but I am gay, after all." I smiled but could see Jerry wasn't amused, so I forced myself to take things more seriously. I was desperate to ask more, but I wanted to be considerate. I got the sense that Jerry felt as lonely as I did. Outside the window, I watched a bag of crisps blow back and forth. Cheese and onion. Not a flavour I liked. It stands to reason that someone who likes cheese and onion couldn't use a bin. I didn't know what else to say to Jerry, so I waited.

"Sorry, was that all a bit of an overshare? Too much from some man who eats the cakes and talks all the time?"

His cheeks were, if I'm not mistaken, a tiny bit red.

"I don't mind at all. But do you always tell random men your deepest darkest secrets?" I asked, hoping he'd make me feel special.

"You're not just anyone off the street. You're..." He grasped for the right words, panic written across his face, "the guy who makes the cakes."

"You don't know my name, do you?"

"In fairness, you've never told me...god I'm such an arsehole today."

"You're not an arsehole. My name is George."

"Hi George, nice to meet you."

We shook hands and continued to look outside the window. Men are so formal sometimes. Jerry made a start on the brownie.

"These are really good," he said after the first bite.

"Thank you. They're my favourite thing to make. I love melting the chocolate. It makes me feel witchy."

He laughed at that, although with a mouth full of brownie. Crumbs jumped onto the table. He swallowed and wiped his mouth on a napkin. I considered picking up one of the bigger crumbs and placing it in my mouth, exchanging saliva as though we'd kissed. I know, I'm gross.

"I appreciate you telling me why you came to No'Man. I like that you come here and can share your secrets." I reached over and patted his arm, then retreated to my side of the table, concerned I'd been overly familiar.

"Thank you. Why are you here? On the island, I mean."

"Good question, I suppose." I inhaled, ready to reel off my answer.

"I had a break-up and had to find somewhere new to live, so it just seemed like a fantastic opportunity to come and bake some cakes and think."

He leant forward in his seat, eyes wide. It was intense under his full attention.

"Must've been a big break-up?"

God, now I sounded petty.

"It was kind of a big one for me. I think he was the love of my life. Pretty embarrassing, really, as he's moved on. Completely."

I smiled. I wanted so badly for him to think I was fine. But it was too fresh. One stupid tear crept from the corner of my eye and made its way down my cheek.

"It's only been three weeks. How has he moved on? I was a good boyfriend. Why am I here, and he's already moved on?" I went to stand, howling now. "It's not just the break-up. I also had a big fight with my mum and haven't spoken to my best friend. It feels like I've lost everything."

Jerry moved over to my side of the table and put his arm around me. It felt good. And it was kind. I turned into his arm, clinging on, and began to wail. I couldn't control my reaction. He stroked my hair until I stopped. When I opened my eyes, it was like the stormy night had passed and a new day had begun. I was embarrassed. His denim shirt was wet where my face had been.

"Look at me crying. I'm sorry, you should be crying. You have real problems, no offence."

I managed to stand and almost reached the kitchen when he jogged in front of me. I stopped, and he looked into my face.

"Do not apologise."

He pulled me into a proper hug. One arm was around my shoulder, and the other was around my waist. He was taller than me, but not much. His shoulders were broad. I tried to adjust my chin and nuzzled my face into his neck. He smelt amazing. I didn't want him to think I was going for a kiss, so I let go.

"I need to go to the loo, but thank you very much. Tomorrow's cake is on the house."

"Free cake and a hug, what a day." He smiled and was still very close. He turned me on only a bit. This constant emotional assault was exhausting. I was embarrassed but also aware that Sam should be here shortly. I needed to wipe my face. I also didn't want Jerry and Sam to meet. Imagine if they hit it off? There'd be no need for me. I couldn't stand to be their matchmaker. I could picture them, in twenty years' time, reminiscing about the kind sexless café manager who introduced them.

Meanwhile, I'd live alone, still wearing the wedding dress I'd inexplicably bought.

Am I Miss Havisham? I *needed* Jerry to go.

"I'm going to wipe my face. I'll see you tomorrow?"

I backed toward the front door.

"Yes, good shout."

He popped back to his seat, grabbed his things and walked through the door I held open.

"If you ever want to talk, I'm here every day," he said, rubbing my bicep. I could see through his smile how sincere he was and I felt my lower lip bobbing.

"Thanks, pal." I waved and closed the door. By the time he'd crossed the road, I was already upstairs.

I did a quick change and threw some water on my face. Obviously, I'd been crying, but I would just yawn a lot when Sam arrived and pretend my eyes had watered. I heard the doorbell ring and ran down to answer it, taking in a huge gulp of air. *Nothing has happened* I told myself, in a bid to feel normal, before turning the latch.

"Hey, you." Sam stood there grinning.

I invited him upstairs and offered him a drink. He accepted a glass of water. I led him over to the sofa. He stretched his legs and arms along the back, relaxing into the space. It annoyed me. His legs jogged in place, betraying nervous energy.

"So, what did you want to talk about?" I asked, as though we hadn't sucked face yesterday. He placed his glass on the coffee table – not on the coaster – and readjusted in his seat to face me.

"About that kiss," he began, "I don't know if you could tell, but that was my first one. With a man, I mean."

"I did think that was potentially the case."

"And I liked it. More than I thought I would."

"Did you plan it? Going up to the viewpoint like that?"

He shook his head.

"I just feel like I want to spend time with you, and when we were up there, I wanted to kiss you."

He looked past me. I followed his line of sight and saw he wasn't looking at anything. I felt the corner of a frayed cushion in my fingertips. The threads bumped along my thumb in a way that felt soothing.

"Is that all you wanted to say?"

"I guess, but that wasn't the only reason I came."

He reached over and touched my thigh. I pushed my knee toward him, and he edged closer. I didn't move, stuck with my indecision. It felt good that Sam seemed to fancy me and was initiating something. However, I was the more experienced gay, and it felt like I was grooming him. It's important to note we were roughly the same age, although I undeniably was a smidge older. Unsure how to start, I decided honesty was the best option.

"I'm not sure what to do here."

"What do you want to do?" His tone was mischievous.

"I don't think you're ready for this, if I'm honest. Finding out who you are is an exciting time, and I think you should enjoy that. But I'm not in a good head space." I took his hand off my knee. "I can't face something that might feel like rejection. Does that make sense?"

"I get what you're saying. I'm not asking you to marry me. I just thought we could do something fun and see where it led?"

He put his arm along the back of the sofa so it reached behind me.

"But I remember those first few times with a man when you're not sure, and it's great, and then you're filled with shame. And that shame shouldn't be there. It's so unfair, and I wish it wasn't. But it will be there, and it'll make you resent me, and I can't handle it."

"I'm not ashamed of what we're doing."

"Sure, but you were scared of your dad thinking we might've kissed. This is all new. Do you even identify as gay or bi? Does that feel comfortable coming out of your mouth?"

I stood. It was dramatic, but I needed to be further away from his pheromones before I continued.

"There's no pressure to feel comfortable now. Pushing you is the last thing I want to do. I'm just trying to make a point."

Sam adjusted his posture. He sat forward, taking both hands and resting them on his knees.

"I think I've come here for something different to what you were expecting."

"I was expecting some explanation for yesterday."

Sam looked at me, his face betraying nothing of how he felt. I looked back as long as I could. It felt as though neither of us knew what to say, yet there was still so much unsaid. He shuffled again and crossed his legs. My heart pounded in my ears. He stood up. I didn't move. He was a T-Rex, and I froze in a bid to remain undetected. He left. I listened for the door closing behind him. I didn't move for a minute. From my window, I stared out to sea. I didn't feel regret for the decision I'd made. But it was crummy having to hurt Sam.

Later that night, I couldn't sleep. I felt guilty for what I'd said to Sam. I longed for the carefree days of just having a boyfriend, but that only reminded me of Rob. I couldn't fathom how he was on holiday so quickly after our break-up. It struck me as horribly unjust. I'd done right by Rob, and I was so unhappy I'd moved hundreds of miles away. He'd disrespected me, broke me, and he was on holiday. He should be in pain, not me.

I lay in the dark, telling myself the most logical things. Rob couldn't have moved on. Surely, he was only better at ignoring his hurt feelings; he was still in pain. If he could move on so quickly, then Rob couldn't be the one, so he wasn't worth feeling this upset over. I turned onto my stomach. All the logic in the world couldn't stop my heart from aching. Seeing Rob so happy with someone else made my sadness seem ridiculous. I wasn't only sad anymore; I was frustrated.

When would Rob's ghost leave me alone?

4

Running a Bloody Café

My midnight wailing meant the whole next day I was sluggish. I couldn't keep my eyes open. Priya convinced me to take a shot of espresso, which tasted awful, strong and awfully strong and had no effect. Whenever the café had no customers, I'd rest my head on the counter, too tired to use my neck. Immediately after work, I kicked off my trousers and socks and covered myself in my blanket. I must've fallen asleep because when my eyes opened, it was almost dark. The front door was knocking. With more agility than was typical post-nap, I bounced up to my feet, stumbled down the stairs, and turned on the hall light. The door was already halfway open when I wondered if I should've been afraid. I presumed it would be Sam or potentially Jerry or Priya. I didn't really know anyone else; it could've been a murderer. It could've been Eileen, and maybe there was a problem with the café. All of these thoughts came to me, but none led me to put my trousers back on. Before I had time to consider other options, my eyes took in the sight before me. Coily black hair, round face, bright jacket.

It was Nat.

"Could you take any longer to open the bloody door? I'm going to piss myself. Move."

She elbowed her way past and helped herself up the stairs. I closed the door.

"Hi, I didn't know you were coming," I called after her. Nat opened the door at the top of the stairs, dropped her bag and jacket on the floor, hiked up her denim skirt and sat on the toilet. I made a show of looking elsewhere, but she'd left the door wide open like she always did.

"Of course, you didn't know I was coming. You're not speaking to me."

"I'm not sure you're speaking to me either."

Nat held up the palm of her hand to silence me.

"You literally ran away in the night. It was bizarre, and I've not heard from you in weeks. Ten days. I'm too angry to talk about it yet."

"You said that moving here would be the biggest mistake of my life, so I think my reaction was justified. But fine, let's not talk about it yet."

"Good."

I folded my arms. Nat finished her wee and washed her hands.

"You're staying here, right?"

"Obviously. They probably don't even have hotels here. As if anyone would come here by choice."

She wandered into the hallway, collected her bag and rested it on the table. I bit my tongue, choosing not to point out that all of the island's economy came from tourism.

"It's a nice place, at least," she conceded.

"I like it." I lifted one shoulder, unsure.

I didn't know what to say. I was still coming around from my nap.

"How are you?" she asked.

"I'm a bit discombobulated. I just woke up. How are you?"

She shook her head.

"That's not really an answer, is it?"

I put the hem of my T-shirt in between my thumb and forefinger and rubbed them together.

"I'm not sure how to answer it right now. Also, I haven't seen you for a while, so I want to know how you are."

Nat put her hands on her hips and grinned expectantly.

"OK."

She swept into the kitchen, fetched a glass of water and flounced on the sofa. I followed her and sat opposite. It didn't seem to fit her, being in No'Man. My old life and my new life weren't compatible. I didn't know what to say.

"What's new?"

Nat filled me in about work, although it seemed as though nothing had changed. Her flatmate was getting on her nerves, but that was typical. She'd been seeing a new man called Emmanuel.

"Emmanuel." She grinned as she said his name. Nat showed me his picture, and he was handsome. Tall, broad, big, and bearded. He worked as a film graphics designer or something; he was the perfect boyfriend material.

"What a hunk," I replied to the picture.

I felt a pang of homesickness. It felt good to chat with someone who knew me. The island was idyllic, but it wasn't home yet. London was too sad for me right now, but leaving had brought its own sadness.

We ate some crisps and chocolate as we talked. I told Nat about Jerry but realised there wasn't much to say except he was famous and seemed to enjoy my cakes. I mentioned Rob's cameo, and she spat with rage, which was extremely validating. I forgot to mention Sam.

We dressed in matching silk PJs that we'd worn on a mutual friend's hen do, and Nat tied her afro hair in a silk scarf. We brushed our teeth together, and I could've wept with how intimate and familiar it was. In bed, it was dark besides the moon's glare that seemed to be on steroids that evening. A strip of light between the curtains illuminated the whole room.

"Apparently people used to celebrate full moons because they were so bright you could work during a full moon."

I spoke into the dimness as moonlight poured onto the floor.

"Lucky I don't need to look too hard for my hoe," Nat said, grabbing my arm. I laughed and shook her off. We went quiet.

"Why didn't you call me?" Nat whispered.

I'd been asking myself this question since I arrived here. Staring up at the ceiling, I searched for an answer.

"I don't know. I felt like I needed to be really sad. And I couldn't handle you judging me for wanting to come here."

"I only tried to give you advice before making the decision. But you're here now and have my full support; you have to know that."

"I didn't want to tell you what I was thinking because I know I've made a mistake. Look at me. What the fuck am I doing on an island? Running a bloody café? Have I ever expressed an interest in baking or living rurally? I knew it was a mistake when I applied for the job. But I needed time to think of my next thing."

"You could've been in touch since you left. I was worried."

Nat's voice was quiet. I could hear the sea shushing away to itself. I'd been a bad friend.

"You're right. I'm sorry I disappeared on you."

"I might be rude for a bit whilst I learn to forgive you."

67

I went to say something, but I wasn't sure what. I wanted to joke and break the tension, but I was relieved we were friends again. The noise that left me was more of a muted cry. In the darkness, the duvet rustled as Nat found my hand and held it.

My eyes were open when the alarm sounded. I'd rested more than I had in a long time. I rolled out of the bed and landed on my hands and knees. I crawled to my phone, turned it off, scrambled for my clothes, and crept out of the room.

"I don't know why you're pretending to be quiet," Nat said as I creaked the door shut.

In the café, I was singing Tina Turner when Priya arrived, and she joined in with half a chorus of 'Proud Mary'. We took bows for one another as Nat emerged from the kitchen in her PJs.

"Customers aren't allowed back there." Priya was polite but firm.

"Sorry, Priya, this is Nat, my friend who's staying with me."

"Hey, I didn't realise that door led to a kitchen. Otherwise, I would be wearing an apron and clothes." Nat pulled at the hem of her PJ shorts.

"Sorry, love, I thought for a minute an undressed stranger had broken in."

We all laughed because someone breaking in, wearing PJs, was quite fun.

Typically, I didn't so much 'take a lunch break' as sit next to the coffee machine and gobble down a sandwich between customers. However, since Nat had travelled from London, I decided to sit in the café and eat with her. The lunchtime rush had subsided, and it was nice to enjoy sitting out front like an actual customer.

"These sandwiches are delicious you know."

"I bake the bread each morning. It's hell."

"Do you sell loaves?"

"I don't know if anyone would buy it, the majority of our customers are holidaymakers, and they mostly don't have kitchens."

I took a bite of my sundried tomato and mozzarella baguette. The pesto was nice; I thought I might experiment with making my own. Nat stared out of the window.

"Some of these men are good-looking. Sorry, that must be hard for you."

"Why?" My mouth was full.

"I imagine the ratio of LGBTQIA-Plus to cishets is not in your favour."

"I do alright."

Nat put down her sandwich and faced me.

"Pardon?"

I swallowed and leant forward and told her about Sam.

"A pirate?" she asked, too loudly for my liking.

I smiled at her joke. It felt like we were the same person sometimes.

"You have to keep your voice down. He's still really new to this."

"You turned him? That's so *Twilight* of you."

"I have always been very handsomely tortured."

Nat gave a little laugh. It felt like we were on holiday. I finished my sandwich and Sam walked past. He looked into the café, caught my eyes and glared at me. It seemed as though he was suddenly aware of a predator watching him. It annoyed me because I hadn't been watching him, but now it looked like I'd been waiting to see him. Nat followed my gaze.

"Is that...?" she asked quietly.

"Sam."

She nodded. Sam saw her head bobbing and steamed off toward the beach. He kicked a bottle into the road and stomped through a flock of seagulls.

"Why is he so angry?" Nat asked.

I shrugged. I didn't want to talk about it here. I cleared our plates and got back to work. I gave Nat instructions on how to climb to the top of the island whilst I finished. She wouldn't be here very long, but at least we'd have another two nights together. I was thinking about the snacks we would get later on, as we'd planned to have dinner. Nat waved goodbye and headed out into the afternoon. She had a bottle of water and seemed determined.

By the time Priya left, I was worried. I checked my phone, but there were no missed calls. The hill path was quite popular; if she'd fallen, then chances are someone would find her. I couldn't believe I was thinking in these terms. She was fine. Of course, Nat was fine, she maybe was a little lost, and her phone battery died. But beyond that, she'd be fine. The door opened, and I flicked my head toward the noise. Jerry was standing in the doorway.

"Hey," he said.

"I thought you were someone else. I didn't mean to stare over at you."

"Who did you think I was?"

"My friend, she's visiting from London."

Jerry walked toward me, and I positioned myself behind the till. I needed to regain some degree of professionalism.

"What can I get for you?"

He squinted at me and ordered his usual.

"Coming right up," I began and saw Jerry going for his wallet, "this is free because last time you were here, I cried."

70

"No, you have to let me pay for my stuff. I'm quite rich, so it looks bad when I don't pay."

"Quite rich?" I laughed. "Honestly, it's fine. There's no one here, and I want to say thank you."

"Well, that's kind of you, but unnecessary."

I told him to take a seat. I whipped up his order, placed it in front of him and scurried off like a woodland creature snatching a nut. Unfortunately, I was without the nut I so deeply craved. By which I mean a conversation with Jerry. With Nat on the island, I must've felt braver because I forced myself to go back and look out the window.

"When is your friend due back?"

"Now. I'm not worried. She'll be along shortly."

I stared, wondering why I lied about Nat. What if she missed her chance to meet Jerry?

"Do we need to talk about the crying?" said Jerry, his tone light and jovial, but his eyes were penetrating and sincere.

"We're fine."

His leg was jigging again. I could see him working up the courage to share something with me.

"I don't want to push you. I spoke about you in therapy today. Not in a bad way, but…"

Jerry was interrupted by the door opening. Nat limped into the café, assisted by Sam. Shit.

"Oh my goodness, are you OK?" I practically screamed at Nat as I swooped to help her and pulled out a chair. Sam and Jerry stood uselessly, regarding each other. This was my biggest fear, the pair of them meeting and falling in love. Nat winced as she sat.

"I fell over. It wasn't even that bad. It slowed me down. Sam found me and offered me a lift down here."

Nat looked pointedly at Sam. She approved. Maybe I'd been too harsh on him. I ought to cut him some slack; I remember how hard it is before you come out.

We all have to start somewhere.

"Do you want ice? Where does it hurt?"

"Only grazed my knee and hurt my wrist. Honestly, I'm fine. But I'm starving, are you nearly done here?"

"Yes, basically, just closing up."

"I invited Sam to stay for dinner if he wants to." Nat looked up at him. He puckered his lips in agreement.

"OK, the more, the merrier," I said. Then I uttered the stupidest thing I've ever said: "Why don't you stay, Jerry?"

Nat looked at Jerry, then did a double take.

"Ah, I don't want to intrude…"

"It's no intrusion," Nat butted in.

Speaking of intrusions, Dianne knocked on the café door.

"Are you closing early?" she asked through the window.

It irked me; there was an implication I was lazy. I'd cleaned the coffee machine, but she said she wanted a slice of cake to go. I wrapped up some walnut and coffee cake and she stood amongst our motley crew.

"Do you have dinner plans?" I heard Nat asking, trying to win Dianne over on my behalf.

"I can't stay, I'm afraid. Going on a date actually."

"Ooooh fancy," I said as I carried over her takeout box.

"Who are you going out with?" Sam asked, as the only person who would know them.

"Jed, he's working the season as a water sports instructor. You wouldn't know him, George, he's sporty. You know what it's like here, Sam. Everyone knows everything eventually." She smiled and looked from me to Sam. Instinctively I shook my head.

"Yeah, people love getting into everyone's business," he replied, an easy smile spreading from cheek to cheek. Just as I was hoping that maybe he was as clueless as everyone implied, he turned and glared at me.

"People do love to chat, even when it's not true or a misunderstanding," I added, entirely unnaturally.

"Can't swing a cat, or kiss a man, without everyone knowing about it," Dianne appeared to say to herself, although I knew it was for Sam's and my benefit. No one spoke for a moment, slipping into a group panic over what to say. Jerry coughed.

"I better get on," Dianne said, smugly. She left with her cake, and we ventured to the flat.

I led Nat upstairs, and the boys followed. I quickly whipped around to tidy. I didn't think it would be too bad, but after changing in the living room this morning, some beautiful silky boxers were lying in the middle of the floor.

"Don't know where these have come from." I laughed to keep the atmosphere breezy. Jerry looked away, but Sam licked his lips. In fairness, it was warm in the flat, so I don't think it was a sexual gesture. I was also fairly sure he hated my guts. After throwing my clothes in the laundry basket, I got everyone a drink, and Nat went to the bathroom to clean up her knees.

"Nice place," Jerry said. He rested his hands on the counter and then moved them to his pockets. I'd hazard a guess that he was nervous, which explains why he was lying. One of the richest people in the world, with several multi-million-pound mansions in different countries, was impressed by my one-bed over a shop. I don't think so. I was extremely grateful that I'd not brought the *My Love and the Sea* film poster to the Isle. I'd hung it on my wall at Uni. It featured a shirtless Jerry standing in front of Reese Witherspoon. He'd gotten me in the mood more times than I could count. Sam claimed the same place as before – his territory. Whenever I dared steal a glance over at him, he just scowled at me. Jerry waited for me to bring their drinks and perched on the sofa's arm. He teetered a second and slid down the arm into the spot next to Sam. I sat at the small table and glared at them.

"Sorry, I don't have anything more exciting than tap water. We were going to the supermarket, but I've not had time today."

It was so uncomfortable. I thought about putting some music on – that would've made things worse.

"Well hung," Jerry pointed at my nude, hung on a pre-existing nail.

"Nothing to write home about," Nat called out from the bathroom, and I gave her a look through a gap in the door.

"Why do you have a nude photo of yourself?" Sam asked. He seemed angered by the picture.

"Why not, I guess? If you've got it, flaunt it, as they say," Jerry jumped in to answer for me. Did this mean we were in love?

"One minute," I said and hurried out to see Nat.

"You never said Jerry fucking Hilk was your friend." Nat punched my arm.

"I told you he'd been in."

"You didn't say you hung out."

"We don't usually. He's just a customer, except for the other day when I cried, and he held me like a sweet baby. Now they're both out there, and they're going to fall in love. I was hoping they weren't going to meet."

I slumped onto the end of the bed, throwing my head back into the duvet. I needed a good sulk, but this was not the time.

"George, there's no way you could stop them from falling in love if that's what was meant to be."

My eyes bulged from their sockets.

"You mean, there's no way they'll fancy each other over you," I moaned.

"Don't be naive. We all know you can fancy more than one person at a time. I mean, look at you and Rob. He clearly fancied other guys when you were together."

"Why have I missed you so much? You're terrible at making me feel better."

Nat finished getting ready.

"Right, let's go out there and have one of the most fun nights of our lives. It's going to be wild," said Nat before adding an enthusiastic "whoop whoop."

"It's going to be shit. I don't have enough snacks, and everyone drinks tap water."

We wandered out to the living room, refreshed and filled with dread. Without much to discuss, I took out my phone and discussed what to order. We landed on pizza, a crowd-pleaser.

"Shall we get some beers in?" Sam asked.

I looked at Jerry, whose brow had furrowed.

"I dunno if it's that kind of party," I laughed, trying to keep the tone light.

"Beer stinks like bad breath anyway," Nat added, saving the moment.

Jerry looked at me and gave me the saddest smile I'd ever seen. I wasn't sure I'd manage to eat much with all the sexual tension in the room. Maybe it was just regular tension. By the time the food arrived, Nat was retelling the story of her first kiss.

"It was the longest and worst kiss ever. He kept licking my teeth; it was like the orthodontist."

"That's the worst," Jerry laughed.

"I've done that before, I think," Sam added. "I'm much better now, though."

I wanted to add that he was right, but of course, I couldn't.

"Who was your first kiss?" Nat asked Jerry.

"Officially, it was Keira Knightley. We were in a film together."

Everyone went quiet. Not very relatable, I suppose.

"It's a bit of a crap story. We did it like ten times for the different takes."

"Keira is well fit, to be fair," Sam added, and I was grateful my face didn't turn green like the jealous emoji. I can't compete with Keira. Who can?

"She is really beautiful." Jerry smiled to himself, lost in memory. "Inside and out."

It occurred to me, briefly, to set the flat on fire and take them all with me. Jealousy is hard to manage. Once, at a gay bar, I saw a man wearing a Beyoncé T-shirt I'd wanted but couldn't afford from her concert. I tried to push into him and spill my drink down him. It wasn't reasonable. I tried to move the conversation on.

"I'd love to film a kissing scene," I piped up.

"No, you wouldn't. You won't even snog someone in a club." Nat pushed my leg.

"That's because club kissing makes no sense. It's hot and sweaty, and you can't chat. It's just gross. No offence."

The group looked confused until Nat added, "I met my boyfriend in a club. We kissed a lot that night."

"That's not strictly true. You met online, went for a drink, dinner and then a club. No judgement, I think that's a lovely evening, but I couldn't do it."

"I think I judge you, George," said Jerry.

My lower jaw dropped open in mock offence.

"Excuse you?"

"I just think you sound a bit like a prude." Jerry smiled and took up another slice of pizza.

"I am no prude; I will snog almost anyone, almost anywhere. But I think clubs aren't for me. I resent your accusation."

We were laughing and having a good time. I did think for a moment we might move into a sexier vibe, and maybe someone would suggest playing *spin the bottle*. We fell quiet. I wished the boys would leave so we wouldn't feel so tense. It never works trying to bring friends together. Sam looked at his phone, and within seconds, everyone was looking at their phones. I was worried everyone would want to leave, which, despite being what I wanted, made me feel desperate for them to stay. Sam whooped.

"What's happened?" Nat asked.

"Spurs just won against Arsenal."

"No way!" Jerry's voice jumped out of him, unable to contain his excitement.

They high-fived. I couldn't decide if their hands lingered longer than they should have.

"Football talk is banned, I'm afraid," Nat told them sternly.

"It's homophobic to mention football in my home," I added.

We laughed, but Sam and Jerry had syphoned off into a conversation around transfer windows, the offside rule, or something equally as tedious. I considered asking them to leave after talking football in a gay person's flat. Nat looked at me and mimed shooting herself in the head, and I laughed, pretending to be fine that Sam and Jerry were bonding.

Everyone finished eating and I collected the boxes on the coffee table. I took the last slice of cheese pizza and had a huge bite. I carried the rubbish to the kitchen, tripped, and the boxes fell from my hand. Everyone laughed, and so did I. It was the only way to wriggle out of the uncomfortable situation. When I laughed, a thick piece of mozzarella stretched into my throat, and I choked. The laughter stopped, and my face grew red as I was retching. I ran to the kitchen sink and spat out anything in my mouth. I dug my fingers in to grab the piece of melting cheese and pulled it from my throat. I coughed and ran the tap until I could breathe again. I felt Nat's hand on my back, patting hard.

"Are you alright?"

My head ducked toward the sink, trying to prevent anyone from seeing my face. Tears streamed down my cheeks.

"Don't look at me," I spluttered. Nat snorted, trying to cover a laugh, as she manoeuvred herself to be next to me, blocking the view of the others. Spit was dripping from my mouth. I was redder than I've ever been. This was embarrassing.

"I'm fine; just give me a second," I croaked.

I heard them retreating, although I didn't remember them following me. I felt water trickle down the back of my head. Once my hair was wet, I cupped the water in my hands and splashed my face. I wiped up with a tea towel and came back to sit down.

"Sorry for the interruption. My death shouldn't detract from the evening. Where were we?"

They all laughed. It was not ideal, but it broke the tension. Everyone began sharing stories of times they'd choked, or embarrassed themselves. It was really beautiful to see them all bonding over my misery. After an hour I went to shower because my T-shirt was soaked. It was nice having them all chatter while I got ready for bed. I did a quick body wash and crossed to the bedroom in a towel, eliciting whoops from Nat as she saw me pass the door. When I rejoined the group, Sam stood behind Jerry, arms held across his middle.

"Are you fucking joking?" I shouted, filled with rage, before the scene in front of me began to make sense. Sam's hands were balled together, and Nat was looking on, holding her phone.

"Now you remember the Heimlich manoeuvre..."

I laughed as though that was what I meant the whole time. They all gave a light chuckle and then got back to their instruction from Nat. I sat at the table, embarrassed but also jealous that Jerry was being held by Sam. Or jealous that Sam was holding Jerry. Being gay can be confusing.

"I better get going," said Sam, "up early for work tomorrow."

Jerry checked his watch phone. "I really ought to go too."

Sam smoothed down his trousers.

"It was nice for everyone to come along. Hopefully, I will see you all soon." I sounded exactly like my mum but not in a cool way.

"Nice to meet you all," Nat added to the chorus from the stairs as I followed them. It was windy outside, and it blew fresh air into the flat. They wandered out and crossed the road, waving. I was about to close the door when Sam patted his pockets and jogged back.

"Have you forgotten something?"

Sam came close.

"I can't believe you told her." He was quiet, but his rage was written in the deep creases that sat parallel between his brows. He must've been holding onto that for ages.

"I promise you I didn't. She guessed it was you and I said that I wouldn't say who."

"That's such a load of shit. Don't speak to me."

With a sudden burst of energy, he jogged away.

"It was in my pocket," Sam called out to Jerry.

They disappeared from view, and I trudged upstairs. I was pissed off that he'd had a go at me. Sam's anger distracted me from my worries; that he and Jerry would fall in love and walk around the island together.

"That's so crap," Nat said as we got into bed that night.

"I know. I can't believe he was so rude."

"I mean for him. I know you didn't out him to Dianne but actually I feel like she didn't need to elude to the fact she knew. It's a bit unfair."

I hummed in agreement. We'd cleared up and were just in bed and about to read our books.

"Maybe I need to give Sam a few days. But I think I'll have to talk to Dianne tomorrow."

***

The alarm sounded and I was filled with jealousy as Nat just turned over. I felt antsy all morning. Priya commented that a dark cloud hung over me. Before lunch, I made an excuse to go to the shop. I marched up the hill in a fit of justified anger, but when I saw Dianne at the till, it was replaced with a fear of confrontation. I hovered around the drinks fridge, waiting for my moment. I pretended to read a can of Coke, so I didn't feel like a creep, but I was unsuccessful. When there were no customers, I went to the till with some chocolate bars.

"Hi-hi." Her voice was flat, a return to her previously unfriendly self.

"Hey, I just, I thought I should tell you, because I don't want you making any accusations. The guy I kissed – it wasn't Sam. I think you thought it was, and he seemed confused after you said what you said, I just don't want you making yourself look silly by assuming."

The lies spilt from my mouth, and I felt like a monster. I hated lying, even to Dianne. It didn't feel right to make her feel bad, but I couldn't think of a better way to protect Sam's secret. I owed him.

"Really? Because I thought it seemed like he knew what I was getting at."

"Do you think, if you'd basically outed him, he'd just sit and smile at you?"

"Whatever," she huffed and silently scanned the rest of my shopping.

Now I had to wait for Sam to visit so I could tell him. I was planning on running a prepared speech by Nat. And who should cross my path but Sam. He crossed the street, and I doubled down and crossed over too.

"Hey," I called out and he glared at me, "I need to talk to you."

"I'm busy."

He wasn't going to make this easy.

"I need to tell you that your secret is safe."

He tried to move past, and I blocked his path. He moved to the other side, and I blocked him again.

"You can't force me to talk to you."

He had a point.

"But I need you to know, your secret is safe. I spoke to Dianne again and told her it wasn't you, and she believed me. You can relax."

"Thanks," he said with a sigh, making me not believe him.

He crossed the road and left. I watched him walk away whilst my chest stopped beating so fast. What could I do? I ate half the chocolate I'd bought on the way back to the café. I hid the bag behind me and stashed the rest in the kitchen, so that Priya didn't judge my chocolate consumption.

Nat meandered down and took her lunch to go so she could explore the island. This time her phone was fully charged. We'd planned a late-night dinner, just the two of us. I had quite a bit of baking to do since I'd ignored my responsibilities whilst Nat was in town.

I wasn't sure if I should expect Jerry just before closing. I knew he'd enjoyed the night before, but I didn't think that meant we were friends now. He seemed to be less keen, now that I'd cried on him. I was disappointed when I had to close up shop before he arrived. But I wasn't surprised. I was back to my no-man existence. Nat called me around six to be let in. She came to the café kitchen and watched me bake for a little while.

"What do you think of the island?"

"It's nice. I can see why you came."

Her answer was vague, which got my hackles up. Nat jumped up on top of the chest freezer.

"I think I could make a home here."

Nat nodded in a way that said, 'I'm not saying anything.'

"Share your opinion. You're dying to."

"Nothing, no opinion. I think it's good for you, for now."

"What do you mean?"

"You know what I'm saying. New house, new town, new job, new island. It's a lot of…new. And if you need that, then I support it. But I'm not sure how you'll feel in a few months."

My face must've been betraying my anger, as by the end of her speech, Nat's hands were raised in the air in surrender. In fairness, I was brandishing a rolling pin and a helluva scowl.

"Why does it always have to be a mistake I'll come to regret? If I do come home, that might not mean this was a mistake. I'm exactly where I want to be."

Nat shifted off the freezer and came around the kitchen counter to put her arm on my back. I leant into her and finished my cakes. We went upstairs to eat pasta 'n' sauce, which was tradition as we'd enjoyed a delicious cheesy pasta 'n' sauce regularly since living together at uni. I was expecting us to watch a film but we ended up talking until late. It wasn't until we had this uninterrupted time together that I realised how lonely I'd been. Sometimes it's nice to talk to someone who truly gets you.

The next day, as she left the café and the island, I hugged her goodbye and almost didn't want to let go. But I had no desire to go back to London.

Not yet.

5

Superstar Dies in Loser's Bed

Nat had been gone a week, and Sam and Jerry were giving me a wide berth. Every time the café door opened, I'd hoped to see either of them or even both. But not together. I'd occasionally see Sam pass by the window, but he made an incredible effort to always look ahead. At one point, he walked into a street light. I tried waving to see if he was alright, but he ignored me.

By the following Thursday afternoon, a figure hovered around the doorway. It was Sam, standing with his hands in his pockets.

"Hey, how have you been?" I asked him. The café was dead, and Priya had gone home. He glanced around to check if anyone was in earshot.

"I heard from Dianne you might've snogged Bill."

I leant forward on the counter.

"You know that's not true, right?" I asked, and Sam shrugged his shoulders. His inability to say something was starting to cheese me off.

"I told her it wasn't Bill. I think she's lied to you to gauge your reaction."

Although it was annoying that Dianne was talking to people about someone I kissed, I was glad my lie seemed to have paid off.

"Yeah, I figured. What a bitch."

Sam's anger was justified; I also had some choice words for Dianne. But I think calling her a bitch was maybe a bit sexist.

"Let's not call her a bitch. Maybe she's a dick. But I guess we all like to gossip sometimes." I surprised myself at springing to her defence.

"Alright."

He moved to the counter.

"Do you want a drink? It's on the house since you hate me."

His mouth moved to one side, subduing a laugh.

"I don't hate you."

Sam corrected the sleeve of his polo shirt that had flipped up.

"Then you don't get a free drink."

I made him laugh, breaking some tension. He ordered a tea, took out the bag and added milk and four sugars.

"Look, Sam, I'm sorry. I shouldn't have told Dianne anything. I thought I could try to make her like me and keep your anonymity. I wasn't always out. I have an idea of how you're feeling. Not that you're waiting to come out or anything."

"I know, mate. I didn't mean to make such a thing of it. I'm confused about stuff, and I don't want people saying something that might not be true."

I nodded so hard my head almost fell off.

"Totally."

"Can we be mates again?" He put out his hand for a shake. I was surprised at how much that hurt my feelings. I don't believe in the 'friend zone' and I was firmly in it.

"Of course, no hard feelings. I'm always here if you want to talk."

I don't know how successful going back to being pals would be. It's not like we were best friends to start. I felt like I'd made amends with him. Sam gave a silly salute as he left. The door slammed shut, and I realised his undrunk tea was still on the counter. What a bum hole! I almost wished we hadn't made amends.

Something about closing time brings the boys to my yard. No sooner had Sam left my sight than Jerry appeared.

"Hey, stranger." I waved with my left hand while I wiped the counter with my right.

"Am I too late for a hot chocolate?"

I considered saying yes and offering him Sam's tea.

"Never." I pointed for him to take a seat and joined him at the table with his drink and Sam's tea for myself. Jerry looked at me, then out of the window. I sipped my drink, getting ready for a chat. Jerry took out his phone. At that moment, I realised I'd invited myself to join him. This was uncomfortable. I took out my phone and performed my finest shocked expression.

Thanks, GCSE Drama.

"Look at the time. I've got so much to do."

I went to stand, but Jerry put out his hand and I squatted over my seat.

"Sorry, I didn't mean to look at my phone."

"It's fine. I actually do have stuff to sort out."

"Can I wait here for you? I'd like to have a chat, maybe?"

Fuck. It was happening. I'm pretty sure he was about to ask me out.

I stumbled back to the kitchen and giggled; I knew there was no way I was about to go on a date with Jerry Hilk. No way. I couldn't think what else he would tell me, but it wasn't that. And still, I fixed my hair in the reflection of the sink, rinsed some water around my mouth, and blew my nose. I got on with a few random cleaning bits and weighed some unnecessary ingredients. When I could think of nothing more to distract me, I returned to the café and sat with Jerry.

"Hey." I was calm and placed my hands in front of me on the table. I felt giggly. Like he might tell me someone had died, and I'd laugh.

"You done?"

I sighed.

"OK, I can't delay any longer. I guess I wanted to say sorry I've not been around as much."

He smiled and his eyes creased. That was all he said. Then it was my turn.

"That's fine. You don't have to come in every night."

"But I want to..." He hesitated. "Coming here is the highlight of my day."

"You do have a sweet tooth."

He smiled and moved his hands to the tabletop. He had a thumb ring that he turned around. Yes, thumb rings can be naff, but this one was sexy. Shut up.

"I love the cakes. I started coming here for a break and cake, but I carried on because I enjoy your company."

My stomach sank to my groin like I was plunging on a roller-coaster or driving over a steep bridge really fast on a country lane.

"I'm glad we both feel that way."

Our hands were close, and our knees almost touched. The space between us felt solid, like the final frontier I couldn't cross.

"I do like coming here, but I need to explain."

"You don't owe me an explanation, honestly."

"Being honest is important, and you're someone I find it easy to be honest with. When you were upset the other night, I liked being there for you." Jerry broke his intense eye contact before adding:

"Because of what my life is like and my reliance on alcohol, I'm not very dependable."

This was embarrassing. *Did I seem needy?*

"I got upset in the moment. I'm not desperate to be taken care of." I sounded indignant, although I didn't mean to be.

"And it's OK to be upset. I think I was just scared of letting you down."

"I don't want to be a dick about it, I appreciate you being honest, but I wasn't asking you to take care of me. I was just a sad person who you hugged."

"It's not like I think you can't live without me; I meant that it felt good to be helpful, but it freaked me out a bit too."

"OK, I appreciate your honesty, even if I'm unsure what to do with it right now."

He pushed his chair back and I had the feeling again; the air was charged. What was he going to do? Jerry leaned on the chair and bent down so our faces were level.

"I'm sorry," he said, his face closer than it had been since the night I cried, "do you want to go for a walk?"

This man was unpredictable. Not in a fun, cute, sexy, pixie dream girl way, more like if a cow were to meander into your kitchen. I couldn't understand what he wanted or what was expected of me.

"Sure." I scraped my chair back.

Before we set out, I ran upstairs to change before catching my breath and locking the café.

This was my first public outing with Jerry. Most of the people who lived on the island, who I'd begun to recognise, paid us no mind; they were used to seeing Jerry. He was pretty ignorant to it, but many tourists seemed to do a double take. We took a different path through town, one that led past my usual beach and onto a coastal path that carried around to another, quieter cove. It wasn't popular as the sun didn't reach the beach after midday. Jerry walked at the same pace as me, and I laughed as we tripped on the same patches of grass. We weren't outdoorsy people.

"What's funny?"

I explained my thinking, and he smirked. It gave me thrills to make him laugh. We continued going around a bend and went quiet as we struggled. We reached the top of the path and walked down to the sand. It wasn't a long walk, but it was becoming less fun.

"This…is quite…a workout, really," he gasped for breath.

I laughed because forming a whole sentence was beyond me at that point. However, as we climbed down, we each found our breath. By the time we reached the sand, things were easier.

"It's a hell of a walk, but the beach is much quieter," he said.

There was a man on the beach with his dog. He dipped his chin in acknowledgment as he reached the path out of the cove.

We began our exploration of the beach by taking off our shoes, leaving them by the stone steps. Jerry rolled up his jeans.

"Have you been to this beach before?" I asked, and he had. This was the farthest point on the island from Greenford Manor, where he was staying. It was an hour's walk, but he had a lot of time for walking each afternoon.

"We're not encouraged to go to the pubs, but other than that, we can wander anywhere. It's not a prison."

We walked to the far side of the beach, toward some caves.

"It does sound like a holiday in many ways."

I was joking, but he didn't seem impressed.

"It's quite intense, the therapy and stuff. Trust me, I'd rather be by a pool, although Greenford does have a pool."

"Why don't you go 'be by a pool' and pay a therapist to talk to you every morning for a few hours?"

He took his time to consider the question. I wasn't being serious when I asked, but I supposed Jerry was wealthy enough to afford that. He probably realised my idea's smart, and now he felt annoyed that he did not think of it himself.

"I needed to change my location. Sometimes going somewhere new helps. Does that make sense? I'm scared I've gone really 'woo-y' from therapy."

"Makes total sense." I laughed at the term woo-y.

The caves were dark and dank, except for the occasional glistening litter – condom and crisp packets – illuminating the way. You could wander inside easily, and then, four metres later, the sandy path turned into treacherous rock. Jerry led, and I followed. He climbed a little at the rocks and put his hand back to help me up the small step. It was a friendly gesture, and I took it gladly.

"I wonder if we're about to find treasure," I joked, "though I suppose the real treasures in life aren't to be found in caves."

Jerry didn't laugh. Instead, he yelped. Then…

"Fuck."

He half fell back toward me, and I caught him.

"What's happened?"

He sucked air through his teeth, and I could tell he was in too much pain to answer. His hand found mine and squeezed.

"You're OK," I whispered. Once his pain was bearable, we edged out of the cave.

"I stubbed my toe."

I snorted just a tiny bit.

"It really hurt." He slapped my arm.

"I know, hurting your toe is the worst."

I didn't mean to sound sarcastic; toe pain is bad. We got to the lip of the cave and inspected his foot. His big toe was bleeding. I definitely would have cried.

"Let's dip our feet in the sea. The saltwater is healing."

"Look, I know it's not a broken bone or anything, but it was dark, and it hurt."

I laughed again.

"Shall I carry you to the water's edge?"

"As if you could." Jerry doubted my ability, which was a challenge. I powered ahead, stopped right in front of him and crouched slightly.

"Jump up."

Yes, I offered him a piggyback.

"Don't be silly. We'll both die."

I turned to face him.

"Jump up." I was serious, and so Jerry jumped onto my back. I carried him for about ten steps before it felt a bit embarrassing.

"That's quite impressive," he said as he slid off my back, "now it's my turn."

"But you're injured." I pointed to his toe. He moved around so that he was in front of me.

"I can carry you." He wasn't joking. I was much heavier than Jerry. This was going to be embarrassing for us both. Christ.

I put my hands on his shoulders and jumped up. He grabbed my thighs, and I put my arms around his neck. He hobbled but managed a step, then another. He was doing it. He was carrying me. I hadn't been carried like this since I was a toddler. I felt like a dainty princess or Rose in *Titanic*. Was I the romantic lead? Without warning, he sighed and dropped my thighs. I returned to a standing position; it could've been much worse after the way he dropped me! My entire groin was tingling, and I was becoming aroused. I adjusted the jumper around my waist.

"You didn't think I could do it." He was grinning, proud of himself. I felt fizzy and self-conscious all at once.

"What are we going to do next, race to the water? See who's the fastest?"

He looked at me with a challenge written plainly in his eyes.

"Go," he shouted and sprang off. I followed and came close to beating him. He pulled ahead at the last minute as I dropped back, wary of the water. Jerry face planted into the waves, water splashing out in all directions. I've never seen someone drop like a sack of shit with quite so much gusto. I gasped. He sprang to his knees and stood, but the damage was done. He was soaked. I was bent over double, unable to breathe because I was laughing.

"Are you joking?" he giggled and wrung out his T-shirt.

I didn't stop laughing for at least three minutes. Each time I thought I'd calmed down, he'd start wringing out a sock, and I would erupt again. I sat on the sand and wiped tears from my eyes. He kicked the water, spraying me in the face. I shielded myself as best I could, but I was soaked.

"Stop!" I managed to say, between gasping for air and laughter.

"Not so funny being the wet one." He lunged, catching me off-guard. He managed to grab my wrists and pin me down. I squirmed, before bucking him off, turning the tables and pinning him down. Our faces were close, and we were gently panting. A seagull squawked, and Jerry bent his face to look around the beach. I realised what we were doing and panicked.

I can't go around wrestling customers.

I was being inappropriate, taking the joke too far. I sat up and looked out at the water. Jerry slumped down next to me. He was close. I felt I should move up. I didn't know if he did it on purpose. His legs were stretched out in front of him, and mine were crossed, my knee almost on his lap. It felt as though we fitted together. I wouldn't say it was relaxed, as every molecule of my being wanted to close the gap. But it didn't feel bad. We sat, looking out to sea until the sun sank further down and the stars began to pop out of the sky.

"We need to head back," I said, "I've got a cake to make."

I helped Jerry up, and we hobbled toward our shoes.

"This is going to be miserable, isn't it?"

"The walk back? Pure hell," he replied with a wink. And it was cold and getting darker. It was uncomfortable, but I didn't stop smiling the entire way.

By the time I got home, my skin was irritated by my wet clothes. I walked like John Wayne in a bid to avoid chafing. Jerry followed me in so he could change. I jumped in the shower and washed quickly so I could begin baking. I found some things for Jerry to change into and showed him the bathroom to freshen up. I always felt so mature getting someone a towel. I went down to the café's kitchen and started my cake. My stomach growled. I heard Jerry's voice, but I couldn't hear what he said. I heard him on the stairs.

"Thanks for these," he said, looking fit in another pair of jogging shorts and a pale green jumper that didn't fit me anymore. He'd rolled the sleeves up, and I immediately thought about sniffing the clothes when he returned them. He moved around the kitchen, opening a few cupboards and peering in.

"I should probably head back to the manor?" he asked, and I wasn't sure what he wanted the answer to be.

"I can make you some dinner if you'd like?"

"I don't want to take the piss," said the man wearing my clothes after using my shower. I realised he'd been looking around the kitchen for food.

"It's no bother, just a bit of pasta and pesto. Although I did make the pesto myself." I shrugged. So casual.

Jerry agreed to stay for food.

"I've called ahead and told them I'd be late. It'll take me an hour to get home, probably."

"Do you have a torch?"

"No…"

"I've never got a taxi here, so I don't know what they're like…" I trailed off.

I was thinking of how he could get back to Greenford, but then I thought of another more alluring offer.

"You're welcome to stay here if you…?" I didn't finish saying 'want' because I was too embarrassed that I'd offered.

"I'm not sure…" he began, and the longest pause ensued. It was excruciating. There aren't enough words in the English language to demonstrate the length of this pause. Please kill me. He added: "It would be allowed. But I might give them a call and check?"

He moved into the actual café to make the call. I had exactly the length of this phone call to freak out. Did I just invite him to have sex? I put my hands on the counter and bent at the waist to make myself at a right angle. Maybe the staff at Greenford Manor would say no, and I wouldn't have to think of the next steps. I straightened up and picked up my mixing bowl again, just in time for Jerry to return.

"All systems are go!" Jerry gave a fake punch for emphasis. "It turns out rehab works best when you don't get squashed by a truck whilst trying to get back."

"Smashing stuff."

"Yep. They can't afford to lose me; I've not paid for the whole stay yet."

I poured the mixed batter into greased tins and put them into the oven.

"Oooh, can I lick the spoon?"

He was on the other side of the kitchen counter, and I held the spoon. I gathered a good dollop together and held it out for him. Instead of taking it from my hand, he leant closer and licked the cake mix whilst holding my eye contact. If anyone else had done this, it would've cringed me out. But I looked into those eyes, and I wanted to fuck him. Or for him to fuck me. If I never saw him again, it would've been worth it. He leant back again and smiled.

"It's good. Do you lick the spoon?"

"Occasionally, when the mood strikes me."

"Right then." He stretched over, took the spoon and bowl from my hands, gathered some more cake mix, and held it up. Again, it sounds cringe, but I licked. I could feel the tension in the air. Like static in the atmosphere before a storm, we needed some thunder to release it. His hand was close to my mouth, and he went to pull the spoon away, so I put my hand over his to steady him. We would certainly be having sex later, it seemed. I took back the bowl and washed it up, sloshing the warm soapy water around in circles – entrancing. I ran through my head when I'd last touched myself. If it had been a few days, I was bound not to last very long. Jerry appeared at my side, took the bowl and wiped it with a tea towel. Amongst all our tension, it felt domestic, which weirdly was also a turn-on. His elbow caught my forearm, sending a tingle of pleasure down to my legs. My entire body was an erogenous zone.

We relocated to my kitchenette upstairs, where I boiled some pasta. When it was ready, we sat across from one another at the table.

Nervous.

"Thanks," he said.

It was getting late, and I wasn't sure what we should be doing.

"Do you want to watch some TV?" I said and cleared the table.

"Yeah, sure."

He followed me into the kitchen and sort of pushed me out of the way of the sink. He washed up. I could see bits of pasta where he hadn't binned our leftovers. I wasn't complaining. It was very polite of him to try. I then led him to the sofa, and we picked out some episode of *Grey's Anatomy* I'd been watching. It was distracting because he kept pointing out the actors he had met and explaining whether they were nice or not. He'd met them all when he auditioned to be a patient.

"I didn't get the part. My agent wouldn't let me. It was for a patient with a botched penis enlargement surgery."

"Of course," I giggled, "that would be bad for the brand."

I was distracted then, thinking about his penis. Not too distracted that I didn't cry, as I typically do during *Grey's Anatomy*. I guess it wasn't typical. I was silently crying instead of crawling on all fours and howling, which is what I prefer when I'm alone.

"Are you alright?" he was smiling.

"I'm fine," I blubbed. He laughed but it was good-natured. The credits rolled, and it was bedtime. He yawned.

"I'll set up in here but let me grab a blanket from the bedroom if that's OK?" I suggested.

"No, don't do that. It's your room; you should sleep in it."

Jerry followed me down the hall and into the bedroom.

"You're the guest."

"Honestly, it's big enough for two."

"If you're sure." My whole body jangled.

He ushered me away. I went to the bathroom, did a wee and brushed my teeth. I washed my bits and bobs in the sink in case we did have sex. I returned to the bedroom, and he was sitting on the end of the bed.

"I have a spare toothbrush if you want?" I offered him. For once, my overeager shopping habits had come in useful.

"Thanks," he said and padded off.

"It's in the bathroom cabinet," I called.

I had to decide what I was going to wear to bed quickly. A T-shirt? I wouldn't usually wear a T-shirt. I usually wear loose boxers to bed, which I call my night-time pants. I had to be careful not to say that to Jerry, as night-time pants sound like nappies. I removed my top, popped on the loose boxers, and climbed into bed. I needed to set my alarm, so I scrambled out of bed to my phone and got back in just as I heard the bathroom door opening, I didn't even have time to put on my lamp.

"Do you want these lights off?" he asked, gesturing toward the hall.

"Yes, please."

The lights clicked off, and he appeared in the doorway.

"Bedroom light off?"

"Unless you're scared of the dark?"

"Only a little."

He clicked off the light and took off his top and bottoms down to his pants.

"Scoot over," he said.

"Oh...I usually sleep on this side of the bed because I'll be getting up early for the café."

"Good point, hold on."

He climbed over me. I could feel his entire weight on my body as he straddled me. He paused and booped my nose. I laughed a lot, which was not conducive to bedtime. But, then, neither was sharing a bed, especially with a half-naked celebrity known for being sex on legs. This was not a normal bedtime. Jerry moved over and manoeuvred under the duvet. I don't know if it was the nerves, but I was practically pissing my pants, like an idiot, for what felt like ten minutes. I'm pretty sure I snorted.

"It was just a nose boop," Jerry said.

"Sorry, I'm calm now." I managed to stop the laughter.

"Good night."

"Good night," I replied. Jerry rolled onto his side, and that was it.

I lay there for about twenty minutes before his breathing slowed down. There was a ten-second pause, and I thought perhaps he had died. The headlines rushed through my head:

SUPERSTAR DIES IN LOSER'S BED

How would I explain this to anyone?

He breathed again. It wasn't until that moment that I thought, 'I'm in bed with Jerry Hilk', and about all the times I'd wished for this. And all the millions of gays and girls around the world who would be so jealous of me. I'm not proud, but I thought if I'd taken a photo, I'd probably get some cash from the *Daily Mail.* Does that make me a bad person? I wouldn't do it, but it scrolled across my mind. I listened to his breathing and remembered he was just a man. An impossibly sexy man. He was sharing my bed but had still not kissed me; that's a pretty strong indicator that he didn't fancy me. I had to give it up that we were just friends. I wasn't even certain that he was gay. Maybe he was secure in his heterosexuality that he didn't need to assert it. It felt like hours before I finally fell asleep.

6

Aroused and Afraid

My alarm sounded, and I felt horrific. I'd barely slept, silently awake, aroused and afraid of waking Jerry. I grabbed my phone, snoozed it and got back into bed. Jerry lay there, presumably awake but not moving much. I discreetly wiped my mouth and tried to return to my normal self. I drifted off again for a minute.

"Good morning," Jerry mumbled. His arm lay over me, his eyes were closed, and he was smiling.

"Good morning," I said. Our faces were too close. The sunlight snuck through the curtain and danced on the wall behind his head. I could hear the sea outside my window. He was sleepy; I was sleepy. I leaned over and kissed him gently on the cheek.

I was groggy; perhaps it was still a dream. Did I just do that? Neither of us moved. His eyes opened. God! What the fuck did I just do? The world seemed to close in around me. It was as if a bomb had exploded in the café, and the only sound I could hear was a high-pitched ringing in my ears.

"Finally," he said, lifting himself on his elbows and hovering over my face. His eyes were molten, and his hair a mess. He lowered down and kissed me. I could feel the stubble on his upper lip. I put my arms around him, drawing him closer. One hand stayed safely by the nape of his neck. The other roamed freely down. We were kissing! Our mouths parted, and he took more of my bottom lip. Slowly, his tongue found its way into my mouth. I wanted more. I had no concern over the slightest whiff of morning breath, nor did I care that I looked a mess. We were kissing as if it was the most normal thing in the world. I didn't know what to do next. Jerry moved his head away.

"Thank you." I whimpered; my gratitude reeked of desperation.

"No, thank you," he laughed.

He kissed me again. My entire body was screaming with sexual energy. I was prepared to do anything he asked me. I'd probably shoot someone square in the face if he wanted me to.

When the kissing stopped, I missed it.

"What did you mean...finally?"

He scrunched his face a little. I wanted to touch every inch of that face whilst I could, certain that this moment wouldn't last.

"I felt like I was dropping hints all day yesterday."

"I couldn't pull the moves on you," I said, unable to meet his gaze.

"But you did, just now."

I pulled my duvet up over my face.

"Don't remind me; I'm such a creep."

"You're obsessed with me." I could hear the mockery in his voice.

He pulled the duvet down and stopped around my stomach. I was topless, and the air hit my nipples. He looked down at my body and licked his lips. I couldn't move. What do you do when you're being appraised?

I felt like a rotisserie chicken.

Under the heat of his eyes, I was juicy and delicious. He paid such close attention to my body, it seemed as though he was going to draw me like one of his French girls! I rested my hands behind my head. It was a bold move I think I'd seen in a film before and found arousing.

"Finally," he said again and reached for another kiss. He put his hand on my chest and straddled me. Through our underwear, our erections were touching. It was intoxicating. My second alarm sounded. It was Nat's voice: 'Wake up, sleeping beauty, mummy loves you.' She'd recorded it as a joke, and now it was mortifying. Kill me. Jerry lunged for it, pressed a few buttons and threw it onto the floor. I almost dove after it, exclaiming 'My baby' before remembering I'd rather shag him than have a phone. I looked up at his chest and stomach. Perfectly furry. I knew he'd waxed for sex scenes!

"I have to go to work."

"Nooo." He pinned my arms above my head and kissed me again. I pretended to squirm.

"You're mine now."

He moved downwards and took a nipple in his mouth. My back arched of its own accord. He let go of my hands, and they lifted, curling into his hair. I felt the muscles in his neck flex.

"I have to go," I muttered. He kissed me again and began to roll away. I followed him until he laid on his back, and I knelt beside him.

"I'm going to set up, but then I'll come back and see what you're doing."

I slid off the bed and stood, energetically waving my arms around like a fanatical conductor to distract from how hard I was. I went to the bathroom to begin getting ready, thinking of gross things to make myself flaccid, like cleaning clogged hair from a drain or how many germs live on a computer keyboard. I greeted him again as I returned to get some clothes and felt his eyes bore into me. My erection threatened to return, so I rushed out to change in the hallway. I couldn't wait for us to be naked with one another. I'd rather be taking clothes off than putting them on.

In the café's kitchen, I was jigging around and singing under my breath while prepping for the day. I popped some frozen croissants into the oven and fired up the coffee machine. The set up went quicker than ever because I wanted to spend more time with Jerry. Being away from him, I wondered if I'd made the whole thing up. With ten minutes to spare, I grabbed a flat white and headed upstairs, half expecting no one to be there.

"Rise and sh…" I started to say.

He turned his head to the door, beaming. Instead of being in bed, he was sitting cross-legged on the floor in his underwear, facing the window…

"Oh, sorry, erm…"

I scouted for somewhere to put the cup.

"I don't mean to interrupt."

"Not at all, I was just doing some meditation, but I'm basically finished."

Did his meditation cringe me out? No, Jerry Hilk was in his underwear in my bedroom, he could've been doing a jigsaw puzzle, and I would've thought it was cool. Did I think Jerry meditated every morning? Absolutely not. It was endearing that he wanted me to be impressed by him. I placed the drink and pastry on the sideboard. He stood, and I examined his body. His torso was soft. Sparse tattoos in various styles, fleetingly once on-trend. His nipples were hard, and there was hair around them. He was tanned, and his thighs were surprisingly thick. His boxers were white and still looked fresh. I'd worn black underwear since I could remember because I couldn't keep white underwear looking new. They looked grey ten minutes after wearing them.

"Is this for me?" he asked and took the croissant.

"Well, if it was for me, it's got your grubby mitts all over it now."

"Shut up," he laughed, breaking a piece of croissant off. He stuffed it in my mouth, getting crumbs all over my lips, which he kissed away. He took a bite himself.

"I could get used to this."

"I only offer this service once; next time you stay, it'll be corn-flakes."

"Next time," he mused on those two words and panic shot through me. Had I overstepped the mark?

"I can handle cornflakes if something else is on offer?"

He stepped closer, and we kissed again. I wanted nothing more than to get on my knees right there and then. But I knew I had to go to work. I peeled myself away.

"There's no rush, but I'll need to open up soon. You can leave whenever, but you might wanna go out the front door. I think that's more discreet."

"I'm not worried about being discreet."

"It's a small island. We don't want to be the centre of gossip, is all I meant."

Except I'd assumed since I'd never heard he liked sex with men, that he wasn't 'out'. I kissed him again, wanting to move on from a potential minefield. The alarm I'd set to remind me to open the café sounded, and I pulled my face apart from his.

"I have to go."

"I'll see you later on then, possibly?" He sounded hopeful.

I nodded – a lot – and kissed him again. I walked from my bed-room, and Jerry followed me to the bottom of the stairs before heading into the kitchen. We kissed again. I knew we were being too much, but I couldn't help myself. I walked out the door and left him behind, where I immediately leaned on the kitchen counter and sighed like a person in love. Was I being too intense?

I went to the café, and Priya was behind the counter, serving a customer. I wiped the smile off my face and rushed to put on my apron. I was late.

"I'm sorry, Priya, I was a bit late getting up and messed up the opening a bit. Can you hold the fort whilst I get things sorted?"

"Of course," she said. I saw Jerry crossing the street from the corner of my eye. Priya turned and must've caught the back of him. Maybe she wouldn't recognise him, wearing my clothes? The most famous man on the island. I watched him disappear up the street, a little bummed out that he didn't look back.

"Get up to anything fun last night?'

"Nothing much," I lied, springing into action.

Although my spring was more of a sporadic movement, I knocked a cappuccino from Priya's hand, smashing the mug on the floor. As foam settled, I looked at Priya with the lie plastered across my face.

The day marched on, and we barely had a chance to speak until she was ready to go home.

"So, are you going to tell me? Did you have a visitor last night?"

Was she allowed to ask me that?

"It sounds a bit like you're asking if I got my period." I tried to joke to change the subject. She did her big infectious laugh but quickly broke out of it and held my gaze.

"I've mentioned my regular customer who comes in every night before closing, right?"

"Once or twice." She elbowed me in the ribs.

"Last night, he was here, and we went for a walk to the beach, got soaked, and he had to stay because it was late and dark. Nothing more exciting than that."

"And you were running late this morning, just on the off chance?"

"Uh-huh." I made a sort of affirmative noise, and she patted my arm.

"Was it just a little kiss, not like a full-on blow job?" She sang to the tune of 'Crush' by Jennifer Paige.

My jaw dropped as she patted for a few painful seconds before leaving to get her things.

"Have a good night," I said.

She turned in the doorway, pointing to her eyes before pointing back at me. She was watching me. I waved her off and served the customers that followed. I needed to do some work tonight. I couldn't get distracted again. I'm not the kind of person to lose my mind over a man, I lied to myself as I stared out the window, wondering if Jerry would turn up early. He didn't, but to my relief, he arrived on time. A group of teenagers sat in the café watching as he came in.

"The usual?" I asked him.

He bit his smiling bottom lip.

"Yes, please."

"Do you want to take a seat?"

"You know, I might wait here for a minute if that's OK?"

His eyes darted to the youths. It must be weird being famous. Imagine not being able to avoid young people or having to be nice to them so they don't beat you up. Whilst I whipped up his order, I could hear them asking him for selfies. I laughed. If only they knew what had happened that morning. He got up to use the toilet, and I heard them discussing how fit he was and whether he'd get with any of them. I wanted to scream he's mine! Maybe even leap over the counter, scratch somebody's eyes out, and rub my scent on him. Perhaps I was feeling territorial? When he came out of the toilet, they went quiet. Noticing that the time was 5.30 pm, I marched to the door and flipped the sign: CLOSED.

"Do we have to leave?" asked a teenage boy with a Nike cap.

"No rush. Finish your drinks and head out when you're ready."

I was proud of my customer service. However, I did cash up the till sharpish so they couldn't ask for more drinks.

By 5.45, I'd done most of my tidying. I knew I'd have to make more cake, so I told the youths and Jerry I would be in the kitchen. I was glad Jerry was there to keep an eye on them. They were not criminals, although one of them had their lusty eyes on my man. It's just that young people do stupid stuff sometimes, and I was keen to stay employed.

When I returned, they were all still sitting there.

"Who's the best dancer in *Just Desserts*?" the kids asked. *Just Desserts* was a musical that Jerry had been in, which I'd totally forgotten about. He played a pastry chef who dreamed of becoming a dancer.

"It wasn't me."

He was warm and engaging. I almost felt rude having to kick them out. I wracked my brain, thinking about removing them without forcing Jerry to leave too. I couldn't just say, "It's closed for everyone except him because he's fit." Could I? Shit.

"No rush again, but I am gonna close-up shop shortly," I said to the group. Then I began to turn away. "Except, sir, don't I owe you a free drink? Would you like to collect now?"

I was a genius.

107

"Sure, can I get a hot chocolate, please, sir?"

His eyes lit up, relishing the pretence. Usually, when you call a man you want to kiss 'sir', it's followed by a gentle spanking or light bondage. I went behind the counter and made the drink. I was only mildly irritated when the teenagers didn't leave. I remember being young and having nowhere to hang out. It's tough. But also, go away!

"Thanks," Jerry took the drink from my hand. "I'm just going to make a call. I'll be right back."

He left his drink and stepped outside. Ten minutes whipped past, and the group showed no signs of going. I felt my cheeks burning. Was I furious?

"Hey gang," I started, like a teacher, and I could see them lose respect for me instantly. I'd lost respect for myself. "Sorry to break it up, but I need to close. I've got cakes that need baking."

Have you ever witnessed a group roll their eyes in unison? It's not as fun as it sounds.

"I'm gonna take Jerry's drink," one of them said; a girl in a crop top, that made me worry she was cold, picked up his cup.

"I might just bin it. It'll be cold if he comes back for it. I'll have to make another one."

"Can I have it?" they asked.

"If you take it outside, sure."

They seemed content with the freebie and filed out as Jerry returned.

"Sorry I gave your drink away, I'll make a fresh one," I called out, so the young people would hear me.

I closed and locked the door behind the group and returned to behind the counter. I heard a bang, so I spun back to look at the front, and the teens were all laughing. They were laughing at me because they scared me. Dicks.

"Do you really want another drink?" I asked.

"Are you joking? The hot chocolate here is amazing."

I made enough for myself too. We walked into the kitchen together, and as the door closed, I felt his hands on my body. I put down my cup and turned to face him. His face was close to mine, and we grinned like idiots. He kissed me. It wasn't as urgent as it had been that morning, but he still took my breath away. His tongue was warm from the hot chocolate. It broke my heart when he moved his mouth away from mine, but then he slowly began to kiss my cheek, jaw, and neck. He exhaled; the feeling of his breath and lips on my neck was amazing. I could feel my underwear getting tighter. I wanted to have sex with him right now. I moved my hands down his back and cupped his bum. I almost didn't know what I wanted to do to him. I simultaneously wanted to touch every part of his body with my tongue while feeling him doing the same. I could barely think where to begin. His face moved away again. He stepped back. My hands held a little tighter automatically until I realised what I was doing and let him go. Jerry moved around the central island, far from me.

"I enjoy doing that," he said.

But I enjoyed doing it less since I was prepared to throw away my business so I could spend all night doing it. I wasn't the one who stepped away.

"I really ought to do some baking, I guess."

"That's a good idea. We can chat without getting…distracted."

"What do you want to chat about?"

"Erm…" Jerry pondered as he moved around and ended up sitting on top of the freezer, sipping his hot chocolate. "I spoke to my therapist about us today."

I gasped as a memory broke. Jerry had told me before about talking to his therapist about me.

"You mentioned me for a second time?"

Jerry smiled and looked down. I think he'd assumed I'd never remember.

"I did mention you before, but that was before we kissed. Maybe leading up to the kiss."

"Wow…and did they say I sounded cute and sexy?"

"For some reason, no. It wasn't a major thing. I was just a bit worried that starting something new with someone might distract me from what I'm trying to do."

I was creaming butter and avoiding eye contact.

"And what did your therapist say?"

"The advice wasn't very extensive. There are no hard and fast rules. The advice was to take things slowly and be honest about my feelings. That kind of thing."

"Really? I watched a film with Sandra Bullock, where she goes to rehab; really underrated, and they suggest that after a year of being sober to get a plant. Then, if it has survived a year later, get a puppy, and then a year later, maybe start dating."

"That is a smashing plan, and I must thank Sandra Bullock for that. Officially you're supposed to be sober after a year, which I am – more than."

"Really?"

"Yeah, this is sort of a refresher course. Staying sober has been…" Jerry searched for the words, "harder, recently."

I wanted to ask him more but could see his leg bouncing around. He hopped up and came to stand behind me as a distraction. He kissed my neck, and my insides went to jelly, but I had other worries on my mind.

"Jerry, are you even gay? Or bi? Or something?"

I needed to know. It didn't seem fair that I didn't want to get into things with Sam because he was confused, but I'd go down the same road with Jerry just because he's famous. Or rich. Or whatever it was, I didn't ask this question until now.

"I'm pansexual," he finally said on an exhale.

"Is it safe for us to be in the kitchen?"

Jerry frowned.

"With all the pots and pans…"

He laughed at me. It's such a cheap joke but a real classic.

"Why do you not talk about it? Or why have you not been pictured with anyone obviously queer?"

"What do you mean? Do you want me to be papped with you?"

"No, of course not. But what if we went for a meal together and someone took a photo on their phone? I don't want to be responsible for outing you."

"I'm careful to keep my private life private because it's my life. I'm not ashamed of being queer. I've honestly never been asked in an interview or anything."

"Yes, but that's because you've been married to women and never been photographed with a man."

I pointed my spoon at him – a perfect gotcha moment.

"Fair point. I suppose I'm purposefully not very talkative about my dating life and my marriage to a woman. But you don't keep marriages private. Also, I was younger then. I'd do things differently now."

My butter and sugar were well-creamed. I tossed in some more ingredients and stirred for a fraction of the time, determined to get something in the oven before talking all night. I tipped the batter into cases, and Jerry offered to put them in the oven.

"Middle shelf, thank you."

"I'm a natural. If the next film isn't any good, I could be a baker."

"You're a master baker?"

God, that was such a shit joke. He still laughed, but I was disappointed in myself. I rinsed out the bowl, dried it and began on my cookies.

"Sorry, I've got so much to do. I've been a bit distracted."

"No problem." He lifted a bit of chocolate from the counter and ate it before I could stop him. "Do you mind me hanging out?"

"Not at all."

I showed him how I liked to prepare my cookies and left him to lay them out on a tray whilst I started on the brownies. It was helpful having him around.

"Melting chocolate? Are you feeling *witchy?*" Jerry asked as I added butter to a bowl of molten dark chocolate.

"Yes, I am. You should be careful."

I finished baking in record time, and we relocated to the flat, where I made a stir fry.

"That was fantastic," Jerry said, impressed with the dinner I'd thrown together. It was quite a crap meal, but I added some pineapple to the stir fry, making it seem like I knew what I was doing. The shop-bought sauce did most of the heavy lifting, to be honest.

"You're very welcome."

Jerry took the plates to the kitchen. I went to get up, and he insisted I stay right where I was. I watched him wash up. I was excited to watch him do the most mundane domestic tasks. Not because he's a Hollywood star, but more that it was like a window into our future together. He does the washing up. I put the kids to bed. He cleans the bathroom whilst I hoover the living room. We collapse on the sofa after a long day of chores and kiss until we could resist no longer and make love. My daydream was so potent that I hardly realised he was finished. He left the kitchenette, walked behind my chair and started to massage my shoulders. We went to lie on the sofa and kissed some more. It felt amazing, but I was slightly worried that I'd cum in my pants if we didn't do a bit more soon. Jerry pulled away.

"I'm enjoying myself. I could do this all night."

"Same," I agreed, although I couldn't survive much longer like this.

"Which is why it sucks that I need to go."

"What? Why?"

Did I sound panicked? I felt panicked between the kissing and the fear of it coming to an end. I worried about the stress on my heart. Physically but also in a metaphorical sense.

"I have a room that I'm staying in. I think it looks like I'm un-focused if I keep staying out."

"Right, I guess that makes sense."

I don't know if it did. Why was he like this? I could feel myself beginning to hate him. This was quite common for me. When I liked a man, it was sometimes easier to be annoyed at him than to feel the full extent of my feelings. Like when I'd scream at Rob for 'not putting away the washing' so I didn't have to ask why he'd stopped holding my hand earlier that day.

"You could. I dunno if this was forward of me, but I checked before I left. You can come and stay over at Greenford Manor some-time."

He was blabbering a bit which was cute. I think he was nervous – as if I'd say no!

"Yeah, I think that would be great. Not tonight, though, up early for work and all."

"That's cool," he said. He was lying on top of me, so I patted his bum.

He sat up, and I joined him in the land of the vertical.

"I guess I should make a move then?"

"Do you want me to walk halfway back with you?"

He agreed, and we set out.

The path led from the town towards a pub and beyond into some winding lanes. I still hadn't explored the little island fully. It was hard to see much, but we each used our phones as a torch to guide our feet. We chatted about London, the things we missed and those we didn't. It was strange to talk about; I felt so far removed from my old home. It was comical to hear how different our experiences had been. Jerry didn't have any stories from the night bus, and I didn't have any experience of using a black cab. It was like talking about London with a time traveller. That's how foreign his experiences were to me.

"I feel like we're in different worlds."

"You're hardly down the mines every day, working in TV! Just because I went to a premiere with Beyoncé, and you only stood outside with a camera."

"SHUT UP – YOU'VE MET BEYONCÉ?" I screamed, and I wasn't even embarrassed.

"Just a couple of times at award shows. It's amazing, but we don't sit at the same table and chat. I don't want to oversell it. I've never been invited on holiday with her."

"If we weren't in public, I'd fully suck your dick just for being in the same room as her."

"Thank you, it's an honour that you would even offer."

I demanded he tell me what she smelt like, who she spoke to, and everything else he remembered. The only break in conversation was when he grabbed my hand, and I instantly lost my train of thought. I looked ahead on the country road and behind. No one was there. I didn't want to ask if that's why he was holding my hand.

"This is halfway."

"Really? Feels like we've not been walking too long."

"I promise. You need to get home. I can't keep you out all night."

He leant in and kissed me – no tongue – before pulling away.

"Well, I shall see you soon," I said.

"Should we…swap numbers?"

I agreed as if it were no big deal. However, I did want to text Nat and tell her I had Jerry Hilk's phone number in my phone.

"When do you think you should come and stay?"

"I could do Saturday night if that's any good?"

It was Wednesday, so not too long to wait. I hoped we'd have sex sooner than that, but beggars can't be choosers. We agreed on Saturday so we could lie in on Sunday. It was oddly formal for a first planned sleepover and potentially doing anal. I didn't even know if he was a top or bottom. This level of mystery must be what it's like for straight people to date. Because usually, I would meet men from Grindr, and we'd have covered the basics before I got off the sofa. Jerry kissed me again, and I walked home.

7

Fattest Person in the Room

For days, all I thought about was staying over at Jerry's. I'd managed not to text Nat about it because I was scared to admit how big a deal I thought it was. Jerry still came in each night for his coffee, and we'd kiss in the kitchen before he trudged back. The next morning, it would be a battle not to tell Priya.

By the time Saturday arrived, it was like Christmas morning. I'd planned the outfit and counted the minutes until work finished. I showered and changed into a jumper and shorts. I sprayed a little bit of Glow by J.Lo and collected the bag I'd packed. It wasn't a serious bag like I was moving in – my book (*Happy Fat* by Sofie Hagen, if you were curious), moisturiser, Vaseline, condoms, toothbrush, toothpaste, lube, and a change of pants. I was ready. I texted Jerry to let him know I was on my way and started walking.

After a minute without reply, I worried he'd given me the wrong number. I cursed myself for not texting him all week. I had been proud of myself for being so cool and elusive. Every day I'd panic around closing time and go to text him, but then he'd come into the café, and I'd regain my composure. I'd been so patient, not texting, but now, I was on a woodland path, alone and without a text. I reminded myself that he was a celebrity and probably wasn't used to giving out his number. I kept walking, even though I doubted he'd turn up.

I called Nat to take my mind off things, although she was getting ready for a date night with her boyfriend. They were going to this restaurant at the end of her road, which I thought was rank, but they both loved it. I should say *their road*, as Emmanuel had recently moved in. I asked her whether he was a good flatmate (yes, he was), what his best housemate quality was (cooked the best Nigerian food ever) and whether they'd been arguing (no, they hadn't). I didn't tell her about my plans, I knew I could trust her, but I didn't want to make the night a bigger deal than I already felt it was. I needed to feel as though it was casual. As we said goodbye, she giggled over something adorable Emmanuel had done. I guess that he'd be in the background of all my calls with Nat from now on,

I considered throwing my phone against a tree. I stopped because I love nature, and it held Jerry's number.

Up ahead was the halfway spot Jerry had told me about. He was nowhere in sight, and still no text. I carried on but mentally decided I wasn't going into Greenford Manor until I received his reply. I pretended I didn't care if he replied, but my heart soared when my phone pinged. He sent me a message:

Shit. Fell asleep. Coming now xx

He double kissed me. That was my first ever text from Jerry Hilk. I was going to get it tattooed on my body in Sanskrit.

I walked another ten minutes until I saw him coming around a bend. He waved, and I waved. We drew closer, shouted hello and repeated ourselves as we came closer still. When I eventually stood in front of him, he looked around briefly before leaning in to kiss me on the cheek.

117

"Good evening," he said.

I grinned like a dolt. We walked and chit-chatted as though we'd been married for fifty years. I was almost disappointed to arrive at Greenford.

"It's just up here." He pointed at the longest drive I've ever seen. So long, I didn't see the manor until the last third of the driveway. I was so sweaty there was hardly any point in showering before leaving. He kept glancing at me.

"Are you OK?" he asked for a third time.

I knew why I was nervous, but he had always seemed so relaxed about sobriety. Today, his need for reassurance gave him away. The manor came into view, and I wondered what the difference was between a manor and a castle. Greenford was definitely bordering on a castle. It was built from large yellow stones, and the hedges were neatly manicured and clipped into cylindrical shapes. The wooden front door looked heavy, and an automatic glass door opened as we approached.

Everything was white except for the dark wooden floors. There was a reception area straight ahead of us with staff standing behind it wearing white scrubs; they beamed at Jerry as we entered. Everyone here knew him better than I did, in a way. For the first time, I doubted whether I'd be able to help him with his sobriety. Being in Greenford with him, I realised how out of my depth I was.

"Do you want to put your stuff down, and I can give you the tour?" he offered. I agreed. He led me to a stairway off the main hall with a dark green carpet running down the centre. Upstairs, things were still all white except for the various wooden sculptures dotted around. We walked along a corridor and up another flight of stairs, where he pulled out a key card, opened it, and beckoned me inside. His room was the entire top floor.

"You can put your bag anywhere," he said as we strolled through the sitting area.

We'd arrived in the middle room. After a quick lap of the floor, two bedrooms were on one side with a shared bathroom and a kitchen. Then there was the seating area, another with a dining table and a master room with a four-poster bed and an en suite bigger than my flat. Running along the entire suite was a balcony with views of the back of the property. The interiors were white and wooden, really committed to the theme. I couldn't quite explain what it was, but everything felt luxurious. The decor looked simple but cost £10,000 for a door knob. Like when a supermodel wears tracksuit bottoms, people think they look cool, despite looking bland. The wooden floors seemed to have magically worn down to just the right amount of distress. The paint had no scuff marks. There were no hard edges. All of the furniture seemed rounded. The towels were impossibly fluffy and also white. The dining table was oval and had the appearance of being worn. It reminded me a little of a theme park, where authenticity is sacrificed to aesthetics.

"Do you want to take a look around? Or go for dinner? Or have dinner sent up?"

"Can we…have dinner downstairs, look around and then, if I'm still staying, maybe have breakfast sent up?"

"That sounds like the best plan, and of course, you're staying. No pressure, there are other beds if you'd rather …"

"I don't think I'd rather anything." I moved closer to him.

"That doesn't make sense," he responded, wrapping his arms around me. We were kissing. I will never tire of reporting that. We kissed until I had to come up for air. I was in two minds about skipping dinner, but I knew I'd have more energy for sex if we ate first.

Also, I'd been googling the menu all day.

We made our way downstairs to the restaurant. It was at the back of the manor, through a pair of French doors leading to the grounds. The tables were decorated with candles inside large jars nestled on stone beds. Food smells wafted from the kitchen, garlic, lemon, bread. The guests had perfectly coiffed hair and wore big sunglasses, even inside. There was a lot of beige and cream clothing and, surprisingly, very few stains. I wasn't going to fit in here. We sat and sipped the weird starter smoothie thing they gave us, although it tasted of death and buttholes. Looking at the other patrons, I was the fattest person in the room by a country mile. Jerry wore black jeans and a cream shirt, but they were obviously designer, so he fitted in well. I was wearing a matching lilac terry cloth jumper and shorts. I'd picked it because it reminded me of wearing comfy PJs. I wore the waistband high, and it felt like I had trapped gas.

"You look cool, by the way," Jerry said as he laid his napkin on his lap.

"Thanks, you too."

"I mean it," he said, staring intently at me. I guess I looked self-conscious. I'd been to nice restaurants before, but I thought Greenford would be like a spa, and everyone would wear dressing gowns. I ignored my slight embarrassment and stared at the menu, although I'd already memorised it. There was an option for a baked goat cheese salad or a simple pasta dish, but I couldn't decide. Pasta would be more filling, but baked cheese was my weakness.

"Why don't we order both and share?" Jerry suggested as if it was nothing. I know we'd kissed a few times, and I was hoping to suck his soul out of his body via his genitals, but I didn't often share a plate of food.

120

"Great idea," I said because I wanted to look cool and relaxed. And as the food appeared, I didn't mind sharing. The goat's cheese came with peppers, red onion, pomegranate, loud crunchy croutons, and a raspberry balsamic glaze. The pasta had cherry tomatoes and oil on it with pearls of mozzarella. It sounds dull, but if you imagine each dish cost around £30, the ingredients were top-notch. I think the mozzarella was buffalo, but I'd never had it before, so I couldn't be sure.

"Fuck, this food is great. I can't believe I cooked for you when you have this every night!"

"It's not that filling, though, is it?"

I tilted my head to the side, slurped my pasta, and crunched my croutons. The waiter walked past, and I flagged him down.

"Do you mind if we get some bread?"

The waiter looked at my stomach and wasn't subtle about it.

"If you're sure you'd like some," they said.

"Yep," I reassured them, and they scurried off.

Fucking dick.

"No one has ever asked for extra bread. You're a rebel." Jerry was oblivious to my exchange.

"It's a nice place. We deserve to feel full," I replied righteously.

"I love that you don't care about eating bread."

This will sound conceited, but I have to be honest. He looked at me the way people in a comedy show audience looked at me. They're smiling, but they don't realise it. All of their attention is on you. And it's as if you can hear their thoughts, and they're saying to themselves 'I didn't know I could be this happy.' And Jerry's face was saying the same thing right then. It felt incredible because I knew I was pulling the same face.

"I care deeply about eating bread. You know you can eat bread *any* time you want."

He took my hand across the table. I moved away.

"What about keeping your private life private?"

"People aren't allowed phones here," he shrugged.

Without a doubt, my phone was in my pocket. I was going to protest, but it was his life and decision. Instead, I replaced my hand and let him hold it. And the sky didn't come crashing down, and everything was ok. It seemed everything was perfect. Emphasis on the 'was'.

My stomach gurgled. I coughed to cover the sound, but my face, contorted in discomfort. It was hard to ignore.

"What's wrong?"

"My tummy." I whimpered, trying to make it sound cuter than it was. "I'll just be two minutes."

I sprinted to the bathroom as soon as I was out of sight. I was up on the first floor when I realised I didn't have the key, so I sprinted back to reception.

"Do you have any toilets?" I asked through huffing breath. The receptionist pointed, and I was off again.

I stormed into the toilets just off the lobby and into a cubicle. I didn't have time to lay toilet paper on the seat or anything. I swooped down my shorts, and a torrent of shit left my body before I'd even sat on the seat. I won't be too graphic. But it was horrendous. I had to rip off my jumper because I was in a real sweat. I lost track of time. I had no idea how long I'd been.

When I felt, finally, as though I could take a break from being on the toilet, I pulled at the loo roll. When I went to wipe, the stall was too small. I had to bend around, scraping my entire hand, arm and shoulder along the cubicle, trying to wipe myself. I grazed the back of my hand on something sharp and it started to bleed. I was filled with rage. Greenford Manor had made me feel too big for the restaurant, and now I was too big to wipe my own ass. Would this humiliation never end? I found an ingenious way to feed my trapped hand toilet paper, but it wasn't good enough. As desperate as I had been to expel that shit from my body, I was now as desperate to go back to Jerry's room and try to feel clean again. I flushed and waddled out of the cubicle, slamming the door in an act of empty revenge.

Looking in the mirror, my T-shirt had sweat stains, and the colour had drained from my face. I couldn't go back to the restaurant like this. I got myself sorted as best I could and left the toilets. Reluctantly, I flagged down our waiter in the doorway to the restaurant and asked him to tell Jerry I was waiting in reception. He appeared two minutes later, smiling.

Explaining to Jerry why I had to leave after dinner was pretty embarrassing, but he just laughed and rubbed my back as we went to sit upstairs. I felt revolting. I considered going home. Back in the room, I had a shower in the bathroom furthest from his room. The products were expensive, and the shower was more complex than my laptop. The water spray came from above and also shot out of the sides. I felt cleaner than ever as I stepped into the lounge wearing PJs; the dressing gown didn't fit.

"You look cosy." Jerry looked me up and down and patted the seat beside him. I plonked myself down, and he immediately leaned in. I felt better, but my stomach wasn't entirely settled.

"I don't think tonight will be as fun as I thought it was," I said, pulling away.

"Oh," he moved back, hurt, "you're not having fun."

Shit.

"No, no, no, that's not what I meant. I'm saying I don't think we're going to be able to have even more fun because I'm not feeling super great. I've had a fantastic night. I'm just annoyed that it's been ruined."

The concern dropped from his face.

"No worries, we can just relax and watch TV. I'm not expecting anything."

And we did exactly that. We watched *Bridesmaids* and chatted throughout. Halfway through, we paused it, and Jerry ordered some cakes to the room. It was awkward around bedtime. It's one thing to fall into bed with someone, but it's much more intimate to potter around one another, brushing teeth before grabbing a quiet moment to do the final wee. Despite my shower and stomach-settling, it still didn't feel particularly romantic. We got into bed, just pants, and kissed again. We talked for a little while, or so I thought. Only when Jerry got up to use the loo again did I realise it was 2 am. He climbed back in, and after another hour of chin-wagging, we finally drifted to sleep.

8

The Incredible Hilk

When I woke, Jerry was still asleep. I stayed in bed as long as I could. I enjoyed the heat radiating from his body until my bladder eventually drove me into the bathroom. Tucking myself back into bed, I spent some time on my phone, replying to Nat and scrolling online. He rolled over, now awake. I lifted my arm, and he curled up into my armpit.

"Good morning," he mumbled, clearly struggling to come around.

"Hello, sleeping beauty."

We took our time getting out of bed. I eventually demanded we get up because things were getting steamy, and I was still not ready for sex. We called down for breakfast. I ordered toast with fried eggs and some vegetarian sausages. I also asked for some fruit and yoghurt. If I played my cards right, I'd get enough good food this weekend that I would only need toast for tea later – ideal since I had nothing else.

Jerry got some avocado with eggs.

After eating and dressing properly, Jerry pounced on top of me on the sofa, and we kissed again. Neither of us seemed to want to progress things further. I wasn't sure how much more I could take, but also, I was beginning to feel scared to make the next move. I wished I'd get out of my own way. Either my mind or my bowels seemed determined to keep me celibate. We eventually wandered the grounds before returning to the hotel bar and ordering lunch. I'm happy to report this meal did not end in diarrhoea. We went back upstairs to his room and napped. It was perfect. I woke in the afternoon, watching the dust swirl and settle in the sunlight, our bodies intertwined on the sofa.

"I should probably make a move home."

"Do you want me to walk you?"

"Sure."

We lounged for a while and kept promising one another that we were about to get up. Finally, I stood. Jerry pulled me back down, and after some additional snogging, I got back up again, and we left the hotel. We walked hand in hand for a little while, with stops for kissing and smacking each other's bums, all kinds of fooling around.

We reached halfway, but it took double the amount of time.

"Do you want me to walk you a little further?" he asked. I need to tell you that I'm aware we were nauseating. It was very early days and exceptionally honeymoon-y.

"You shouldn't. You'll only get to the café, and then I'll have to walk you home, and we'll be exhausted."

"True," he took my hand, "why don't I stay with you?"

I was too excited to question why Jerry wanted to spend two nights in a row. Were we honeymooning? Or was this his addictive personality? Was that a real thing? I was too blissfully happy to care.

We got back. I showered, he showered, we had some tea, and finally ended up in bed. We chatted, and kissed. He was on top of me, our lips met, and his tongue gently touched mine. I ran my hands down his back and under his pants. His bum felt furry and firm. He brought his knees up, lifted my thighs and moved his hand under my shirt. He moved to kiss my neck, and my breathing was heavier, louder. I ran my hands up and down his back. Jerry continued to move down my body with his kisses. It was happening. He tugged at my underwear, and with a bounce, he pulled them down. I was nude. I thought to cover myself up, but before I could move, he bent his head and kissed my stomach. He moved further down my thigh and kissed his way up. He dug his mouth right where my leg met my torso, and my body tensed as a wave of pleasure rose inside me. I was about to ask him to stop because it felt too good when he opened his mouth, and…I moaned, clutching at the bedsheets.

"Hold on," I said. He looked up at me, then, with a grin, released me from his mouth.

"You OK?' he asked.

"It's too much. I need to focus on you." I smiled, getting up onto my elbows, ready to move. I grabbed the back of his neck and pulled him into a kiss, laying him on his back. I pulled off his boxers right down to his feet. Then I stopped and looked at him.

"What?" he asked.

"Nothing, just enjoying myself," I said. I bent and brought my mouth to Jerry's body, mimicking his actions. Jerry confirmed his enjoyment when he groaned and ran his fingers through my hair. His body reacted to my actions, involuntarily arching. In hindsight, I never thought, 'So, this is sex with Jerry Hilk.' Following my instruction, Jerry flipped onto his front. Moving to lie on top of him, I started kissing his earlobe and then down his back. I grabbed his butt and kept kissing. He called my name, and I couldn't wait any longer. After getting a condom, I began thrusting slowly, then stopped to kiss him. We moved in tandem, losing and finding our rhythm repeatedly. Waves of pleasure swooshed through my body, threatening to spill over.

"Oh my god," I breathed – such a cliché. My eyes rolled, my pelvis thrust forward. I was legally blind for at least 15 seconds. No memory of the noise I made or what my name was, just waves of pleasure. As I came back to my body, still feeling sensitive.

"Your turn," I was able to say eventually, as I kissed him, then focussed on his body.

Before long, his breath became ragged, and I could feel his toes tensing. I almost worried that he wasn't enjoying himself, but he called out, clutching my hand. He finished. I placed my hand on his stomach. He twitched, and I laughed.

"I'm very sensitive right now," he laughed.

"Noted." I kissed him on the cheek, slow, so as not to shock him.

Our heart rates returned to normal. Jerry looked into my eyes.

"I can't believe that was my first time."

My eyes went wide, and my mouth dropped.

"Just kidding," he said with a smile.

I laughed so much that I had to clutch my stomach. He kissed my cheek. I loved that he made me laugh. I'd had sex with men before, obviously, but they'd never made me laugh like Jerry did. Later, I waited in bed as he fetched us some water. He came back in naked and I stared at him.

"Stop looking at me," he laughed.

"Why would I ever do that?"

"You're being a creep."

"Alright, sorry then." I covered my eyes.

He lay next to me. We kissed and began to get drowsy. At one point, I got up, brushed my teeth and set my alarm, and Jerry followed suit. Then we had sex again before falling asleep.

128

We continued to see each other every day. Most evenings, we'd meet up and eat together, and then I'd walk him halfway. And yes, the sex was mind-blowing. Priya noticed a spring in my step and tried not to complain when I didn't make enough cake.

"You seem more relaxed, more at home," Priya said during a quiet moment.

"Did I not seem that way before?"

"I wasn't sure if you felt settled. Some people move here, and their lives are so different that they can't get on. We all dream about making big changes, but the reality sometimes doesn't match up."

"You're so wise, Priya."

"I'm wasted in this café. Right, empty cups at empty tables." She sang to the tune of 'Empty Chairs at Empty Tables' from *Les Mis*, using all the bass her voice could muster.

Priya bustled out amongst the tables, and I watched her for a minute. Even wiping tables, she had a commanding presence. She held court with the customers: firm but never rude. She was wasted in the café, but I couldn't quite place her elsewhere. Over the weeks, Priya had mentioned living in Paris, Istanbul, New York, and old York, but I'd never imagined her anywhere but No'Man. She'd become a life coach for me, but I think she was too charismatic to be doomed to listen to other people's problems.

Priya walked into the kitchen, and when she walked back out, she'd scooped her copious black hair into a pineapple on her head. She did a box step and jazz hands and then took her place behind the counter.

"You're the best."

"I know." She smiled.

I started baking, which I was getting better at. I was now so practised at the café nothing took me long. I let my mind wander and realised I'd not clued in Nat about my recent sexcapades. I found her on my phone and gave her a call.

"Hello, baby," she answered.

"Hey, my love, do you have a bit of time?"

"Yes, of course," she said with a strong hint of concern.

"Nothing bad. I thought I'd tell you something. I've been seeing Jerry."

The line went quiet. I didn't know what to make of her silence. I heard heavy breathing and maybe a door close. Then...

"NO FUCKING WAY!!!!!" she screamed. "Sorry, I had to leave my desk to react. Are you kidding me? What's he like? How long? What's happening?"

I explained how we'd been spending time together and answered all of her probing questions. 'Was he circumcised?' 'Should I call him the incredible Hilk?' 'Is he interested in some kind of wife swap agreement?' that kind of thing.

"I knew something was up. You kept calling me on these random walks. I know you don't like walking."

"Sorry for the secrecy; I wasn't sure what to say yet. I'm not sure what he's thinking about everything."

"Inexcusable. You must always tell me first; how else will you really know how you feel about things."

"An excellent point. And obviously, you can't mention it to people. I feel this huge pressure to keep his secret. He doesn't want his business being known by everyone."

"Of course, no need to alert the media until you know what's happening for the two of you."

"I also want to say sorry if I've gone a bit quiet."

"You haven't, really. I could tell something was up, but you're entitled to two weeks of less in-depth texting. Our love is long-lasting and long-distance. Just keep me in the loop. You don't have to figure out everything on your own."

I heard Nat's boss Thandi in the background asking questions.

"I have to get back," Nat said to me.

We said our goodbyes. I drummed my hands on the counter. It felt like I'd arrived at that point with Jerry where I could no longer continue doing what we were doing without asking some questions. It felt too soon in many respects. I didn't want to seem clingy. But his need for secrecy meant I had to ask the questions and figure out who I could let in. I was nailed to the spot, chewing the inside of my cheek, when Priya popped her head into the kitchen.

"Can I get a hand, George?"

I jumped into action on the till, chatting to people and serving them as quickly as I could. It stayed that busy for the rest of the afternoon. Even as Priya left, I could barely wave as we had so many customers. I reached the sweet spot where I could serve customers whilst making drinks orders. I was in my zone. It felt as though I'd grown extra arms. I was making great drinks and even greater chit-chat.

I'd hit peak barista.

Customers had begun to thin out when Jerry arrived. He joined the end of the queue, and I smiled at him from behind the counter. As it always happened, he was the last person to come in.

"The usual, please," he said when he got to the front of the queue. I was being gushy and giggly as I put his order through the till, with a discount, because we were regularly fucking.

"Could you do me a favour and turn the sign to closed, please?" I asked, and he obliged. All the customers were served, I handed off

Jerry's drink, and we headed into the kitchen and set up for my nightly baking.

"So, Jerry, how are you doing?"

"Well, George, thank you for asking. I'm doing swell," he laughed but abruptly stopped when I didn't. I continued to knead the bread. Jerry took a few seconds, surprised by my conversational interruption.

"And, how are you?" he asked.

"I'm totally fine, feeling good. The only thing that could impact my mood is what we're about to talk about. But no pressure."

"You're scaring me," Jerry said, sliding from his seat and standing in front of me.

"I feel like it's too early to ask this. I don't want you to think I'm *kneady*." I smiled, pushing my palms into the bread. Jerry let out a loud and singular "HAH."

"Still…I kind of want to ask you, what are we doing? And I am usually so much more chill than this, but I'm also aware that your time here is finite, and my time here isn't."

"So, we're finally doing it – the 'what are we?' conversation."

Jerry drummed his hands on the counter, presumably because his leg was busy standing, and he couldn't jiggle it.

"I can't have the conversation alone. You have to agree to take part. Don't feel forced."

"I can have this conversation; this is what I've been waiting for. Is it too soon? I don't know. But I've been practising."

"Practising?"

"You've come up in therapy. Just once or twice, don't get a big head about it."

"You're obsessed with me." I was smiling like an idiot and joking, but I also felt reassured that he'd given us some thought.

132

"As if you haven't told all your friends, you probably write Mr and Mr Hilk all over your notebook."

"I actually haven't. I only told Nat today. I didn't want to get ahead of myself because I feel this may be short-term for you."

My cheeks were a little red, and I could feel sweat prickle on my lower back. Jerry put his hand out behind my elbow, ushering me closer.

"I don't want it to be. I don't know what we're doing necessarily, but I'm having a good time and I'd like to be a bit more formal."

"Like refer to each other as m'lord?" I make jokes when I'm unsure what to say. Don't judge me – it's usually endearing.

"I was hoping you'd refer to me as sir."

I bowed my head in a mocking submission.

"Yes, sir."

"Seriously though, I am serious about wanting to be serious. Let's be monogamous.'

"Yes, let's be," I agreed, which was easy, not just because I had no other options. "One thing I'm wondering now, how long are you going to stay here?"

"I've got another month planned. But I'll start having weekends away from the island in two weeks. It's like a staggered release."

"That's sensible."

"We could do a weekend away together? If you can get any time off?"

Oh my god, it was happening. I'd dreamt of a mini-break with Jerry since I first saw him on the ferry. Who am I kidding? Since I was fourteen, I've fantasised about going for a mini-break with Jerry Hilk! He was in a film opposite Amy Adams, where they fell in love in a house in the Cotswolds, and I wanted to be her so badly. I even bought the same giant oversized straw hat she wore in the film. I looked ridiculous.

"That could work." I didn't want to give too much away. "I guess what I really want to know is what happens after this month?"

"Dunno. I want to keep trying. It might not always be easy, but we've got something good here. I don't often feel this way about someone after knowing them for such a short time."

"That is reassuring," I said just in time for Jerry to snog my bloody face off.

The conversation seemed done; although nothing concrete had been decided, it was good to know we were on the same page. And that was it. We were official, sort of. Did I panic daily about whether we'd stop seeing each other? Of course. But for the most part, we were fine. We started to hold hands in public more often. We went for dinner at both the island restaurants and Greenford Manor.

***

The next week, in a full honeymoon-y type daze, Jerry took me on a date. It had been warm, but the evening brought in a cool breeze. I'd thrown on an oversized pink jumper, and we walked hand in hand to the ice cream shop to get a scoop each. I had a lick of his. He had a lick of mine. He made me laugh, and I dropped my cone. He promised to get me another one but first moved in for a big kiss. Jerry returned to buy my scoop and I saw Dianne had clocked us. She was juggling shopping bags, purse, and phone, looking overwhelmed.

I felt particularly smug the next day when I went into the shop.

"You're awfully pleased with yourself," she said scanning through my milk, bread and eggs.

"Sorry, I'm in a good mood. I'm not just trying to annoy you."

"You don't have to try to be annoying," she said without a smile. She wasn't making a clever joke; she was being a dick.

Emboldened by the lust in my life, I looked her square in her eyes.

"What is your problem with me, Dianne? I can't work out if you're homophobic, fatphobic or just mannerphobic?"

"I'm not any kind of phobic. I just think people should earn what they get."

"I've got literally nothing, so I don't have to earn anything."

"You're so ungrateful as if that café is so beneath you. I would've been so much better at managing it than you."

"Well, next time, make sure to apply."

"I did, you arsehole."

Dianne swiped my feta cheese through the till and shoved it down the conveyor with such force it left a small welt on my hand.

"I didn't know that, but it explains a lot," I shouted back, slamming my card on the card reader. Once I heard the beep, I stormed out of the shop, my chest rising and falling too quickly to breathe. I don't think I'd ever had a screaming match with someone I didn't like, not as an adult. I walked down the street, away from Dianne's view and sat on a bench. I waited to calm down. It took a long time, and I was glad I gave myself the time. It was nice to take a moment on No'Man. The sea breeze had a soothing effect.

I wanted to call my mum. I hadn't spoken to her since before coming to the island. I used to call her every time I had a bad day. Eventually, I left the bench, but things with my mum hung heavy on my mind. Seeing Jerry was the first good thing to happen in months, and I hated not being able to tell her about it.

That night, as Jerry drifted off to sleep, I called her. I turned my phone over and over in my hand but couldn't bring myself to press the call button. I read her texts to me, asking for a call. Guilt sat like a weight on my chest. But each time I thought to call or text, our last argument flashed through my mind.

***

I had been at home for the weekend. That Friday, I had a very challenging work week. It wasn't horrific, just incredibly boring. I'd been threatening to quit and work as a freelancer for a long time, so I printed my resignation letter and handed it to my line manager. My mum flipped out.

"You can't quit your job without another job to go to," she screamed.

She had a good point in fairness, but the damage was done. I needed support, not maternal rage.

"I need a change. I'm going to get something else, but I need to do something."

"Of all the stupid things you've done. I can't afford your rent, George. I can't afford to keep you."

"I never asked you to. Can you stop shouting at me about something that hasn't happened? Just because you've never taken a risk in your life."

"What a luxury to take risks." She was on her feet. "I couldn't take any risks because I had you."

"Doesn't it make sense then that I quit my job now rather than when I've got kids?" I screeched back, standing up to match her.

"Do you think you're even remotely responsible enough to be a parent? You're still acting like a child."

"Eat shit, Mum. I don't have kids, so I don't have to think about them, but how dare you imply I'd be anything other than an incredible dad."

"You never finish anything. You never stick with anything. The first sign of trouble, and you run off. That's hardly responsible behaviour."

I was shaking. I had no idea that my mum saw me this way.

"You're just sour because you can't tell your friends I work in TV anymore."

"No, now I'll have to tell them you're unemployed. You're right. What a shame."

"I'm not ashamed."

"Well, you should be."

I didn't reply for a minute. I glared at her catching my breath.

"Well, I'm not," I whispered.

"Don't you dare twist my words" Mum shouted. I stood, took my already-packed bag and walked out.

***

Nat eventually told Mum that Rob and I had broken up and I had moved to the island. Would Nat tell her about Jerry and me if I waited long enough? I put down my phone and climbed into bed.

I couldn't sleep. My brain searched far and wide for incidents of humiliation and shame to replay on a loop. I got stuck remembering a time I bullied my neighbour when we were eight. Guilt pinned me to the pillow, and I stared up at the ceiling. To move my thoughts on, I scoured my mind for something even more tumultuous. Rob, and his dumping me, had been my go-to sad thought, but I realised that I'd not thought of him in weeks. This bit of good news allowed me to move. I turned away from Jerry, who was peacefully asleep and nudged my bum toward him.

Since Rob was no longer triggering, I thought about Sam. I'd told him we couldn't be together since he wasn't out, and then I promptly started having sex with Jerry, who was famously not out. I rubbed my eyes in the dark, stifling a loud yawn.

Behind me, Jerry stirred, but then his breathing deepened.

Back to Sam: I'd not seen him in the café for a week, and the last time we'd crossed paths had been a Sunday. It was the first time Jerry and I had held hands in front of everyone, walking through town. My palms were sweaty with nerves, and it didn't help that it was now properly summer. I'd seen Sam walking toward us, but our agreement meant I couldn't wave. I usually managed to catch his eye and nod, but he'd avoided my gaze. I wouldn't have thought more of it, except he crossed the street to avoid us. Jerry didn't notice it, but I felt his snub.

The moment began to loop around my mind again, and I wished I'd stopped him or done something different. Each day with Jerry was a honeymoon fantasy, and our nights were even more dreamy. But whenever I couldn't sleep, the list of people I'd hurt would loom. I was about to give up on sleep altogether. In the dark, Jerry reached his arm out for me, pulling me into him.

Finally, my mind went blank.

9

A Fucking Helicopter

Before I could catch up with myself, my weekend away with Jerry had arrived. I'd not seen him the night before, so I could bake up a storm before my departure. Priya arrived early on Friday, ready to open the shop, but I'd already channelled my nervous energy into setting everything out. I didn't know what else to do whilst I waited for Jerry.

"Not much for me to do, really." She stood behind the counter, strumming her fingers on the till. I wondered if I should wait upstairs. It felt naughty that I was out of uniform. I felt like a layabout for leaving her, but I think Priya desperately wanted me to go.

"You keep looking at that door," Priya noticed.

"Sorry."

Priya shrugged and sang Madonna's 'Holiday' under her breath. I was the one headed on a trip, but I think Priya saw my time off as a holiday from me. I took a sip of the hot chocolate I'd made. I felt silly, but a part of me didn't believe he would turn up. I checked my phone:

On my way xx

I had packed a bag. I wasn't sure where we were going, but Jerry said to pack some swimwear and not much else.

"Trevor is due at ten. Call me if you need anything. I'll have my phone on."

"No offence, pet, but I worked here for years before you turned up. I've even knocked out a few of those cakes myself. I doubt you'll know anything about this place that I haven't already discovered." Priya laughed but kept her gaze on me. It was a total power move, and I was tempted to expose my belly, lay down, or do something 'beta'.

"Sorry. It's not that I worry about this place without me. I think I'm starting to worry about myself without the café."

"It's just a job. Knowing you, you'll be doing a few different jobs over the weekend."

Her innuendos were shocking.

"Priya! I've never in my life…"

"Don't play coy with me. Do have fun, though. Your lift's here."

Outside, a taxi pulled up, and Jerry bounded out. I waved to Priya and handed him my bag. He flexed his bicep as he strained to carry my unmentionables. Have I mentioned he's hot?

"Why don't we get a taxi to and from the hotel all the time?" I asked him.

"I like walking."

"And the first night you had to stay at my house 'because it was late'?"

"I wanted to stay."

He kissed me. It was only a casual greeting, but it still gave me a thrill.

"Do you have your passport?" he asked for the eighth time. I confirmed and rolled my eyes.

"We're ready," he told the driver and hopped in.

I hesitated.

"We can walk to the ferry," I whispered, hovering at the car door.

"We're not going to the ferry. Will you get in?" Jerry grinned at me with his mischievous face, and clutching my forearm, he pulled me into the car. I did as I was told, and the car went in the opposite direction of the dock. We travelled inland and part way up Pal-Dominar's point before turning into a field. In the middle sat a helicopter.

"Are you joking?" I turned to Jerry. Had I been drinking, I would've done a spit take: "A fucking helicopter?"

"We're not going far."

"I don't want to be a brat, this is really nice, but I feel like it's a bit overboard. You don't need to impress me. This isn't a *Love Island* final date."

"I know, but you are my type on paper..." he joked, but I didn't laugh.

"It's not mine. We're just borrowing it because it's the quickest way of travelling. It's not even as expensive as you might think." Jerry slid over and put an arm around me, coaxing me into being OK with his extravagance.

"Shall I pay half?" I offered.

"It's probably a bit more than you can stretch to."

A knock on the car window indicated we ought to get out.

"I hate you," I said, showing gratitude in my own way.

We walked over to the helipad. What even is my life?

Strap-in and take-off happened in less than two minutes. For years, I'd had the sneaking suspicion that things took longer for us paupers, and I was right. Within the blink of an eye, we flipped around through the air, flew off the island and above the ocean waves. Jerry's voice came through on my headphones, a little loud and with so much crackling I wondered if it would be easier without them.

"What do you think?"

"I've never been in a helicopter before."

He took my hand as I stared out the window. The entire time I was guessing where we were going. I was fairly certain we were headed for France as I didn't think we could go super far without a plane.

"Are we going somewhere after the helicopter?"

"Just wait. What's wrong with you?"

"What else are we supposed to talk about?"

"The view?"

And it was a stupendous view. The sea was sapphire, with the waves seemingly in slow motion. It felt like we were outside of time. In the distance, an abundance of green and spots of terracotta – it could only be France. Jerry rubbed his thumb over mine. We flew above a beach, and into the countryside. The houses were small, with a patchwork of different roof tiles, even a thatched barn. Without any graduation, the roofs and houses underneath became sprawling estates with wings, tennis courts, pools, and helipads everywhere. Jerry shifted in his seat as we descended.

The house was all white stone or plaster; I'm not really an expert. I could see trees, a fountain and a perfectly manicured maze. The helicopter landed, and everyone unbuckled. The waiting staff rushed forward and opened the door for us. I hobbled out and turned back to help Jerry down. He held onto my hand as we ducked out of the way of the blades, which were dwindling now.

"Where are we? Is this a hotel?" I leaned into Jerry's ear to ask.

"This is my friend's house. We're borrowing it for the weekend."
He picked up the pace toward a woman wearing a suit, brown hair
in a tight bun on her head, and a serious look on her face.

"Good morning, Mr Hilk. I'm Sara, the house manager. I can
show you around if you like?" Sara spoke a bit like a royal family
member. I was mildly disappointed that she wasn't French.

"Yeah, sure," Jerry answered. More smartly dressed people appeared by my side.

"We can take your bags to your room if you like?"

"I'm fine, thank you," I said while Jerry said 'sure.' No one knew
what to do. I gave in.

"OK, thank you," I said, passing my bag to an athletic elderly
man with salt-and-pepper hair and fantastic posture. He wore all
black.

"I'm the pilot," he said, clearly not wanting to take my offered
bag.

"I'll take it," a different man appeared behind me, also wearing
all black.

"Sorry," I muttered. God, I'm such a twat.

We followed behind Sara; hands still clenched together.

"Sir John regrets that he and the family won't be here this weekend but insisted you treat the place like you would your own
home."

Sir John...did I know any sirs? Is a 'sir' a lord? I wanted to ask
Jerry again where we were.

"Does that mean I can run through the house nude?" I asked
aloud, trying to make Sara like me.

"You wouldn't be the first." She turned and smiled – success.

She took us on a tour around the house. We marched past the
pool with cherubic statues dotted around, although their bespectacled

faces seemed familiar. We took the stairs to a patio area, entering the house through some open French doors (or just doors, in France) which led into the lounge. There was no TV, which I thought was dickish. I was being judgmental because I was jealous – don't make a thing about it. Where the TV ought to have been was an elaborate oil painting of two nude men. I wondered if it was a famous picture, there was something familiar about one of the men, but it wasn't a strong likeness. On the other side of the room was a balcony with a view of the nearby town. To my left was an open doorway leading to a dining room and beyond. We followed Sara through to a corridor, and she showed us upstairs. Along the stairwell was an embarrassment of celebrity photos: Elton John, Princess Diana, Freddie Mercury, Adele, the Spice Girls, George Michael, Elton John again, and Lady Gaga. We were shown the cinema room, which made up for the lack of TV. It was air-conditioned and had a sort of daybed sofa in the middle. We also saw the games room, an elaborate bathroom filled with awards and a gift-wrapping room, all before we arrived at our bedroom. It overlooked the pool, and you could see fields for miles around. The room had a four-poster bed and an entirely marble en-suite with a bidet and a painted mural on the ceiling. I squinted to see it looked a bit like Elton John.

Hold on.

"Why is there an Elton John mural on the ceiling?" I whispered to Jerry.

"It's his house."

What the fuck?

I was going to be sleeping at Elton John's house?

It all made sense, the photos, the oil painting, the cherubs. There was even an EJ print over the furniture in the cinema room, which

I'd assumed meant 'Entertainment something in French beginning with J'.

"Would you like to take lunch on the patio?" Sara asked.

"Yeah, that would be great, thanks."

"Chef has prepared a lobster and pear salad."

"Oh, I'm really sorry, I don't eat lobster." I panicked that I would starve and was being rude all at once. "I'm a vegetarian."

Sara's smile grew wider, and I thought she was probably doing what I do with annoying customers, pretending not to be annoyed until one of my arteries burst.

"Not to worry, I will find out what else Chef has prepared. Will you be having dinner at the house?"

"No, we'll go for dinner in town, if that's alright?" Jerry looked away from me, concealing his meaning. Suspicious.

Sara said that was fine and closed the door. I looked around the room for my bag but couldn't see it. However, my book was placed on a desk opposite the bed.

"Where's my bag?" I was still whispering.

"They've probably unpacked it." He gestured to an exquisite vintage wardrobe that was probably worth more than everything I owned. "What do you want to do first?"

Before answering, I fingered through my clothes, checking the underwear they'd put away wasn't holey or gross. I'd packed a cow print thong, which I thought would be funny for Jerry, and my cheeks flushed with heat at the thought of some member of staff handling it.

Jerry flopped down on the bed.

"Has your time on the helicopter taken it out of you?"

"I'm exhausted."

Jerry pulled me down on the bed.

145

"This is so extravagant, Jerry. You didn't need to go to all this trouble."

"I was offered the house for the weekend, and I said yes. It was as simple as that."

I propped myself up and came to rest my head on Jerry's chest.

"It's too much for me. The staff here earn more than I do. I should be waiting on them."

Jerry kissed my forehead.

"It's a lot, but it's just for the weekend. I don't have any staff at my house. But this is a holiday home, so let's enjoy ourselves."

I kissed him and went to get up.

"Wait," he pulled me back down, "I know what I want to do first."

He kissed me before he pushed my body away. I had my back to him. I was confused by his manoeuvring. Before there was a chance to complain, he closed the gap between us and kissed my neck. His arms circled me. I didn't know what to do with my hands, so I stroked his forearm, feeling his muscles flex. Being under Jerry's intense attention was blissful. We undressed ourselves and one another. Jerry kept his focus on me, and before long, I was struggling to compute how good I felt. Jerry's actions made my body feel so good it almost hurt.

"Fuck me." I could only utter the words.

He flipped me around until I was on my back, and he was on his knees between my legs. He did as I'd asked and held still for a moment. Almost unbearably slowly, he began thrusting. Jerry worked up his rhythm, and I responded to his movements. Before long, my toes curled around Jerry's ears. We both seemed to hold our breath as our pleasure hit a crescendo. Afterwards, we ended up lying together on top of the sheets, Jerry's body warming my torso and the sun warming my face.

I fell asleep, and when I woke, I traced dust falling and rising in the sunlight. Without a rush, I turned to find that Jerry was smiling and had only one eye open.

"I fell asleep," he said.

The grogginess faded from my mind, and I realised we might've missed the spread the chef had prepared. Isn't that a dick move? I rolled up and searched for my phone.

"What are you doing?"

I was ravenous, and it was important we didn't miss our lunch. I looked at the time, and we'd probably only been asleep twenty minutes.

"I want to go to the pool and have something to eat."

He pushed up to a seated position, a drowsy look on his face, betraying he wasn't ready for action.

"Great idea."

We shuffled through drawers and found our things. I took my book down to the pool, *Bridget Jones's Diary*, and I was glad to see Jerry did the same with *Wuthering Heights*. We still enjoyed chatting, but I didn't know if I could sit by a pool on holiday without a book.

On the patio just above the pool, food was set out. It was the fanciest picnic I'd ever seen, with bread, salad, cheeses and many things I didn't recognise. We sat down, and a tall, willowy woman came to the table.

"Would you care for something to drink?"

Jerry asked for water, and I asked for a Diet Coke and some crisps. They brought over a bottle with ice and a glass. I had to keep reminding myself this was a house, not a hotel. I just drank from the bottle. I saw one of the waitresses' eyebrows rise in judgement. Jerry raised his glass.

"To us, on our first holiday."

I clinked his Fiji water.

"What is so good about Fiji water?"

"You tell me." He offered his glass, and I took a swig. It was alright.

"I think I prefer the tap water in London. It's just what I'm used to."

"Tropical rainwater, collected in a rainforest, filtered through volcanic rock, the world's best water, and you prefer tap water? You're impossible."

After lunch, we left the table, and I felt terrible for not helping tidy up. Jerry sprawled out on a deck chair by the pool, but I couldn't wait. I was desperate to be underwater, so I took off my top, tied up my trunks and jumped in. I surfaced and Jerry called "Aren't you going to wait for your lunch to go down?"

"No, that's just a myth."

Jerry smiled at my expense, rolling his eyes as though he knew better. The water was glorious. I swam the length of the pool and back, enjoying the fact no one else was in the water, and there was no pressure to swim anything other than breaststroke.

"Shame we can't skinny dip," I muttered as I swam past Jerry.

"Who says?"

"The fact that one hundred people are working here. We can't just take our clothes off."

"Fair enough. But we could skinny dip after dinner tonight if that's something you're deeply into."

"Oh, Mr Hilk, you spoil me."

I swam back down to the far end and returned.

"Where are we going for dinner? I don't have anything that nice with me."

I mentally sorted through my clothes and remembered that it was all T-shirts and shorts. I have one jumper for perpetuity.

"Don't worry, we'll sort something."

I continued swimming, trying to ignore the nagging feeling that the holiday was about to take a turn. Eventually, Sara came to check on us, and Jerry asked if we could order a taxi to town for later.

"Also, George here has forgotten to bring appropriate dinner attire. Do you think we might send someone out?"

I could feel the heat rise in my cheeks again; I was the colour of beetroot. I wondered if I could enjoy the rest of the day without feeling out of my depth.

"Of course," Sara replied.

"Just a shirt each, and some trousers and smart shoes, maybe a jacket?"

"That sounds too much, honestly. Why don't we just stay in?" I tried to cover up with my towel. My worry was twofold. I didn't want to ask too much, and also...

"What sizes are we thinking?" Sara asked.

I was dreading that question.

"I'll go for medium or large, and George...?"

I didn't mind saying my sizes aloud, but I also knew that a quiet provincial town wouldn't make anything in my size.

"I like a 4XL top. I'm a size 11 shoes, and I wear a short leg."

"Perfect."

Sara's face remained the same. No reaction. She was prepared for anything.

I hardly look like I wear XS. Jerry asked for specific styles and mentioned some shops he knew, including high-end designers:

Balmain, Chanel, Givenchy, and Dior. I knew they wouldn't stock my size. I sat quietly. When Sara left, I swam again and prayed to the universe that the evening would be salvageable. But I couldn't escape the dread of what was to come. The best-case scenario would only be that nothing fit and was sent back. What if I couldn't return the clothes because they burst at the seams? What if I'd managed to close a shirt up, but then it snapped open at dinner? I considered how much swimming I could do in order to fit something, a shadow of thought from a time when I would punish my body.

I didn't want to feel like I should change my body, so I got out and asked for more crisps.

10

An Alcoholic Has-been

After a few more lengths, a spot of reading and some poolside snacks, the sun began to set, and Jerry suggested we go inside to get ready. I heaved out of the water, dried off and trudged to the room.

"Are you alright?" he asked, stroking my back.

I made all the right noises, but I walked slowly up the stairs like someone heading to the guillotine. The room was cool as the sun had dipped below the tree line. Designer bags were on top of the wardrobe, and the new clothes were hanging up. There was a nice collection of shirts, trousers and shoe boxes, which mildly lifted my spirits. The clothes were split into two, with mine on the left. I could tell, as the clothes were longer, larger and there were fewer of them. I took them off the hook and slipped into the bathroom without speaking. The shirt was so long it hung down below my knees. I tilted my head. Was this a legitimate option? The tiles under me felt cool. I considered lying on them and waiting for morning.

I started with the trousers. I held up the first pair – smart, plain black. They'd probably fit. In the shower I wet my hair and rinsed the pool water off. I dried off, moisturised, fluffed around my hair, and cut my fingernails. I looked at the clothes and scrunched my nose. I couldn't put it off any longer. I put on my pants and then the right leg of the trousers. They were tight as I pulled up to the knee. I put my other leg through, and they wouldn't go any further up my body. I'd gotten so good at ordering my clothes online I'd forgotten the pain of trying on too-tight trousers. I whipped them off and tried another pair. These were linen trousers in a sand colour. I wouldn't have picked them myself, but the softer material made me believe they would fit. However, they wouldn't do up when I came to button them together by at least two inches. I started to get hot, exacerbated by the steamy bathroom. The final pair of trousers were navy chinos. It was a miracle I could get my foot through them. The hole in the trouser leg was so tiny. I managed so far but couldn't get them beyond my thighs.

Fuck.

I looked in the mirror and crinkled my face, tears building up. But they never fell. I lobbed the trousers from around my feet across the room.

They smacked the door and crumpled on the floor.

"You alright?" Jerry called in.

"Fine."

I gathered myself and stepped into the bedroom.

Jerry walked past me and went to shower. I surveyed the clothes. I had another look in the wardrobe in case I missed a smart pair of elastic waist bottoms.

Nothing.

Jerry returned in a towel.

"I'm not going to dinner."

I wanted to sound empowered, but I sounded like a brat.

"What's up?"

"I asked you what I needed for this weekend, and you never said I needed to bring trousers and a shirt and dress smartly."

"I thought it'd be less stress if we just got some stuff here?"

"For you, maybe, but they don't make clothes for people like me just for fun. Nothing here fits me." I lifted my pile of clothes, holding them to my body as if to demonstrate.

"Are you sure?"

My eyes widened like a predator about to devour its prey.

"Am I sure the trousers will not fit beyond my bottom? How would I not be sure?" I took a breath. I didn't want to shout at Jerry.

"I don't want to be a dick because you've gone through a lot of trouble to make a nice weekend, but how could you not see that I might struggle with this. We're not the same. I'm fat."

"I don't think you're fat."

Jerry shrugged.

"Why, are you stupid?" I'd say I was almost screeching.

His mouth hung open. I heaved in a breath before carrying on.

"Of course I'm fat. And that's OK. I love my body, and you seem to enjoy my body. But dressing my body in clothes isn't the same as it is for you."

He crossed the room and tried to hug me.

"No, I need to make sure you hear me. I am fat, and the world is different for me than it is for you, and sometimes you'll have to do things a little differently because of it."

Jerry took a big inhale, placing both hands on his chest, before he stepped back to sit on the bed. I felt reassured he was really listening.

"I understand. I wasn't thinking, and I'm sorry. Do you want to stay in? Or we could eat somewhere else? Or you could punch me square in the face."

I laughed and felt bad being so harsh, but I wanted to be heard.

"I'm not sure about dinner. I've only got this shirt, and it's so big it's basically a dress."

I held it up for Jerry, and it skirted my calves.

"It's a sexy and masculine dress," he joshed.

"I can appreciate that. I'm going to wear this."

"What with?"

"Pants. Probably some shoes."

Jerry tried to hide his laugh, but that only egged me on. I put on the shirt and pulled out some of the shoes. They were green velvet backless loafers. I bloody loved them. I slid them on.

I was ready.

"Ready when you are?" I said to Jerry, who was only wearing his trousers.

"Are you really not going to wear shorts or something?"

"Nope."

Jerry finished getting ready, and he looked incredible. But I felt incredible. I was wearing a shirt dress, but I wouldn't say I looked feminine. This wasn't about dressing as a man or a woman. It was about gender non-conforming.

I followed Jerry to the front entrance, which I hadn't used yet. There was a split staircase down to the front door. I skipped over to the car and opened the door for Jerry before walking to the other side. I felt light and unrestricted; despite the tumultuous time it took to get ready, I felt more confident than ever. Jerry hadn't seen me walk around the car and slid toward my door to make room. We laughed as he moved back, and I got in.

"Sorry about that," he said as I sat.

"Not to worry, that was just a rehearsal. We'll try again when we get a taxi back later."

I winked. My confidence was sky-high, bordering on arrogance.

The taxi rolled off. It was a twenty-minute drive through the beautiful countryside, past lavish houses, which ended as we arrived in a cobbled town with hanging lights instead of street lamps. Everything was exposed brick and felt expensive instead of quaint. We pulled up to the restaurant, and someone opened our door and directed us to the entrance. They asked if we wanted to sit inside or outside. I said "Outside," while Jerry said the opposite.

"Just sometimes people take your photo if you're outside," he explained.

"Of course," I conceded.

The wait staff were tripping over themselves to be cordial with Jerry. It was obvious they were fans. It was sweet, except for how they only looked at him when serving us and only addressed him when they asked if we wanted sauces, water for the table or more napkins. I was a man wearing a dress, but I could've worn a welly on my head, and no one would've noticed. I appreciate I couldn't compare to a movie star, but I looked terrific. I thought at least someone would've noticed. I felt like an ignored housewife or something. I didn't need our waiters to like me, but their indifference felt a little rude. This was what it would be like to eat at restaurants with Jerry. I could handle it, but it would've been nice if someone had complimented my outfit. We ordered pasta dishes and diet cokes. The food was incredible.

"After this, I was thinking, shall we get some ice cream?" I suggested, having seen a gelateria about two minutes before the car stopped.

"They do dessert here?"

"Yes, but the ice cream place down the road looks incredible, and we can wander around the town a little?"

Jerry agreed.

He paid for dinner, which made sense as I couldn't afford the tap water. I made a mental note to take him for dinner somewhere affordable next time, maybe if Greggs opened up on the island. We walked out into the town, and the ground glistened underfoot, reflecting the hanging lamps.

"I think it rained," I said as I went to take his hand.

Jerry moved his hand around to pat me on the back.

"I can't here. Sorry."

I understood why. I hadn't been thinking when I reached for him. I felt silly. We passed a group of teenagers who spotted him. It was different to before. I think people had gotten over seeing him on No'Man Island. I could tell he was getting uncomfortable, and felt bad for him. The ice cream shop provided some cover. I insisted on paying and bought him a scoop of pistachio and caramel. I went for toffee and mint.

"Who likes mint ice cream?" he laughed.

"It's fresh. You're so uncultured!"

We scooted into a booth with our scoops, the patio doors open so we could see the village square.

"My daughter loves strawberry. It's such a cliché, but she does love anything pink."

I knew he had a daughter. Anyone with internet access knew he had a daughter. He'd even mentioned her before, but not in great detail.

"That's cute. I can relate. What's her name?" I pretended not to know, as if his life wasn't public knowledge.

He grinned, going along with the fib.

"Her name is Dorothy. I know, such a cliché, but it's her great-grandmother's name on her mum's side. I call her Dottie."

"A cliché?"

"A friend of Dorothy…I'm literally the father of Dorothy," he explained, and I laughed.

The door opened, and Jerry looked up, worried, but it was just a mother and her toddler son, entirely uninterested in the pair of us. The fantastic little boy, with overly expressive wrists, was running circles around his mum. She struggled with a slipping tote bag and hands full of a phone, purse and hand sanitiser. I almost stood up to help, but she righted herself, ordering a scoop of chocolate for each of them.

"Fabuleux," the little boy laughed, licking his scoop.

"I'm sorry if tonight hasn't been so good," he said.

"Are you kidding? It's been great."

"Don't make me feel better."

"Has it been the best time we've ever spent together? No. Has it been better than the time I had diarrhoea at Greenford Manor? Almost certainly."

"I just wanted it to be the best weekend away ever."

"I just wanted to get with Brad Pitt. Sometimes you don't get the movie star you want, but the movie star that's nearby instead."

Jerry shook his head, laughing.

"You're such a dick."

He put his hand over mine and let it rest a second. It was a small gesture, but it made me feel like we were still a team. Before he could pull his hand away, the teenagers burst through the door, brandishing their camera phones. I'd seen Jerry with teenagers in the café, and he handled fans well, but this was different. There were too many of them, and English was their second language, so it was harder for everyone to communicate. He took some photos and smiled. In the end, I agreed to take their picture, and they all got into the frame. The ice cream shop cashier was getting moody, so Jerry bought them all a scoop each, and we left the mayhem behind. Jerry flagged a taxi. He was jigging his leg in the car, sweat streaming down his face.

"Jerry," I started to say.

"I'm sorry, I didn't know that would happen. I know it's a lot. I didn't mean for..."

Jerry stopped mid-sentence, leg bouncing like a bucking bull.

"It's fine," I stroked his arm.

"It's not. Don't say you don't mind. It always gets in the way."

Jerry's voice was gravelly, holding back tears.

"Hey, look at me," I told him, pulling on his arm and turning to face him, "I'm not going anywhere."

Jerry turned and looked out the window. We got back to the house, and as Jerry closed the front door, I stepped in front of him.

"Right, what are you thinking?"

"It's dumb."

Jerry went to step around me.

"Not to me."

"I've had people in my life before, friends, girlfriends, people who are very into the camera, the fans, the parties and all that stuff, and it can be misleading."

Jerry turned his head, but I darted sideways to hold his gaze.

"Sometimes it gets in the way. And sometimes, when the novelty wears off, and it's just me, it's not enough."

"You think you're not enough?"

Jerry didn't answer for a moment, tears threatening to spill over as he looked at me.

"I seem successful from a distance, but...I'm a divorced single dad and an alcoholic has-been."

Jerry bit his bottom lip and looked up to the ceiling. I pulled him into a hug.

"Jerry," I spoke into his hair, "you're more than enough."

He sniffed, composing himself.

"Anyway, I'm sorry for the ruined evening.

"You do not need to apologise, tonight wasn't perfect, but you don't control everything. You're not responsible for us always having a good time. I like being with you, whether in a fancy restaurant in France or a supermarket queue. The important bit is you. It's OK that you come with adoring fans."

He looked at me as he put my hand in his. He stroked my thumb with his.

"You're really sweet."

"I'm just being honest. I'm proud of your success, and that comes with fans. I don't rate you, but at least some people do."

Jerry laughed and dropped my hand.

"Why do you have to ruin it?"

We went to the cinema room, and I insisted we put on *Bridget Jones's Diary*. It's a great film. I'd seen it so many times that I didn't have to follow it whilst we kissed and did…other stuff. The credits rolled, and I put my T-shirt back on.

"I can't believe I just came in Elton John's cinema room."

"This is also where he hosts his famous sex parties."

I spun to face Jerry, my jaw hitting my chest. His face was expressionless, believable.

"I'm kidding," he laughed, but it was a fake laugh, leading me to believe the sex parties were real. Could I get an invite?

We walked out of the room, and I headed toward the bedroom.

"Do you want to go to the pool?"

I bit my bottom lip and followed him. The doors were closed, but Jerry wiggled them open. We stepped outside, and it was cooler than before. I could smell some kind of flower.

"Can you smell that?"

Jerry breathed through his nostrils. "Nice."

"I've never been able to smell flowers like this. They write about it in books, and I always think *what a bunch of shit*, but I can really smell them. I wonder what brand?"

"Flowers don't come in brands. They come in species."

We walked toward the water.

"Jerry, we don't have towels or swimming costumes."

"There's no one around," he said, undoing his belt buckle.

"Sure, right now, but there are about ten thousand people working here. I bet there's a night gardener."

He continued to undress. I joined him until I was down to my pants, matching Jerry.

"Full monty," he said and pulled them down. The sight of his body still took my breath away. The water reflected an eerie light on him, making this feel more like a fantasy. I followed suit and ran straight into the water. Being underwater is almost like wearing clothes. Jerry jumped in after me and clung to my back. It felt intimate like I'd been granted a visa to his body; we no longer needed added bureaucracy to touch. I dipped under, feeling water reach everywhere, and Jerry's arm still slung gently around my neck. Under the water, in the light, I turned and kissed him. It was cold and weird but still sexy. When we rose to the surface, I was panting for breath. Jerry was, too, his legs wrapped around my waist.

"I feel like a mermaid," he said, laughing.

"Because of the scales?" I asked, and he replied by brushing his lips against mine.

Standing in the shallower side of the pool, I lifted him and jumped into the water. Jerry let go, and we laughed as we broke the surface.

"Race you," he said, swimming off to the other side of the pool. I dove forward and kicked my legs into action. I'm glad to say I won.

"How did you beat me?" He wiped his hair off his face.

"I'm incredible."

We paddled about, until I saw Jerry shiver and insisted we get out.

"How are we going to do this?"

"What do you mean?"

"Well, I suppose, dry off for a bit and then put our pants back on?"

"Or we can just run in?"

"I can't run naked through Elton John's house."

"You heard what Sara said? You'd be the only guest not to." He kissed me and jumped out of the pool. I swam to the nearest stairs and hobbled out, using my hands to protect my modesty. I grabbed my clothes and ran after Jerry to the glass doors. In the living room, he stopped, and I almost ran into him. It was dark, and no one was around. He turned, and without saying anything, he knelt.

"What are you doing?" I asked and stroked his cheek. Jerry brought his mouth to my body. It shocked me, being cold and then enveloped in warmth. It was enticing. I leaned against the nearest sofa and surrendered. I felt his hair in my fingers, my other hand holding his. He stood up abruptly.

"Let's go," he smiled and ran up the stairs.

I gathered up the clothes I'd dropped and rushed after him. Once we got in the room, I closed the door.

"Your turn," I told Jerry.

I won't say we made love all night, not because it's inaccurate, but it's a bit gross to say. We did have sex a lot. I woke up naked and in a hazy sunlit room. It was the tired that follows sex, the only type of exhaustion you're not upset about. I stretched out and opened an eye to see Jerry, but he wasn't there. I brushed my teeth before throwing on some trunks and a T-shirt. Jerry wore a dressing gown in the living room, and I saw a flash of his pants underneath. I smiled, but his face was filled with concern.

"Good morning," I called out.

A woman with big hair and a stern look turned around on the sofa, and I realised she was talking with Jerry.

"This is him, huh?"

"Yes, this is George. George, this is Patricia. She's my publicist."

"Nice to meet you." I waved. Something from my old life working on TV said to shake her hand. But I was nervous, and she didn't offer her hand either. She turned back to Jerry.

"All for him, huh?" I heard her say and knew I wasn't supposed to hear. Jerry glared at her; although I didn't understand the intention behind his death stare, I could tell it was about me. I wanted to leave the room.

"Can I get anyone a drink?" I asked, but they both ignored me. I backed out and headed to the kitchen, struggling to remember where it was. I found it but there was a chef and wait staff. They stared at me for what felt like a minute. Finally, they all straightened up and went into action.

"Are you ready for breakfast?" a young hunky waiter asked me.

"No, thank you, sorry, pretend I'm not here. I was going to get some water."

162

The waiter ran three steps to the fridge and removed a water filter. I just wanted to be alone, but there was a server everywhere, and they insisted on doing their job. I appreciate wanting to keep a customer happy, but I'm sure I wasn't this irritating in the café. He poured a glass of volcanic Fiji water.

"Would you like ice?"

"No, thank you." I reached out and took the drink. "Thanks for this. I think breakfast won't be for a while, so…you can chill out, I guess? Sorry."

I walked back toward the living room, as it was the only staircase I knew of to go back to bed. I couldn't figure out what was happening, but the holiday felt over.

"George, can I chat with you for a minute?" Jerry called out to me as I was trying to sneak past. I padded into the living room and sat on the adjacent sofa to Patricia.

"What's up?"

"I don't want you to freak out," Jerry said slowly.

"A photograph of both of you went viral last night. It's all over the internet," Patricia stated. I was annoyed, Jerry bought those arseholes ice cream, and they'd sold a photo of us.

"That's annoying." I shrugged.

"Annoying?" Jerry's face beat down at me. I'd never seen him so serious.

Patricia held her phone up for me to see. The photo wasn't from the gelateria. It was from No'Man, outside the ice cream shop. It was the first time we'd kissed in the street. I instantly knew Dianna had taken the photo. She'd commented that my oversized pink jumper looked like a dress. The photo wasn't overly damning. I was only kissing his cheek.

"I didn't realise it was this photo. But I look nice."

"You look like you're wearing a dress," Patricia spat at me – obviously not a fan of my style.

"Still, no one knows who I am. It's quite blurry. It feels like a bit of a non-story."

"This could end Jerry's career, and you *think* it's annoying." Patricia leant forward.

Livid.

"I feel like that's an overstatement. What does this photo prove? That we know one another. And even if it did come out that we were seeing each other, so what?"

"Grow up. Jerry is known around the world. This getting out that you two are an item that changes things. Yes, love is love, but do you know how many openly gay celebrities go on to become icons?"

I looked around at Elton John's house. I wasn't sure what made someone an icon, but the irony of the location wasn't lost on me.

"I'm going to go check something. Give you both some space to figure out the best way to give no comment," I said, sarcasm whooshing out my mouth before I could stop it. I had no idea what I would do, but I needed to be away from them. I stood up and sidestepped Patricia to get to the stairs. I hated her, of course. She was doing her job, but this was my life. Did Jerry think this was OK? I went into the bedroom, the location of last night's bliss and everything felt different. I picked up the clothes from last night, made the bed and got our things in order.

I picked up my phone, and there were about 100 missed calls and texts, mostly from Nat. Before we spoke, I googled Jerry. It was a mistake.

I went straight to the *Daily Mail* because I wanted to hurt myself emotionally. **'JERRY HILK CAUGHT IN GAY LOVE AFFAIR'** wasn't so bad. The next sentences were more brutal:

Hilk caught out on holiday with another man – totally unlike his typical beauties.

I scrolled down to the comments and saw the word 'FAT'. I decided not to read anymore. Fat isn't a bad word, but I'd need more resilience to read the comments. I called Nat back.

"What the hell?"

"It's really fucked."

"Is everyone losing their minds there?"

"I'm actually on holiday. It's only Jerry and his publicist, who's a real meanie. But yeah, they are freaking out. I think it's such a nothing story, though. We wouldn't even have put this on the show."

"Are you joking? Check your emails; they want to invite you to Wake Up UK for an interview."

"You're kidding."

"Not at all. It was bizarre. They made me call you, but I presume you were asleep."

"I was, but then I woke up, and Jerry was downstairs..."

"I'm sure they'd have you on the show tomorrow," Nat interrupted, laughing.

"I feel bad for Jerry." I chewed my lip.

"You've not read the comments, have you?"

"No, I just saw the pictures. What are people saying?"

I heard Nat exhale.

"I need to preface this by saying that this isn't how the whole world feels, just some prize idiots sitting behind keyboards. Ultimately none of it matters, and I think you're incredible. I'm only telling you about this because I'm afraid you'll read this on your own."

"Alright, I get it. What are they saying."

"There's a fair amount of 'Jerry is gay now'. A few people in the comments say Jerry is better-looking than you. That's the gist of it."

"Oh right," I said, putting her on speaker phone and returning to Google. There was one article from a gay news website saying that Jerry's lover wasn't what you'd expect, implying that he was slumming it with me. I clicked back on the *Daily Mail* and started reading the comments. People were writing that I was the ugliest person alive:

How on earth does Jerry fancy that?

This rancid whale shouldn't be on land, let alone with Jerry.

This fat ox should kill itself and set Jerry free.

"Are you there?" Nat asked.

"Yep." I meant to sound relaxed, but I think I came across as snippy.

"I know it's shit. People are dicks. Most of them don't even mean it. They think they're being funny. And it's not going to change how Jerry feels about you."

"You're right, but they are so nasty." I wiped my eyes. "Quick, tell me something about the real world, something important. How are you?"

"Erm, I wasn't expecting this. What's on my mind? Do you think I should stop making lunch every day? I spend hundreds of pounds on snacks to top up my lunch anyway. An extra sandwich won't bankrupt me."

"Good question."

"No, it's boring. I can do better."

166

I could hear Nat's mind whirring through information.

"Guess who's leaving?"

"I have no idea."

"Raquel. She's got a job as a magazine editor for one of the weekend supplements. I can't remember which one. But it means her job is up for grabs."

"Are you going to apply?"

"Don't be stupid. She's like four people up from me."

"She's two people up from you."

"Is this helping?"

"It was for a minute. Now I remember again. I don't want people at work to know."

I took the phone off speaker.

"You don't work here anymore, so that's probably alright."

I walked toward the balcony. The window was open, and the tiled floor just beyond the threshold was already warm.

"Are you going to be alright?" Nat asked.

"I think so. It's weird, but I feel far away from everything. Also, everyone is only writing what I've already thought about myself."

"Don't be so horrible to my best friend, please. Where are you? Do you want me to come?"

"I'm in France, in Elton John's house. I wish you could come, but I don't even know where I am."

"Oh my god, Elton John's house! That is quite the holiday upgrade. You remember when we stayed in Paris, in the hotel with no toilet."

"There was a toilet, but it was shared with all the rooms on that floor."

"And it was rank." Nat's passion for how repugnant that hotel room was had never wavered. We were quiet as a million thoughts rushed through my head.

Eventually, she spoke up.

"This is just a hunch, and I don't want you to be mad at me," she ventured.

I hummed, not really agreeing to control my feelings.

"You're the funniest person I know, and I don't know why, but…" she inhaled before speaking super-fast. "Your comedy career hasn't ever really gotten you noticed. Is part of why you're upset because you're finally getting some attention, and it's not what you've worked at your whole adult life?"

I didn't know how to respond. "Yeah, I'm really easy to find online. I've got an open Instagram and Twitter. I've been written about by some insignificant media when I've done comedy shows. Finding out who I am shouldn't be hard, yet, nowhere has anyone mentioned my name, only my alias."

"What's your alias?"

"Hideous beast."

"I'm not saying your career is my life's goal, but I've flyered with you for hours, and I'm cheesed-off."

"But does this sound bad, like I wanted to get found out?" I dreaded the thought that Jerry might walk in.

"Absolutely not. It's not like you want to be famous so you don't have to queue at restaurants. It's like a barometer of success in comedy. Or at least it seems it. You want to make people laugh, more than just me in the living room."

"I feel like a loser. I'm in my thirties and crying to my best friend that I want to be a different kind of famous. What a twat."

"Well, you're my top favourite twat."

"That's the kindest thing anyone has said about me in 12 hours, but the bar for that is really low."

She laughed, which helped. A knock at the door, and Jerry peeked his head into the room.

"Do you need anything else?" I asked Nat.

"Has Jerry come in?"

"He has, but I'm not rushing you off the phone. You called to chat with me. What else is up?"

"Do you want me to come back?" Jerry asked.

"I'm good. You go, tell Jerry I said hi," Nat said.

I said goodbye and hung up. I sat on the end of the bed. Jerry waited; I don't know what for. Then he joined me.

"What's going on?" he asked,

"Just chatting to Nat about being the ugliest person alive."

"Please don't read the comments."

"Please," I mimicked, "don't hold private meetings on Saturday mornings about me and then hide them from me."

Jerry put his face in his hands. He exhaled.

"I've just realised how this must've seemed. I woke up, and she was here. It's her job. Sorry, she's spikey this morning. She's gone now."

"I don't think you realise how this felt." I stood, ready to get into my stride. "I woke up and went to find you and stumbled into a war committee meeting, and I was the enemy. It was like a less jolly version of 'How do you solve a problem like Maria', and I was Maria. Except I'm hideous to look at."

Jerry smiled. I knew he wanted to laugh. I glared, and the mirth left his features.

He stood and moved around to face me.

"This must be horrid for you, but I've kept this secret my whole life. Now here we are, two months into being together, and I'm jeopardising everything I've worked for."

"But the thing you're dreading, that's me. I know you don't mean it, but everything you're afraid of, that's just who I am, and I can't hide it."

"I feel like you're putting words in my mouth." Jerry turned away, but I moved around, gearing up for a fight.

"Tell me that the picture wouldn't be less damning if I weren't fat, wearing trousers and if I were thinner or more straight passing."

"Sorry that my whole career is hanging in the balance because the world doesn't want to see me holding hands with a man in a dress."

"But here's the thing, Jerry. You like a man in a dress. I know we don't say it, but maybe even love. You don't have a problem with me in a dress, but you hate people knowing that about you. And I know, with my whole brain, that this says more about you than it does me. But my heart, which isn't protected by logic, that really fucking hurts."

His mouth hung open, and he stared at me. His arms, tense with gesturing, suddenly slacked by his side.

"I don't want to hurt you. I never did."

"How can you like me when all I am is everything you hate about yourself?"

"I don't hate it. I'm just scared of things changing. I'm not sure how I feel about the photo, maybe it'll end up being good, but I want things to be my decision. I have a daughter, and now she's asking me questions I'd rather answer in person. It's a lot to deal with."

Jerry's eyes were wet, pools collecting in his bottom lids, waiting to drop.

"I don't know how to process all of this. Can we not fight about it right now? Please."

His face was serious, mouth downturned. There were bags under his eyes; even in our short morning, he was tired. I didn't want to let it go, but he needed me. I stepped forward and gave him a stiff hug. He melted into me; I could feel his tears wetting my neck. I patted his back, and he muttered the words 'I'm sorry' over and over again. His breathing returned to normal, so I stepped back, moving him to sit on the bed. I grabbed some toilet paper for his nose, which he blew. I took the paper away and flushed it. It was so wet and gross. Suddenly I realised how rank that was. I washed my hands before standing in the bathroom door.

"Shall we go to the pool? Or have breakfast?" I said, thinking we should return to some normality, and I was starving.

"Don't you want to go home or something?"

"They have the internet at home too. I don't see what the point of that would be. Unless you want to go home and see Dorothy?"

Jerry closed the gap between us and put his arms around me.

"She's on holiday too. I don't want to ruin her time with her mum. I'll give her another call later on. Let's go down to the pool."

Jerry grabbed his trunks, and we got some towels and headed downstairs. I practically tackled a waiter and ordered scrambled egg and toast, which I would typically never be arsed to cook. I was learning to take advantage of having an actual chef make my food.

My phone rang again.

"I'm just going to take this."

I walked toward the pool's edge, leaving Jerry with our empty plates at the table.

171

"Hi, Mum."

"You're alive!"

"Yep."

"That's all I get? You're all over the news. How could you leave the country and not tell me?"

"I'm thirty. I don't need permission to go on holiday."

"George, we had one argument. Are you planning to never speak to me again? I'm your mother."

"You're only calling because you saw me on the news."

"I was giving you space, don't turn this around on me. How have you not told me any of this? You're out of the country. You're in a relationship again. Who are you?"

I looked across the view at green rolling hills, terracotta roofs, and blue skies. I couldn't take it in. Instead, I relived the last time I'd seen my mum. We were so angry with one another. Mum's face was red, and I was carrying my bag out of the front door. A bird flew into my peripheral vision, bringing me back to the moment,

"Since I've thrown my life away, I suppose it doesn't matter what I'm doing."

Yes, I sounded petulant. Mum sighed.

"If you're going to be like that, how are we supposed to have a conversation?"

Jerry hovered back by the deck chairs. I moved as far away on the patio from him, in case I wanted to shout at my mum.

"I don't know how to have a conversation with you. You hurt me."

"And you hurt me. But we've always worked through things before."

I didn't reply. It felt like our argument had been so awful. How could I just let things go?

"Will you at least tell me where you are and how you're feeling?"

"I'm in France, at Jerry's friend's house. I feel fine. It's a bit strange, but I'm ignoring it now."

"Good, just ignore it. No one will care by tomorrow."

"Well, anyone who did care has already tweeted their thoughts. I'm the ugliest person alive."

"No, you're not. What are you talking about?"

"Nothing, just don't look online."

"Listen to me. I'd happily spend the rest of my life hunting down the people who have been unkind to you. But most of them will be anonymous. They only want to go online and be nasty. They don't see the beauty in anyone or anything, or even themselves. Their opinions, they can't touch you."

My eyes welled up.

"That's not to say it won't have an effect, just don't forget who you are in all of this."

I tried to say goodbye, but my mum wouldn't hang up without a promise – that I'd come home soon for a visit.

"I want to get back to being us and how we are."

I promised and hung up. Jerry asked who that was, and as I told him it was my mum, a bubble of a cry rose in my throat. I smiled and said I was fine, and my mouth did the turn-down wobble thing. I tossed my phone on the chair, threw off my T-shirt and jumped in the pool. The water was cool and clear, and I felt weightless as my hair floated from my head. When I broke the surface, I found Jerry had joined me.

"George?" Jerry wiped his mouth.

"I'm honestly fine…I'll be OK," I blubbered.

Jerry swam closer.

"Take a second. It's OK. And before you start again, go under the water and wipe your nose."

My eyes went wide, and my hand covered my face.

"I've got a bogie? In Elton John's pool?"

I dipped under and wiped. I considered staying under for the rest of my life before coming back up for air.

"Could today get any worse?"

"It can always get worse," Jerry said with a faux ominous vibration in his throat. "Now, are you OK?"

Finally, the tears that had welled behind my eyes found their escape. Jerry leapt up and wrapped his arms around me.

11

Loomy Doomy Feelings

When we returned to No'Man, things were much the same as when we left, but our argument still hung in the air. To add to my looming dooming feelings, I knew my time with Jerry was ending, and I wanted to do something big and boyfriend-y to say goodbye – something to get us back on track.

"I'm thinking we should have a goodbye talent contest for Jerry's leaving?" I said off the top of my head to Priya while decorating a cake at the counter.

"It could be like a goodbye extravaganza party," Priya said, slapping the countertop and furiously bobbing her head.

"I don't have enough friends on the island to consider it a party. And Jerry has fewer than I do. And people drink at parties. I was thinking of something smaller and cuter. Just a few of us, but doing something silly, like juggling."

"That sounds boring and a bit embarrassing. If you're gonna do it, you have to commit. Otherwise, it'll be rubbish. If I were Jerry, I'd dump you."

"Harsh, I think he does enjoy my company at least a bit."

"But you need to go all out. You need an event."

"Like the summer fair? Is there an autumn fair?"

"Why don't you host an open mic night here? People can dedicate their performance to Jerry if they want."

I adjusted my perch on the counter.

"That's absolutely not a party. I think it would be weird."

"Tell him about it in advance. He can prepare a monologue. You can tell some jokes; he'll be impressed if you're good, disgusted if you're bad. It's going to be great."

I told her I'd think about it, and she went off to wipe some tables, singing 'goodbye my lover' by James Blunt, but she was singing in a jazz style, like she was in *Chicago*. I was relieved when she left for the day and hadn't mentioned it again.

***

But the next day, Priya came running in.

"Good news," she began before taking off her jacket, "I've got you a PA system for the goodbye gig."

"What?" I muttered, unpacking milk bottles from a crate into the fridge.

"Things are coming together. I've got a mic and speaker-type thing. Just need a bit of bunting, put the chairs in rows, and we're sorted."

"Oh right." I stood and brushed my hands down my apron. I'd prepared my excuses last night, getting ready to tell Priya the goodbye gig wasn't my style, it was too big and public, and Jerry and I were private. I looked over at Priya, with her excited little grin. I didn't have the heart to take the goodbye gig away from her.

"It's all going ahead then," I said.

The lack of excitement in my voice did nothing to deter Priya's jumps for joy.

And that is how the goodbye gig was born. I made a list of things that needed sorting. If it was going ahead, it had to be a good night. I raided the cupboards in the café and found some bunting. I borrowed some lights from the school to make a spotlight and a few 'disco-y' type lights they assured me were plug-in and go. Priya's daughter put together some flyers for the front of the store, and we spent an afternoon handing them out to people. I suggested we include the hashtag #goodbyeJerry and everything.

My only remaining worry was serving drinks. Although I don't drink, I was worried about hosting comedy in a sober venue. Typically, open mic nights rely on some alcohol to loosen the audience up. However, since it was in Jerry's honour, and he might bring friends from Greenford, and the café didn't have a licence to sell booze, it would be a dry night. I bought some crates of soft drinks to change the vibe. I was impressed with how the planning had gone, feeling smug that I'd not forgotten anything.

***

A few days later, it occurred to me that I hadn't told Jerry. He'd asked me to accompany him to the dentist because he had some mild tooth pain. I was surprised there wasn't a big hotshot Hollywood dentist Jerry would demand to see.

"I'm in too much pain to wait to see Dr Howard," Jerry whimpered.

I needed to distract him. Jerry hadn't mentioned being afraid of the dentists, but his leg was bobbing around, almost like the leg knew how much he wanted to jog out of there. There were no other patients, considering it was probably out of hours. The receptionist was around the corner of the L-shaped room and I felt confident patting Jerry's leg to calm him. I needed to distract him. I could see Priya had put up one of her flyers, and I decided, for better or worse, now was the time to mention the gig.

"Have you seen this?" I pointed to Priya's daughter's poster with the words:

> Join us as we say goodbye to one of the island's most-loved guests at the café where it all started

"No." Jerry cupped his face before jumping out of his seat to read up close.

"Don't be cross with me. This wasn't really my idea. Priya wants to throw a talent show as a goodbye party. I'd host it, and we've got people coming to perform their talents. Priya is going to perform something, and so could you. Or not. It'll be short. What do you think?"

I braced for some outrage.

"That sounds bloody adorable."

"Really?" I gasped.

"Sounds like an episode of *Gilmore Girls*. Can I invite people from Greenford?"

"Of course." I grinned like an idiot.

He put his hand in mine and led me back to the seats – the first time we'd held hands since the photo incident.

"I'm very flattered by the effort of a goodbye gig."

"I wanted to do something nice, but it was Priya's idea. She's been the driving force."

"Oh...never mind then," he grinned.

"What?"

"Well, I thought it was a really boyfriend-y thing to do."

He still held my hand and carried them both to rest in his lap.

"I had the same thought." I tilted my head to one side, innocent of any ulterior motive, running my thumb down his index finger and across his palm. The frostiness of the last couple of weeks was thawing.

"So, shall I ask Priya to be my boyfriend?" Jerry was smiling and playing with my hands.

"You could…but she has a husband, so she might say no."

"If she says no, do you think I should ask you?" he said.

"It's a bit of a risk, but you're welcome to ask."

"Shut up," he laughed and pulled me into a kiss.

And it was that simple. We were boyfriends. The kiss was short and sweet as the receptionist called him to see the dentist. I waited twenty minutes, and when he shuffled out, he finally smiled.

"I had an injection. It kills."

"That sounds awful. Do we need to blend your food for the rest of the week?"

"I've always hated the dentist, but you've just made that fun."

"If you enjoyed that, just wait for the enema I'll give you later."

"I can hardly wait for my first-ever boyfriend's enema," he said, grabbing my bum.

Later, when I told Nat we were official, I expressed a slight gnawing concern that Jerry had come along so soon after my previous relationship.

"Shut up and just enjoy it," was her advice.

Typical.

***

The goodbye gig took up most of my mental space for a few days. Trying my best to get everything together in time, I barely had time to mope about Jerry leaving. I didn't have time to think about my argument with Dianne. I'd forgotten to prepare myself when I went to the shop for some goodbye gig essentials. She was there, on the till, like a dark cloud on an otherwise brilliant day. She looked up when I entered and then avoided any eye contact. She was the only cashier open, so I had no choice but to engage.

"Hi," I started.

"Hi-hi," she replied, "you've caught the sun."

"I was on holiday."

"I think I saw some holiday pictures," she said with a sneer, "and the comments."

I looked at my purchases, wondering if I could leave without them and storming off again.

"I hope you enjoyed yourself. It's been horrendous, in case you were concerned at all."

"Oh no." Her voice was flat. She was not betraying even a flicker of sympathy.

"You have no idea what it's like having people all over the world hate you for no reason. And I can't even reply or defend myself. Here, however, with you, I don't have to take it."

"Keep your knickers on."

"I shan't keep my knickers on. Where do you get off trying to ruin my relationship? Even if you hate me, do you know what you did to Jerry?"

She didn't reply. I glared and Dianne slowly swiped through my shopping.

"£14.97."

"Thanks," I said, despite myself.

I swiped my card and went to leave.

"I'm sorry for Jerry," she whispered.

"What?"

"I didn't mean to upset him."

"But I'm fair game? You don't have to like me, but you don't get to try to destroy me." I was worked up, and I rolled my eyes at myself. "I know that sounds dramatic, but that's what it feels like."

"You *know* what you did." Her jaw jutted forward.

"Get over it. I'm all for people having their feelings, but not every little hurt gives you carte blanche to be nasty." I snatched my shopping and flounced out of the shop. I'd never said carte blanche before and didn't feel confident I'd used it right.

The sun shined on No'Man and I felt triumphant.

***

When the night of the goodbye gig came around, I was in full-on panic mode. I had not performed stand-up since the night I was dumped. All week I had barely slept thinking about what my material might be. I decided to treat it as a new material night, but I had some classic jokes to fall back on if things weren't going well. As MC, I was mostly worried about preparing the audience for the acts and ad-libbing. I'd MC'd before but wasn't the best at it. I stared at my ceiling, imagining punchlines about people from the island, mainland, or anywhere in the world. At 6 am, I got up and decided to make some cakes to take my mind off everything. Several hours later, Priya arrived carrying a big box she had stashed away. It looked like an instrument carry case but was distinctly box shaped.

"What's that?" I asked.

"It's for later. It's a secret.' She shrugged her shoulders and smiled as she enjoyed teasing me. Whenever I alluded to the box, she'd sing

181

a song about secrets, one from Little Mix, one from Madonna, even the titles from the *Pretty Little Liars* TV show.

As soon as the lunch rush was done, Priya prepared for the show. I didn't mind at first as we weren't busy, but when she began to move tables and chairs that customers were still sitting in, I had to step in.

"I will finish my coffee in peace," Mr Sharp grumbled.

"Maybe we'll just move the tables and chairs when we're closed?" I said to Priya, ushering her to safety behind the counter.

We closed on time, finished the transformation for the goodbye gig and stopped to eat a sandwich an hour before the show to appreciate our handiwork.

"I can't believe how different the café feels," I commented.

The 'stage' area, which was just the floor marked with some tape, was up by the counter. We moved the tables and chairs into little rows and put a spotlight up on the stage. I changed the café's music system to a playlist on my laptop, which I could control remotely. I felt very professional.

"I only need to put up my bunting, and then we're sorted," Priya said between bites of coronation chicken.

I felt my stomach flipping around and made an excuse to change clothes to run upstairs. I was familiar with the terror-induced diarrhoea that comes with stand-up, but using my own toilet was a novel experience. I had 15 minutes before people were due to arrive, and I kept saying aloud it was plenty of time. Despite how calmly I spoke to myself, my forehead was beaded with sweat. I felt a single drop slide right down my back. I pulled a crying face in the mirror, but that was all I had time for. I got ready and went back downstairs. It almost felt like a real venue. There were soft drinks chilled in the cabinet and some snacks lined up along the counter. Priya was pouring some nuts into bowls, so I grabbed some crisps and began to help. As we carried the bowls around the room, people began to arrive.

There were several regulars, coupled with bizarre props to demonstrate their talent. There was Jean from the hairdressers over the road with her hula hoops and Malcolm from the yoga studio, who was planning to juggle machetes. We were friendly and waved them to take a seat wherever. Ten minutes before we started, Jerry turned up with some of his friends from Greenford. We'd saved them some seats that were near the front. Jerry's chair was decorated, by Priya, with some tinsel and an extra cushion and came with a footstool.

"This looks incredible," Jerry said, leaning in and kissing me on the cheek.

"I hope you're ready to be entertained," I replied, checking my list of performers and seeing that they'd all arrived.

"I'm very ready," he said, lifting a tiny ukulele.

"Are you joking?" I asked.

"Just bring me up at the end, so I can say thank you for coming," he said, relaxed, just like you'd expect from an actor who'd performed on the West End and Broadway. I smiled at him, barely concealing my envy. I'd had nervous diarrhoea at the thought of telling a few jokes, and he looked cool and collected. Jerry sat with his friends, and I settled behind the counter, ready to change the lights and begin. I waited five minutes while a pair of late arrivals grabbed some drinks and their seats. Then it was time. I turned on the spotlight, turned off the house lights and shouted to the room.

"People of the audience, please welcome to the stage your host for the evening, George Elizabeth Barnes," I announced. They began clapping, and there was cheering as I reached the stage. There were about thirty people in attendance, and only ten would be performing, so the sound wasn't riotous but was as much of a buzz as I remembered. I picked up the microphone and moved the stand toward the back of the stage.

"Thank you," I said as the claps died down, "how are we doing tonight?"

They applauded again.

"I don't really care, of course. I'm just building rapport."

They laughed a little.

"My name is George, and I'm a Gemini vegetarian, which is true but is also a quote from *Legally Blonde*. Reese Witherspoon and I have an awful lot in common. We're both powerhouse women in Hollywood obsessed with Nicole Kidman."

I got enough laughs; people knew what to expect. I did an official welcome and then started in on the audience. I did the classic "Who came from furthest away?" bit. We found some tourists from Norway who seemed nice. I did some classic material about female masturbation. It was a bit blue, but the joke was that it was my attempt to redress the balance of gendered jokes in comedy. I finished my set by reminding people I'm a platinum gay.

"That means I was born via caesarean, never once touched a vagina, not even by accident. But I don't like the term platinum gay because it sounds like I think it's a good thing, but I like vaginas! Not in a sexual way, more like gynaecology is a hobby. And as such, I'll be doing some free smear tests after tonight's show."

I got a good laugh then and introduced the first act. There was a couple who did sketches together. They were regulars at the café, and I was worried they'd be terrible, but the crowd laughed. I hovered behind the counter as they performed, and when they bowed, I rushed on stage to introduce the next act, the guitar man. He was talented. If you're into music, that's just a man and his six strings, but his song about drug addiction was a bit of a Debbie Downer.

After that, I made some jokes to lift the mood again. We had six acts in the first half, finishing with Priya. I introduced her, and she came up with an accordion. I'm not joking. She performed three quite short songs. They were all hilarious. There was one about dreading the menopause, and the next was about the trouble with living on the Isle of No'man. And she finished with a ballad about how she wished she'd married George Clooney, but changed the words to Jerry Hilk, she explained before launching into her song:

"Oh, I wish I was a bride once more with a veil in my hair
But instead of my poor husband at the end of the aisle,
Jerry Hilk would be there
I wouldn't live in squalor, Jerry would buy Gucci for me to wear,
Oh, I wish I was a bride once more with a veil in my hair."

She finished with some gusto on the accordion, and everyone clapped. I joined her on stage to announce the break and played music for some ambience.

"That was incredible, Priya," I told her as we hugged.

"I'm a bit rusty, but I am very good," she smiled.

We almost managed to get to the end of the break before people started asking for hot drinks, and Priya hopped behind the counter with me. We made quick work of the queue before I jumped back up on stage. I asked everyone if they got drinks and picked on some more people before launching into some material about some particularly bad sex I'd once had. I did feel a bit shy in front of Jerry, but the crowd were eating it up. We whipped through the next few acts, finishing with Jean, the hula hoop woman. After she performed, I joined the stage again.

185

"Wow, that was phenomenal. Let's give her a round of applause. No'Man's answer to Shakira, and that's no lie," I said as a nod to Shakira's 'Hips don't lie' that had been playing. I helped Jean clear her hoops off the stage.

"We have one final treat for you all before we head home. Please welcome to the stage, Bafta and Oscar-winning actor, and the second-best shag I've ever had – just kidding in case anyone writes for the *Daily Mail* – Jerry Hilk."

The crowd erupted into applause as Jerry bounded up to the stage.

"I just wanted to say a huge thank you to you all for coming out tonight. Who knew we lived amongst so much talent? Thank you to George. You've been an adequate host; disappointing there weren't more costume changes. I want to dedicate a song now to someone who has been a shield to me over the past few weeks, and unfortunately, I don't think I've done enough to make them feel the same. I hope what I'm about to do won't totally embarrass me and will go some way to showing what they mean to me. I apologise now for being so cringe…"

Jerry held up his ukulele, and everyone clapped again. I wish every audience were as easy. I clenched internally. A man playing a guitar or ukulele is my idea of hell. He strummed, then cleared his throat. Everyone seemed to lean in. He fingered away at the instrument, and the tune was familiar, but I couldn't work it out until he started to sing:

"I should be embarrassed, it's corny to say,
But you're the sweetest part of my day.
Life is full to the brim with stuff so plain or salty,
My time with you, honey, so sweet, it exalts me."

I held my breath, waiting to be horrified and embarrassed. He sang 'A Slice of Love' from *Just Desserts*. I felt relieved that he wasn't singing Oasis or Coldplay. Don't get me wrong, it wasn't good, but his performance was fun, at least. His voice was gravelly and cool, cooler than if it had been musical theatre-y. As he got to the chorus, people were swaying in their seats. Priya twirled behind the counter, and even Mr Sharp was tapping his foot:

"Give me another slice of your love, honey,
just an hour with you makes me feel funny,
down in my pants, I wanna take your hands,
and share all of our dreams and plans."

The whole café started to sing along. It was adorable. Jerry was smiling, and he never missed a note. I could see the charisma oozing out of his pores. He stopped, and the room fell silent. Transfixed. Jerry turned toward me and began to strum again, gazing directly into my eyes. I cannot stress enough that I would've made fun of this moment if I wasn't in it. But honestly, somewhere between 'Give me another slice' and 'down in my pants', I think I fell in love with him. The crowd cheered, and I was again aware that people existed outside of Jerry and me. He repeated the chorus, this time facing outwards and much louder. The whole café joined in again at the top of our lungs, enjoying a rousing sing-along.

"Give me another slice of your love, muffin,
For you I'd ride out any tumble and roughin',
I'd do or die whatever I can, I'd stop at nothin'
so please give me another slice of your lovin'."

187

We sang in unison, except Eileen, who obviously didn't know the words and so riffed. I had half a mind to ask her to stop ruining the most romantic thing that had ever happened to me. The song finished, and everyone cheered. The show had come to a roaring end. I ran over to Jerry and hugged him.

"You're amazing," I whispered into his ear, and he kissed me.

I said my goodbyes to the acts and cleared up. Things were back to normal almost, when Jerry's taxi arrived. We'd agreed that he would spend one final night in Greenford before giving up his room and coming to stay with me. But after his performance, I was reluctant to let him go. We hugged again.

"See you tomorrow," he said and left.

Priya looked over, eyebrow bobbing.

"Tonight was perfect. I'll see you tomorrow," Priya said, giving me the briefest but loveliest hug.

"You're perfect," I said back to her.

Priya's gorgeous husband was waiting outside with her accordion, and I watched the pair of them mooch off home, hand in hand. I returned to work, cleaning what we'd used, replenishing the drinks cabinet and setting up partly for the next day.

Priya was starting early so I could be off and spend time with Jerry, but I felt guilty as we'd all had a late night. I knew Jerry wouldn't be early at my house, so I got up at my usual time and started to set up.

"I wish I'd stayed in bed another hour if you were gonna do all this." Priya pointed all around.

"Sorry," I said, unsure how to respond. This was the most cross Priya had been with me.

Trevor came in on time, so I sequestered myself in the kitchen and made a couple of cakes. Jerry arrived mid-lunch, and I let him in through the flat doorway.

"Sorry I'm late," he said, smiling and taking off his sunglasses.

We ate some lunch and went for a walk. We wandered the entire way around the island, stopping for dinner at a pub I'd never been to before.

"I can't believe you're going, and we've just discovered this place."

The tables were sticky, but there was a sea view, and the food was smashing. I had tomato soup with bread and butter and a side of chips, which Jerry kept pinching.

"You're right. Maybe I'll change my mind."

"Don't tease me like this." I was smiling and joking, but doom loomed over us.

Everything was for the last time now.

We continued our walk, quiet and a little breathless as we climbed the cliffs, only chatting again when the path led downhill and to the beach. We'd arrived at the same spot we'd had our first date if you'd call it that. I suggested dipping our feet.

"I'm going to get athlete's foot if I keep getting my feet wet and dry like this," Jerry whispered into my ear, hugging me from behind.

"That's so romantic."

"Let's come back here every five years, the beach where we started falling in love." He kissed my cheek. "Romantic enough for you?"

My mouth hung open. He wasn't being serious, but part of him believed that in five years, we'd still be together. In fact, he thought there would be multiple five years. Also, falling in love? We hadn't said 'love' yet, but it was on his mind.

"What do you mean come back? I might still be here, making cake and cappuccinos."

"You might, and I could be retired from acting. Just a washed-up old has-been, telling all the kids at my ukulele lessons about the good old days when I was a movie star."

"Would you call yourself a movie star?" I jibed at him, and he stuck his tongue out at me.

"I mean, I wouldn't call myself a movie star. That would be em-barrassing."

I laughed at him. The sun was setting, and he pulled me into a kiss. Did people really do this? Kissing at sunset? I suppose thin straight couples did it all the time. Jerry has been in films where he'd gotten to do this. But I couldn't believe, at that moment, that I'd gotten to do this.

We raced the rest of the way home and, as you can imagine, had sex – a couple of times. Each time it felt like the end of something. Soon, it was dark, and we were lying in bed, top and tailed and tangled up in the sheets. His head was curled up on my stomach.

"Are you nervous I'm leaving?" Jerry asked, playing with my hand in his.

"I don't know if I'd say nervous. I don't feel sure that everything will work out. But I'm hopeful that it does. But if it doesn't, there's probably a good reason for that." I was lying. To be honest, I did not feel that relaxed.

"You make it seem like we don't have any control over it."

Without seeing his face, I couldn't read his expression. How could I know what to feel if I didn't know what Jerry was thinking?

"It's too soon in our relationship. If we'd been going out for a year, it would make sense to plan to see each other and discuss the future. But it's such early days. I think all relationships take work, and if we're meant to be, then we'll both want to put in the effort."

Neither of us spoke, and we fell asleep. Waiting for the guillotine blade to drop down, severing our togetherness.

I felt extremely melodramatic.

The next morning, we were leisurely, but there was a tense atmosphere. I started getting ready, and Jerry began being annoying. I was trying to make French toast, but he was at the sink and flipping the bread. I snatched the tongs.

"Do you want me to go and wait at the helipad? I feel like I'm getting in the way?" he asked.

I took the frying pan off the heat and hugged him.

"Not at all. It's just that you're a terrible sous-chef," I said, but I know I probably should've just apologised for being pissy. I plated up our food and worked hard at being cheery. I hummed as I sat, which would've been an indicator that I was not OK. I've never been a hummer.

"At least we don't have to worry about cooking together for a while," I was trying to look for silver linings, but instead, I could feel tears gathering behind my eyes.

We ate, dressed, and kissed some more, but there was no avoiding it any longer. I put my shoes on to go with him.

"You don't have to walk me to the airfield?"

"I don't mind." I shrugged. My bottom lip quivered but I ignored it. I didn't want to be ridiculous; he was moving home, not dying. We walked hand in hand to the airfield, and he kissed me.

"I'll see you soon. This isn't goodbye."

191

His face rested against mine, but I could feel him smile.

"No, of course not. I'll see you soon."

He walked away and turned as he stepped onboard, waving at me. The helicopter took off and I felt this sinking feeling in my stomach, but also, I felt relief. It's like knowing you're going to be sick, it's not nice as it's happening, but it's nice to see that it's already out of your control.

Whatever was going to unfurl, it had begun.

***

It was hard when Jerry left. I realised I'd depended on him to fill what would've been many lonely hours. It wasn't like when I'd broken up with a boyfriend but was still at home and could see everyone I knew. Priya invited me for dinner to try and make something with the tagine she'd bought on holiday in the summer. It was nice, if not authentic. Despite keeping busy, Nat could tell something was up with me.

"You're still feeling glum?" she asked over the phone.

"Sorry, I don't have much to report. Go to work, chat with Priya, and bake. I never have anything to tell you about."

"Jerry's not your whole life. Come on, George," she chastised.

"Of course not. I don't have much else going on here."

"Maybe there's not enough happening on No'Man?" she mused, sparking an idea.

"Why don't I come home for a visit? Just for the weekend?"

"Oh my god, yes! You can see me, invite your mum for lunch, and you can see Jerry."

"But wouldn't that be inviting Jerry to meet my mum? Don't you think that's too intense?"

"Or, is it a good way to show you're serious?"

"You're a genius."

I would've leapt down the phone and kissed Nat if I could. When she hung up, I excitedly kicked my arms and legs, bashing my knee on the wall. It hurt so much, but I didn't care; I was going home.

Shut up; you know what I mean.

I hobbled over to the calendar in the kitchen to pick the right dates. I texted Nat and Jerry to make sure they were free, and then, incorporating my knee injury into my movement work, I danced around the kitchen.

12

Bickering is Foreplay

The weekend was upon us.

I caught the boat to the mainland and walked to the train station. Jerry had offered to send a helicopter, but I declined, being so independent and all. I lugged a weekend bag around, a dead weight swinging around my neck. It was heavy, and I felt like a martyr for heaving side to side to get through doors and off the ferry. I noticed other people with much larger luggage. A child was carrying a guitar and a bag, and a mum held a baby, bag, and pram under her arm. I was being pathetic.

OK, yes.

Very pathetic.

I spent the entire train journey unable to sit still. Phrases from my argument with Mum kept popping into my head. As I ushered each thought away from my brain, a worry about seeing her would pop into my head, like whack-a-mole, anxiety popping up from a new place. It was exhausting.

Pulling into London Victoria felt like returning home. A feeling I attempted to deny as I was loyal to No'Man now. It was easier to ignore as I headed to Kensington, and the familiarity faded, replaced by dread. Following a map on my phone, I managed to find Jerry's house. It was a tall white building sandwiched between identical houses with a postage stamp-sized front garden, paved over with a few manicured potted plants. I messaged him, and he came to the door. He was wearing ripped jeans and a white T-shirt.

"Hey baby," he said, pulling me into the hallway for a kiss.

"You didn't have to dress up for me," I said, fingering the hole in his jeans. I thought I was being funny, but then worried I was being nagging. Although, for a multi-millionaire, he could've worn something a bit more remarkable.

"Haha, I'll change before lunch, promise."

Once inside, I could see the black-and-white tile on the floor and the open doorways leading to other rooms. I went to kiss him again, but Jerry held me back.

"Dottie is here," he whispered.

"Ah," I mouthed.

And that was all the heads up I had time for as Dorothy entered the hall. She had that stretched quality that kids have when they're almost not kids anymore – long limbs. Her dark brown hair was in a ponytail, and her outfit was extremely pink, with a baby blue cardigan. She looked cool. Was I intimidated by a tween?

"Hello," I said, using the voice that my favourite teachers used when trying to be nice.

"Hi," she said in a voice even tinier than she was.

"Have you and your dad been doing anything fun?"

Dorothy shrugged, all the while not taking her eyes off me. I felt very appraised. None of us spoke.

"Dorothy's mum is coming to get her, and they're going to the Natural History Museum." Jerry sounded excited as he brought her in for a side hug.

"Natural history sounds fun," I said.

"She's doing a school project about the differences between reptiles and mammals," Jerry explained.

Dorothy's head bobbed up and down.

"Well, firstly, mammals tend to be more adorable. You should write that down."

"You absolutely should not write that down," Jerry smiled.

"Your dad's right. I'm not very good at science. You probably know way more about reptiles than me," I said, wondering how we came to this place in our conversation.

"Reptiles are cold-blooded, and they lay eggs."

"Wow, that's clever. I didn't know that." I was genuinely impressed. I don't often think about animals in that way.

"Are you and my dad boyfriends?"

I opened my mouth to answer but stopped. My eyes darted toward Jerry, who came to life.

"Do you remember we talked about this yesterday? George is my boyfriend, and it's OK if that takes some getting used to. And if we spend more time together, you'll get to know him a lot more, but it's very early days."

"Your dad said he didn't know if I was cool enough to hang out with you. He's going to test me today, and he'll let me know if I pass."

Dorothy smiled at me. I think she thought I was funny. Little did she know that I was planning on becoming her new mummy. Jerry crouched down.

"And even if I have a boyfriend, or a girlfriend, or get married, or have any more children, or even a pony, I'll still always love you."

Dorothy dove in for a hug, and I thought it was sweet. I didn't want to be inappropriate, but nothing is fitter than a man being a good dad.

Phwoar!

They hugged, and it felt like they forgot I was there, which was probably only right. I stared at them, smiling to myself. I almost went for some popcorn, thinking I was watching Jerry in a film. I had to say something.

"Hold on a second. Are you getting a pony?" I interjected. Later, when I thought back, I wondered if I was a narcissist because I'd interrupted. I can hardly blame myself for being a narcissist. I'm incredible. There was a beep from the street.

"Sounds like Mum is here."

Jerry took Dorothy out to the car.

"It was lovely to meet you," I called after Dorothy.

I watched as Jerry chatted with her mum and then watched them drive off.

How did Jerry *ever* fancy her and me? Dorothy's mum was also an A-list actor, gorgeous and talented. I'm not certain Isabella Jergen and I were even the same species.

"I'm sorry," I said when he returned, feeling stupid because I'd interrupted.

"What for? You weren't early. Dottie's mum was late. But it's no problem. I want you to get to know her, but I think it's too soon, especially as I've just returned from Greenford."

"Won't her mum be cross? That I was here?" I ask, prying. I wanted to know more because she was Jerry's ex, but I was curious about Isabella Jergen. As well as being jealous of her, I was a fan and afraid of her hating me.

"Izzie? Not at all. We've been doing this for a while now. There's not really anything to worry about."

I bobbed my head, neither a shake nor a nod, in lieu of saying something.

"Where were we?" He tilted his head before stepping closer and kissing me. I pulled my lips away for a second.

"We need to go and meet my mum," I tried to explain, but the kissing was relentless.

"We have time," he said, dragging me into the living room, where we had sex on a green velvet sofa. It was exquisite, up until the moment I made eye contact with a doll whilst being entered. A sight too explicit for the poor Cabbage Patch baby. I found myself putting on the performance of my life, in case any of the toys were secretly a nanny cam.

If I was going to have a sex tape leak, it would at least be tremendous.

***

Our taxi arrived at the restaurant, and we were ten minutes late. Mum stood at the bar.

"Mum," I called, and she turned around.

As I saw her, my earlier concerns disappeared, and without thinking, we hugged. I realised how scary it might be meeting with your estranged son and his new Hollywood boyfriend, so I felt grateful she was there. I didn't care what had happened anymore; I just wanted to make sure she had a nice lunch.

"They wouldn't let me sit down until all the party were here," she said, without letting go.

"That's ridiculous. What buttholes." I broke free of her embrace to introduce Jerry.

"You must be Tina." Jerry leant in to embrace her.

"Oh, sorry, yes, Tina, Jerry." I pointed at each of them. It was not the slickest introduction.

Following the waiter to our seats I decided to be a bit of an arse-hole to him for making Mum wait. Being rude to waiters is completely unacceptable, but what can you do when they are rude to people you love? Also, the extent of my rudeness was that I didn't smile. I still said please as I ordered a drink. I'd probably say I was being courteous but cold. No one else said anything, as the whole thing was entirely in my head.

"How was the train, Tina?" Jerry asked.

"It was absolutely fine, thanks. I used to commute into London all the time, a little trip down memory lane."

"What did you do?" Jerry asked, and I began to relax a little.

"I only worked in a shop. It was a long time ago. It's where I met George's dad."

The conversation flowed nicely, without much input from me. I only piped up as the food arrived because my mac 'n' cheese had a watery bottom.

"You're so fussy," Mum laughed. Jerry joined in.

I almost lost my pupils, rolling my eyes at them. Thankfully dessert was better. I couldn't afford two failed courses. We'd even begun to have fun until the bill arrived.

"Shall we split it?" Mum suggested.

"I'm happy to split," I agreed. It wasn't an extortionate amount of money, although it was a little fancier than I was used to.

"Why don't I get this, and someone can just get a round of drinks later?" Jerry offered, reaching for his wallet.

"You can't get everyone's meal," said Mum, "that's very generous, but I'd like to get my own if that's OK?"

I was torn. I knew Mum wasn't loaded, and Jerry was, but I didn't want Jerry to feel like we'd invited him so that he would pay. Meanwhile, the waiter approached our table with the card machine. I was still unsure of what to do. I was tempted to get up and hide in the toilet until it all ended. Jerry reached for the card machine.

"I'll get it," he said, shoving in his card before we could stop him.

"Will you send me your bank details?" Mum was firm, and I sensed she was borderline livid.

"It's fine," Jerry brushed it off.

The meal had taken a bizarre turn, although I secretly found it amusing that Mum had asked for his bank details. We filed outside and Jerry offered us back to his house for coffee, which Mum accepted.

Jerry offered a tour, to which Mum and I agreed. He moved into the living room. The sofa was messed up, with my stuff scattered everywhere, cushions on the floor, and toilet paper lying conspicuously in a guilty pile. In the time it took me to notice what was going on, Mum turned back to the hall.

"Can I spend a penny first?" she asked Jerry, who pointed to a door down the hall. I was beetroot red.

"This is not OK," I whispered, although Jerry sniggered. I put the cushions back whilst Jerry cleared away anything unsavoury.

Mortifying.

The cistern flushed, so I perched on the end of the sofa in a bid to look casual and waited. Mum re-entered the now tidy living room.

"Much better," she said. I sensed she was laughing but couldn't even look at her.

"This is the front room, I tend to watch TV in here mostly, or rather, my daughter does. Although, she's got me into *Moana*," Jerry continued in earnest. "If you'd like to follow me."

He disappeared from view, and we followed down the corridor, past a formal dining room and into an elongated kitchen leading to the garden. I also saw the toilet attached at the back of the kitchen with an ante-chamber room for sanitary reasons. None of my old flats had designated sanitation areas. This place was fancy.

We walked out into the overgrown garden. It was devastatingly beautiful; several trees with low-hanging branches, shrubs surrounding the roots, and potted plants. The pavement gave way to grass, and you could see glimpses of stone walls that kept the garden private. A large wooden table and six seats were on the paved section.

"You've kept the furniture in good condition." Mum ran her hand along the table.

"There's an awning that comes out when it rains." Jerry shrugged.

He moved back inside to continue the tour. We followed him toward the front of the house again, but this time, Jerry stopped at the cupboard under the stairs. He opened the door into a dark space.

"Is this where you murder us?" said Mum.

"Not today," he smiled and turned on a light switch, "this is the best part of the house."

We followed him down carpeted stairs and found ourselves in Jerry's secret hideaway. There was a small kitchenette, with fridges full of soft drinks and an old-fashioned popcorn machine, which was empty.

"Great idea, but it's rare I ever have enough people over to use it," Jerry explained, laying a hand on the machine.

"This can't all be for you?" Mum said.

"No, you're right. I host film nights occasionally, especially when I'm producing the film. There's an edit suite just through there," Jerry said, pointing to a door, "but the best bit…"

Jerry had gone all Willy Wonka on me. I half expected I'd turn into a giant blueberry or he'd make us lick the wallpaper. Jerry skipped over to the other doorway. He paused for a moment, and then, with a flourish, he opened the door. Inside was a cinema. The chairs looked more comfortable than your average cinema, don't get me wrong. The carpet was thick and luxurious, the seats large and toward the back the cinema chairs had morphed together into a sofa cinema hybrid. Around the screen, which was almost the entire width of the room, were massive speakers. He pointed to some at the back and along the ceiling. It was cosier than Elton John's cinema room, perhaps more lived in. Certainly, there was less Elton John paraphernalia. Can you believe I've got multiple A-lister's home cinemas to compare? I had to hope Jerry would never leave me because I couldn't go back to sharing a cinema.

"Full surround sound," he said, bobbing his eyebrows, chuffed with himself.

"Don't your neighbours complain?" Mum asked.

I'd gone quiet because I was impressed but also a little mortified. I couldn't tell what my mum thought of this millionaire's mansion.

"It's soundproof," Jerry explained.

"You really could kill someone down here if you wanted," Mum considered aloud.

"It wouldn't be a great idea. It would take ages to clean blood out of the carpet," Jerry replied, which I found funny and a little chilling.

Watching Jerry play host in his natural habitat was like seeing him in fancy dress, but I liked seeing the home he'd made himself. The house was neutrally decorated but with touches of him, like film posters outside the cinema or the family pictures which trailed up the staircase. Seeing my boyfriend's bedroom for the first time was also peculiar whilst standing next to my mum. The house was so tall, Jerry's room was quite far away, and we were exhausted. I thought about setting up shop in the bedroom forever.

"I think I can tempt you downstairs with some coffee in the garden. I have cake."

Mum and I bolted out of the room, motivated by cake. Jerry made some cappuccinos and grabbed me a bottle of water. He brought out some Portuguese custard tarts that had been delivered fresh that morning.

"This is lovely." Mum replaced her cup and rubbed her hand on the polished table top. A bowl of limes was in the centre; one cut open purely for the smell. Jerry and I sat opposite Mum, and he rubbed my foot with his own.

"So, you two are an official couple now?"

Jerry looked at me, and I looked back at him with a falsely passive face as if I didn't care what answer he gave.

"Well, yes, we're certainly on our way there. I wouldn't say we're Instagram official or anything."

"What's Instagram official?" Mum sipped her drink.

"I don't really know, I just meant that we're not going around telling everyone, but we might be soon."

"What Jerry means," I stepped in, "is that we're seeing one another, and it *might* be about to get a bit more serious."

"I won't place an engagement notice in the local paper tomorrow then," Mum chuckled to herself. I laughed too, but Jerry's eyes widened in terror.

"She's joking. People do that, but we're not doing it."

I must've sounded snappier than I realised as Jerry looked at me.

"I probably ought to be making my way home. I'd rather not get the train too late."

"Actually, why don't I book you a taxi?" Jerry offered.

"No, it's fine. I can take the tube."

"Honestly, I'll book a taxi to your home." Jerry whipped out his phone. "I have a car service, so I get an excellent rate."

"That's too generous."

Mum was uncomfortable. I was uncomfortable too, but I felt much better knowing she didn't have to get the train. I wouldn't worry about Nat getting the train, but my mum seemed so out of her depth in the city.

"I'll split it with him. That's such a good idea. You get taken straight home. I think it's genius," I added to the conversation.

Mum agreed, and Jerry called for a taxi. I stood with her as she put on her shoes.

"It was great to see you." Her eyes started to fill.

"Thanks for coming. I'll be home for a longer visit at Christmas. I promise."

"Of course, we miss you at home."

I thought Mum was losing it for a minute, but then I remembered Willy, the pampered loser labradoodle. I don't think Willy missed me, and I certainly wasn't missing him.

I like dogs, but Willy was an arsehole.

I hugged Mum, and we walked out to the taxi. I borrowed some of Jerry's slippers, which felt really couple-y, and I cringed at how much of a loser I was for enjoying such stupid things.

When I came back in, Jerry opened his arms to hug me.

"I will pay toward the taxi – you don't have to offer to pay for stuff, but I did appreciate that."

"It's honestly fine. And I didn't want to waste time coming back from the station alone when you're back for such a short time."

"Let me get dinner tonight?"

"What are we doing for dinner?" Jerry asked.

I grinned, knowing what was in store for us.

"Pizza."

It's what I dreamt about on the island, a decent pizza delivery from a well-known brand. The pizzas I got delivered to the café were alright, but they didn't fill the hole in my heart that yearned for top-notch takeaway.

***

I had enough time to change clothes and unpack my massive bag in Jerry's room before Nat and Emmanuel arrived. Jerry came in from the kitchen just as Nat and Emmanuel took off their shoes. I hugged Nat and embraced Emmanuel, a solid man with a masculine yet floral smell – a great combo.

"Fantastic to meet you, Emmanuel," I said loudly and directly into his ear.

"Thanks for having us," he said.

"Oh, I'm not hosting. I just opened the door!"

I introduced Jerry to Emmanuel and Emmanuel to Jerry.

"It's fate, because Nat and I are so similar; it's like you two are destined to be best friends too or something…" I added, hoping to make fun of the pressure to get along.

Emmanuel laughed loudly.

We did the tour again, but I jumped in to explain things this time. It was fun to pretend I lived there, but not in an obsessive way.

"This set of drawers is vintage. It belonged to Andy Warhol's hairdresser." I pointed at a random set of drawers.

"That's a lie," Jerry explained, and I laughed, thinking myself hilarious. Emmanuel agreed, chuckling away.

"We have the largest collection of bedding in Europe because someone struggles for a dry night." I stroked Jerry's back, enjoying my joke more than I ought to.

"Still lying," Jerry added.

Emmanuel laughed more. He'd be great for an open mic, I mentally noted, as we walked down to the basement.

"It is haunted by the ghost of Queen Anne. She's harmless, except for the thing with the maid. But we never talk about that,' I said.

Jerry gave up, and we retreated upstairs and into the garden. Jerry made everyone drinks. Emmanuel helped deliver them, so I had two minutes to chat with Nat. I could hear Emmanuel laugh from the kitchen.

"What do you think?" Nat whispered to me, bobbing her eyes to Emmanuel through the window.

"Amazing, so nice, really fit, nice laugh, can totally see us being sister wives if the situation ever arises," I whispered.

"So, you like him?"

"Full disclosure, it's quite soon to tell, like maybe he's wildly in-appropriate, but it hasn't come up yet. For the moment, I'm deeply impressed. What do you think?"

"Nice place, doesn't feel too bachelor pad-y. He's being nice, you seem very comfortable with each other, no red flags."

"God, we are so good. I'm impressed with us and the men we've allowed into our lives."

"We're amazing," Nat said, a little louder than the rest of our hushed conversation.

"I'm not going to disagree with you," Emmanuel said as he de-livered a drink and kiss on Nat's cheek, then giggled.

"I wouldn't disagree that Nat is amazing," Jerry challenged me with his eyes.

"Nasty," I said under my breath.

Bickering is *foreplay* to me.

The night crept in, and we moved inside as it got cooler. We settled in the living room with music channels on in the back-ground. Nat and I love watching music videos.

"Do you know her?" Nat asked Jerry as each new video came on. This time she was asking about Lady Gaga.

"I always liked her, but she slated my film *Just Desserts*, so now, I'm not as keen." Jerry answered each question as though he were being interviewed, although he was more honest than usual. "We didn't date, but my team thought it would be helpful if we were rumoured to be dating."

"Does that happen a lot?" Emmanuel followed up.

"More than you'd realise," Jerry said, very mysteriously, but re-fusing to answer any follow-up questions.

It was getting late, so Nat and Emmanuel decided to stay the night. Jerry had a ton of spare eco-friendly toothbrushes that he'd been sent as gifts and lots of dressing gowns. It was almost as though he regularly had groups to sleep over. I wasn't jealous.

"It's so handy you have everything for random people to stay over."

"I have events that run late, so it's not uncommon for my manager to stay over sometimes. Is that weird?" Jerry replied. We were in the upstairs hall gathering things for Nat and Emmanuel.

"Not at all," I lied.

We all went to bed, and Jerry started kissing me, but I told him to get off.

"Are you alright?" he asked.

"Yeah, just in a funny mood and not up for it."

"We don't have to have sex. I wanna get some close-up time with you before you head back tomorrow."

I smiled without showing my teeth, seemingly in agreement. I don't know why I was feeling like this. It was like we'd done so much getting to know one another, but I realised I'd only just scratched the surface. I was annoyed at myself for being too afraid to ask some of Nat's questions. Too worried to acknowledge the fact I knew of Jerry before we'd met for fear he'd see me as only a fan, someone who'd embarrass him at parties. I turned away from Jerry, and he cuddled up behind me. I threw back the covers to avoid getting too hot before falling asleep.

The next morning, I was in the kitchen, looking through the cupboards foraging for food as Nat came in.

"Good morning."

"How did you sleep?"

"Dreamy, this house is so comfortable. Emmanuel is still asleep, which rarely happens, so I'm just enjoying it."

"Jerry's asleep too. He does tend to sleep later than me."

I was on tiptoes looking for cinnamon in a top cupboard when I heard a glass clink. Out of instinct, I stopped what I was doing, worried I'd knocked something over. I didn't see anything, so I leant unnaturally to the side and spotted a bottle of vodka.

Oh god.

I didn't say anything to Nat. I put it back and pretended I didn't see it. I closed the door and said something about the cupboards being bare.

"Are you alright?" I asked.

"Yeah, it's great that you're back. I love it. I didn't realise how much time has passed since you left."

"Time marches on, I guess," I was being glib.

"What do you think, being back? Are you missing London? Or desperate to get back to the café and coast life?"

"I miss you. And I miss London. I'm not desperate to get back to work. I'm sorry I missed so much of you getting to know Emmanuel. He's perfect."

"I love him. I know it's a bit overly emotional, but I love him so much I can't imagine my life without him. It could be the honeymoon stage talking, but I hope we get married one day."

Emmanuel walked into the kitchen silently, not laughing for once.

"What?" he asked, still sleepy-eyed, wearing a dressing gown that Jerry had found for him.

"Just talking about having French toast. Nat's really into it," I lied, getting up to start breakfast.

"Can't wait," she smiled, the fear leaving her eyes as Emmanuel settled his bum in a seat and his head on the table, clearly having not heard Nat's gushing declaration.

"Do you want tea?" I offered.

"If my future wife is having one, then I will."

Nat put her face in her hands, and I giggled as I popped the kettle on. Without lifting his head, he put an arm around Nat, and she used her spare hand to caress his head. They were so cute I could've died. Jerry wasn't down yet, so I popped upstairs to get him. I left the kitchen and all jovial feelings drained from my body.

That *vodka bottle* played on my mind.

"Breakfast is ready," I told Jerry, popping my head into the room.

"I'm coming," he replied, although he didn't move.

I went back downstairs.

"He'll be down shortly," I said.

After eating I dished out Jerry's portion because I didn't think it would be nice much longer. I cleared the table, and Emmanuel helped to load the dishwasher as Nat went for a shower.

"Thanks for breakfast, mate," he said.

"No worries. Thanks for your help."

"It's been good to meet you. I can't believe it's taken this long. I know how much you mean to Nat."

My face flushed.

"If you move back to London, you can always stay with us. I know you probably know that, I just feel like I should say," Emmanuel said with a shrug.

"I'm not moving back."

"Yeah, I know, but when you do."

"What has Nat said?" I quickly picked up the chopping board and knife and cut my finger. The conversation ended as I was bleeding rather a lot. I ran it under the tap and then grabbed some kitchen roll to wrap around my hand.

"You OK?" Emmanuel was putting away the last bits.

"Yeah, just gonna go get changed." I stood up, fully intending to talk to Nat, but Emmanuel followed me, deciding now was the perfect time for him to get ready. I had to climb the stairs and change in Jerry's room. He was still lying in bed, looking at his phone now.

"Have they gone?" he asked.

"No."

"Good, I need to come and say goodbye."

"Hmmm."

I was furious. I dressed as quickly as possible, spraying on deodorant in a rage and shoving my T-shirt over my head. Jerry slowly got up and found a dressing gown, but I was packed, dressed, and storming out before he reached the door. I slammed it behind me and took all my things to the front door. I heard Jerry come down and go straight to the kitchen. Emmanuel joined me.

"I'm gonna head to the train station shortly. Are you guys headed home soon?" I asked, my voice breaking despite my best efforts to fill the silence, wanting to pretend everything was fine. Nat came downstairs.

"I think we should be heading off," Nat said, then ventured off to the kitchen to say goodbye to Jerry. I smiled at Emmanuel to dispel the tension, but I don't think he was convinced. Nat returned, I hugged her briskly and said, "See you soon" as they opened the door. They left, and I waved before slamming the door. I walked back to the kitchen.

"They're gone now."

"Can't believe I've slept in so late."

Jerry sat with his legs resting on a chair with a cup of coffee in his hand.

"I'm gonna head out." I rested my hands on one of the chairs.

"What? Your train isn't for ages."

I went to the cupboard and took out the vodka bottle. Jerry stared at it.

"I…" He opened his mouth to lie, then closed it again, looking at my face.

"Thought so."

"You won't understand this because it's bad, and I can't deny it. I haven't drunk it. It's my 'just in case' stash. But I shouldn't have it. You're right to be mad at me."

"I don't know you. I thought I did, but…"

"You know I have a problem with alcohol. I haven't hidden it from you. I mean, this one bottle, but I've been honest about everything else."

"I thought you were recovering, but you're still in the thick of it. I'm not negating all your hard work, but I didn't realise how hard this is for you. I thought we were starting this new wonderful thing, and everything was perfect. It's not."

"It's not perfect, but it's pretty bloody close. I love…spending time together. I haven't drunk anything, and I can get rid of that." Jerry grabbed the bottle and tipped it down the sink.

We stood silently, waiting for the vodka to drain.

"I appreciate that. I don't think it's enough. It's not just this. When we were on the island, everything was straightforward. But now I'm here, and I don't know how to be in a relationship with you. You can't take me to the station now. How crap is that?"

"What?"

"I'm trying to explain. I think we're kidding ourselves that Jerry Hilk and some coffee shop person were going to make a go of things. What're we gonna do when you're tempted by a drink and I'm in the middle of the lunchtime rush? Who will cover for me at the café if you need a plus one for the Oscars? I can't be there for you and be in my life."

"This is coming from literally nowhere."

Jerry threw the bottle into the recycling, making me jump as it smashed. He slumped down in the kitchen chair and put his head in his hands.

"Thank you for the weekend."

I walked out of the kitchen. I collected my bag and stepped outside, closing the front door. I waited ten seconds, which I'd seen on *Sex and the City*, but Jerry didn't follow. I counted to twenty as I had a slow realisation that perhaps I'd acted too rashly. This is why I don't trust myself to make decisions. Jerry still didn't come, and I couldn't go back, so I pressed forward. I walked two streets toward the tube, found a bench, and cried for ten minutes. It was very not *Sex and the City* as I wiped my nose on my sleeve, and two teenage boys pointed at me as they walked past. I looked at my phone, keen to get myself off the bench and to the train station.

Nat had texted me asking why I had been acting weird. I replied that I couldn't chat, but that Jerry and I had argued. I went underground and surfaced at London Bridge to a flurry of messages from Nat. The last one said she was at London Bridge. My flare for the dramatic meant I considered ignoring her text. I decided that was too mean, so I asked to meet outside M&S food. I went into the shop to get some cookies.

Men come and go, but you can depend on baked goods.

While waiting for Nat, I sighed and bit into the chocolatey, gooey goodness. Another tear rolled down my cheek, mixing with the cookie crumbs. Nat appeared, and I swallowed my last mouthful.

"Hello," I muttered in a tiny voice. She hugged me.

213

"Sorry," I blubbed, "I'm such an arsehole."

"It's OK. We're all arseholes, really."

"I think we just broke up. I woke up this morning and saw all the ways this wouldn't work. All the resentments we'd have, the compromises."

"You just broke up with him. It feels sudden."

"I know, but I feel so certain this would end in disaster in a year's time, and I can't face it again…"

"What did he say?"

"Nothing. I think that's what made it worse. This isn't just me panicking; he must feel the same."

Nat rubbed my back, slowly leading me toward a bench. An elderly couple saw us coming and left. My raw display of emotion was off-putting.

"There there, you'll feel better soon."

"I've done it again, haven't I?"

Nat bit her lip. People kept milling past, only glancing at the grown man in tears.

"I've run away again. I don't know how to undo it."

"You don't always run away," Nat began to explain.

"I didn't leave Rob. He dumped me. I should have sprinted to the next borough of London. Now, I can't keep hold of anything."

My tears fell freely, and Nat put her arm around my shoulders. We didn't speak for a while, and I cried freely. I forgot to feel insecure about weeping. It was Nat who started us up again.

"Emmanuel told me what he'd said. I think he phrased it all wrong. I don't think it's inevitable that you'll come back. I'd love for you to come back to London, and I always have space for you. But I know you'll make your own decisions."

"I was in such a bad mood earlier. I think it was a funny five minutes. It's so nice what he was saying. I'm so lucky to have you as a safety net. And you have me if you need me."

We locked eyes. Nat moved her head inward, and I did the same. Our mouths were breathing space apart. It seemed as though we were about to kiss. We both started laughing.

"One day, I swear it's going to happen."

"In your dreams," Nat laughed.

And just like that, I felt so much better.

13

Back to No'Man with No Man

I got off the train and boarded the boat. Sam was working, and I didn't want to interrupt, so I waved. It was comforting to see a friendly face after ending things with Jerry. Even though Sam wasn't my bosom buddy, he looked happy to see me. It was out of season and there were only five passengers – a family I didn't recognise and me. I assumed they were tourists looking for a cheap trip. Halfway between shores, Sam came up and tapped my shoulder.

"Hi-hi. How was your weekend?" he asked.

"That's a complicated question," I laughed, "how was yours?"

"Boring, work, the normal. I did stay on the mainland last night. I went to"—he looked around before leaning closer—"a gay club."

"Wow! How was that?"

"It was scary. I guess it's like a normal club, but it feels more sexual."

Sam responded to something on his radio. I took a swig of water and resisted the urge to look at my phone and see if Jerry had messaged. Our lack of communication was like a phantom limb. My phone was a constant reminder that he wasn't talking to me. I couldn't message Jerry after how we ended things, but surely if he cared, he would message me. Sam and I chatted about various clubbing experiences, although I hadn't been 'out out' for around 100

216

years. Then Sam got up so we could dock. It was a mixed feeling, being back on the island. It was familiar, but I can't say it felt homelier than London.

I stepped ashore with Sam's help, waved him off and walked up the street. I had a feeling that I wasn't the country mouse I was trying desperately to be. I'd been away for the weekend, and everything was the same upon my return. Dark clouds closed in from the ocean, and the summer was giving way to autumn, but even the change in weather wasn't as thrilling as it would've been in London. Nothing on the island had held my attention. I hadn't even swam in the sea since I'd moved.

When I reached home, I dumped my stuff, changed into my swimming trunks and returned to the beach. I walked along the coastal path, away from where the boat docked and around to a quieter section of water. It was actively cold, I wanted to pull my jacket tighter, but I had to force myself to remove it. I took off my shoes, dumped my towel and removed my jumper and T-shirt. As the air hit my chest, my skin pimpled. With as much gusto as I could manage, I traipsed into the sea. My feet were fine in the water until the cold lapped up my calves, and the shock was almost unmanageable. I tied the string around my trunks tighter and carried on wading.

Come on, George. One, two, three.

I dipped my face underwater. Nothing registered but coldness. Water swirled around my arms, into my armpits and through the hair on my head. I broke the water with my face, and I don't want to oversell it, but I felt reborn. The sea carried me in and out of the shore. I jumped as waves arrived, riding them onto the beach before paddling back out. The light faded, so I dragged myself out of the freezing water. Drying myself on the sand, I felt cold in every part of my body.

I walked home quickly, making my face warm and red, but my body was still cold. I made a hot drink and checked my phone when I got home – still no messages from Jerry. I put on *Sex and the City* again and let it make me laugh and cry.

***

I'd been back a week and still hadn't heard from him. I'd spoken to Nat about it almost every night and spent a particularly slow day talking it over with Priya. I was desperate to make a new friend to talk about it more. I can't understand these men who don't like talking about their feelings. It's the best. Hard times, and not enough people to talk about Jerry with. I took myself to the pub and sat alone for 40 minutes, trying to make a friend, not trying so hard that I looked at anyone or smiled. Dianne came up and stood beside me at the bar after I'd been there a while.

"You doing OK?" she asked.

"I'm not, so please don't put yourself out trying to ruin my night. It's already a steaming pile of shit," I said before swigging my cola.

"I just wanted to say I'm sorry for the photo thing."

I almost choked, spinning my head to see if she was being sincere.

"Quelle, surprise."

"You look fucking miserable. It's hard to watch."

"Careful, you're almost showing empathy," I said with a hint of humour.

"I'll quit while I'm ahead," she laughed.

218

Dianne sat back down, and I returned to my malaise, although it was harder to be unhappy after her unexpected defrosting. I thought about joining her and making Dianne my friend, but then I thought better of it and just looked at my phone and thought about texting Jerry, as I did every other minute of the day. I searched my wallet and found a 2p coin to flip. Heads, I ignore him, tails I text. It went too high, and I missed the coin, which hit the floor and rolled under the table next to me. The middle-aged men stared at me with faces like thunder as I crawled on my knees to pick up the coin. My knee rested in a puddle of spilt pint, and it was all for nought when I saw the coin show heads. I trusted its answer and didn't text Jerry. I wanted so badly to talk to him. To tell him I'd been rash and stupid. But I felt that he had to speak to me if we had a future. I needed to see that glimmer from him before I could apologise. Instead of texting, I went to the bar and ordered an Appletiser. Bill served me.

"Thanks," I said and squinted my eyes, "it's Bill, right?"

"Yeah, and you're George?"

"Yes, ten points to you," I smiled.

Maybe it was wrong, but surely it was no harm chatting to Bill if he made me feel better?

"Cool, we're closing soon, just to let you know."

Bill turned and served someone else. His demeanour was weirdly abrupt. I tried to imagine he was saying, 'Wait for me, I wanna flirt with you,' but it was clear he didn't want to hang out with me, especially when he started chatting up a group of women at the other end of the bar. I was fine.

"Get home safe," Bill said after handing me a glass of tap water. Once upon a time, I would've considered that as his way of expressing care for me. But now I could see it was just a person ending the conversation, hoping I'd leave and possibly never return. After necking back the water, I forgot to go to the toilet, so walked home as fast as I could, for fear I was going to piss myself. It wasn't just the piss. Every branch snap sounded like a murderer coming for me. I wasn't scared of death, but the thought that Jerry would hear about my urine-soaked body turning up in the woods was too embarrassing. Back home, I flipped the coin again to see if I should text him.

Still no.

***

Several weeks later, my wish for some flirty validation came true. It was a cool Sunday afternoon, and we were firmly in autumn, headed into winter. There were barely any leaves on the trees and few tourists as I strolled through town. The off-season holidaymakers were mostly outdoorsy types with sensible walking shoes or the occasional stubborn ones wearing shorts and a determined smile.

After work, I forced myself to walk by the sea. Although I was acclimatising to the freezing water, it was still an effort to get in. I undressed quickly and walked into the water only to stand knee-deep for twenty minutes, daring myself to go further. After about seventy '1-2-3' attempts to get myself in the water, I managed to wade further in and dive under the waves. My mind emptied, thinking only of the cold. I bobbed up, gasping for breath, keeping my body under the water, and acclimatising. I forget how quickly the water feels OK. I paddled around a bit, dipped under the waves some more, and jumped into the bigger waves. I got out when I could feel the water moving me further out. I was enjoying the sea, but not enough to die in it. I wiped myself down. I put on an extra-long shirt and took off my swim shorts and towel, confident that I wasn't revealing everything to the world. I did put on some pants, but I left my legs bare. I looked like I was wearing a shirt dress again, and I was still loving it.

On the way home, I wondered if this was a sign that I was nonbinary or gender fluid. I'd met gender non-conforming people in London and always admired how comfortable they seemed. I certainly felt comfortable in my dresses. Did that mean anything? Was I not a man, or was I deciding that being a man was something other than not wearing a dress? As the sand underfoot turned to stones, I decided I felt most comfortable being described as a man. Clothes don't maketh the man, is that what they say? I think it's good to check in with yourself every so often in case you feel differently.

I rounded the coastal path out of puff and saw Sam disembarking the ferry. I waved. He was chatting to Mr Sharp in the hut, who was always such a dick for no reason. Some people say Londoners are rude, but at least you don't see the same rude person every other day. Sam waved back, and I could see Mr Sharp roll his eyes. Unnecessary. As I got closer, Sam hovered and waited.

"Ahoy there," I called over. What the hell is wrong with me?

"Ahoy?"

He smiled but didn't laugh because it wasn't funny. It's fucking stupid. I carried on walking toward him.

"What are you up to?" he asked, tilting his chin toward my hessian bag.

"Just been for a swim."

"It's freezing. Are you stupid?"

"Spoken like someone who grew up in a seaside town, where the beach is always available, and you can pick and choose the optimum conditions."

By the time I finished my rant, I stood directly in front of him. I stopped, but I wasn't sure if he wanted to chew the fat.

"I'm heading back to town, done for the day," Sam gestured for us to continue walking and fell in step with me. It felt unnatural to be in sync like he was doing it on purpose, and I didn't trust why.

"What's new?" I asked.

I felt a bit like I'd forgotten how to have a conversation.

"Not much. Was out last night, at that place, again."

His eyebrows bobbed up and down as he recalled his experience at the gay club. He was excited; I almost felt proud of how far he'd come. It didn't escape my notice that he didn't just say 'gay club'.

"Did you get any action?" I asked and berated myself for asking such a silly question, the same as my mum would've asked. I wondered if I embarrassed Sam the way mums tend to do.

"Nah, got some numbers and stuff. It was fun."

We walked, and he raved about his night and the friends he'd met there. He used more hand gestures than I'd ever seen from Sam. He even stayed at some random guy's house instead of paying for a hostel. It sounded like a nightmare to me, but Sam was pumped. I stopped outside my door, and Sam carried on talking. I invited him up for a drink. He followed me upstairs, and I felt that sexual weirdness that happened the day we'd first met. I dismissed it now as I did then. Sam went off into the living room. I went to the bathroom. I considered washing my bits in the sink, as I'd been in the sea. I was being ridiculous, as there was no way Sam and I would have sex. But better to be safe than sorry, I thought, turning on the tap. Before heading into the kitchen, I looked at my reflection and told him to calm down.

"I'm so glad you're finding the gay scene really welcoming," I told Sam, thinking I was hardly surprised as he's a young, good-looking white man with abs. As an older fat gay, I didn't want to be bitter. Did I ever feel welcomed into the gay community the way Sam had been? No. Did I have friends who loved me regardless? Yes, I had Nat. I suppose, for a short while, I also lived the fantasy of the world's sexiest man being in love with me. Yes, for a short time, I had that too. I took the mugs through and sat on the sofa. Sam was telling me about some guy who'd come on to him while he was in the toilet.

"I said no, but I'm not opposed to the idea in the future."

"You think you might like golden showers?"

"No! I mean, someone offering me their number while we're pissing."

"I dunno. It sounds like you might be interested in piss play. And fair enough, no judgement here."

"Have you ever done it?" he asked.

It was happening. He saw me as the older gay mentor, and to be honest, I didn't hate it.

"Once I let a man watch me wee, and then he sucked my dick. He enjoyed it, but it wasn't for me."

I'd told the story as part of my set in stand-up, but with more embellishments.

"That's gross."

We laughed. He was disgusted by me now.

"When are you headed to the club again?"

"Next weekend, wanna come?"

"Absolutely not."

I slapped my hand on his thigh. He nudged closer.

"Are you sure?" his voice was lower, almost a whisper.

"What are you doing?"

I jerked my head back, shocked by his closeness.

"You didn't want to do this before because I was new to it, but I'm more experienced now." He looked into my eyes. "I know what I want."

Sam leaned in and kissed me. I kept my mouth still, trying to decide what I wanted, which was made more complicated by the very sexy man trying to attach himself to me.

"Don't you want to?"

His eyes were intensely focussed on me. His breath warmed my lips.

"I'm not sure."

"Let me see if I can convince you."

Sam kissed me again. This time I opened my lips, mirroring his. I felt his tongue dart into my mouth. I felt his teeth sharply on my lower lip. The sensation was pleasant until it started to sting. I murmured an ow.

"Sorry," said Sam before diving in again, tongue first, as if it wasn't a separate kiss. Why was this kiss so much worse than our previous attempt? I wanted to suck his soul out through his dick the first time we kissed. Yes, he was still gorgeous, but the kiss wasn't good. I was brainstorming how to calm down on the kissing when Sam leaned back and whipped off his shirt. His body *was* incredible, but it wasn't anything I hadn't seen a million times before on TV or in magazines. I'd never touched proper abs, and they were softer than I expected. When compared to my own, his body made me feel really wide. I kissed his neck. He didn't make a noise or anything.

"Do you like this?" I asked.

"Yeah, if you like it," he answered. I stopped. He pulled me onto my feet, and we kissed. We needed to slow it down, but I felt Sam's hands plunge into my underwear. He pulled away, and I thought he was freaking out, but he pulled down his trousers and yanked at my waistband. He undressed me and then positioned me to sit next to him. We were both naked and side by side whilst looking out into the room.

"What do you want to do?" I asked, confused, as we stared at the black reflective TV screen. It was as uncomfortable as it sounds.

"I just wanted to try something."

He put his arm around my shoulder; his body was giving off heat. We kissed, and I got on my knees and went down on him. Instead of grabbing the back of my head, he seemed to tap along with my motion. It felt like he was hitting the back of my head each time I moved back, so I waved his hand away. Two minutes later, he stopped me and pulled me up onto his lap.

"Can we use a condom?" he asked.

"Absolutely, I wasn't expecting to need them…" I wanted to joke about usually having them in a bowl on the coffee table, but Sam wouldn't appreciate my humour right now. Everything about our interaction made me feel unsure.

"OK. Now?"

I went into the bathroom for condoms, lube and a spare hand towel for good measure. When I returned, he had adjusted himself onto his knees, facing the door. I started kissing his neck. When I moved away to put the condom on, Sam kept putting his arm behind him, grabbing at me to check the condom.

"It's on, I promise." I wanted to sound reassuring, but I just sounded annoyed. Sam rested his head on his hands, and he stopped making any noise.

"Is this your first time?"

"Yeah," he seemed shy.

"We can stop. It's OK to stop."

"I want to..." he insisted, "to do it."

"OK, I'm gonna start just now. If you say hold, I'll hold in place. If you say stop, then we stop."

"Go ahead."

I moved forward, but we couldn't get into a rhythm. Our actions felt jarring. Something about this entire escapade felt wrong. It was Sam's first time, so I let him choreograph things.

"Can we try it the other way?"

"Sure, of course." I sounded much more enthusiastic than I felt, and we switched places. I made the right noises, but as Sam couldn't see my face, I kept rolling my eyes. After two minutes, he stopped.

"Are you OK?"

"I've...finished," he said, backing away from me. He pulled the condom off and stared at it for a long time.

"Are you going to cry?" I spoke before I had the chance to stop myself.

God, I'm a fucking dick.

"I'm fine."

I took the condom, threw it in the bin, and Sam still hadn't moved.

"Sorry," he looked sheepish.

"You don't need to apologise."

"OK."

I smiled and went to the bathroom to break the tension. When I returned, Sam was fully dressed and sombre-looking.

"Are you OK? You don't need to rush out."

He shrugged and looked out the window.

"Something I used to do, after I'd had sex with a man and was filled with shame, I'd drink a diet coke. I read somewhere they use coke to wash blood off the pavement in America. I don't think it's a healthy way to handle how you might be feeling, but if it helps, you can use it.

"Thanks." Sam laughed. "I might go get some."

I walked him to the door and closed it. It might've been unfair, but I felt cross with Sam. Sex had been his idea, and I wished I'd said no. I didn't know what else to do, so I sat on the stairs. Sam leaving felt lonelier than if I'd just spent the afternoon alone. I missed sex with Jerry. I took my phone from my pocket and searched his Instagram and Twitter. I know he didn't use them very often. There was a picture of him at home drinking tea captioned 'easy like Sunday morning.' Was that a dig at me? I started to cry.

The light faded fast. I peeled my face, sticky from crying, off the hall carpet. I didn't know what to do until I woke up the next day for work. I wasn't answerable to anybody. I crawled up the stairs and turned on the hall light. In the kitchen, I drank a huge swig of water.

I needed to get my feelings out. I thought about calling Nat but decided not to spoil her Sunday night. It was no use spilling my feelings to Nat or Mum. Not that I'd want to tell my mum about my sex life. All my feelings were for Jerry, and I needed to talk to him. I took out my laptop and typed a draft email:

I don't know what I'm supposed to say to you. There's nothing I'm supposed to say…

227

I deleted the message and started again:

Jerry,

I miss you. I know that's embarrassing to say, but it's true. I
don't know what we got wrong. I guess it's telling that neither
of us has been in touch. I've been too embarrassed, and I feel
as though the longer this goes on, the more certain I am that
this has worked out for you. I'm sure it will work out for me
in the long run. We wanted different things. What my life will
ultimately look like is entirely different to how your life
looks. I understand that. Well, in my logical mind, I get it. But
my heart has some catching up to do. Getting over you hurts.
What we had might not have been everyone's idea of
perfection, but I now realise it was perfect for me. Even
though we could find each other deeply annoying, and
sometimes you said the wrong thing…All I can think about is
how much I love you.

George x

That message didn't feel complete, but I had to stop writing. Too
gushy, too honest and a little bit over the top. Yes, I certainly felt
Jerry was the love of my life at times. But I couldn't give it all up
like that, especially when he wouldn't return the favour. Jerry was
moving on without me.

Maybe I didn't need to write him a letter at all.

However, the next night I made another attempt, and the following night, another. I was on my fifteenth unsent message when
I told Nat about my new habit.

"That's good, get it out," she chirped over the phone, most likely
relieved I was making an effort to deal with my neuroses.

"No, it's getting sick. I write an email every day bearing my soul
and ripping out my still beating heart, and then I do it again the
next night."

"That's a lot of editing. There's a reason we work to a deadline in news. Are you ever going to send it?"

"It's not even really editing. I start afresh all the time. I should say something to him. Eurgh, it's such a mess. Let's move on."

"I'm coming to visit this weekend, but I'm not bringing Christmas presents because you're coming for actual Christmas, right?"

"Yes, I'll be home on Christmas Eve, so we'll have lunch, like every year."

"No need to sound so tired of me checking plans!"

"I'm sorry, I'm just tired, full stop." I sounded like a moody teenager; I was sick of myself, to be honest. We talked about Nat's job, Emmanuel, and Christmas, and I had to try so hard not to bring up Jerry again because I'm awful. I'd exhausted Nat and Priya with my cycle of Jerry chat. I was excited to meet new people so I could tell them about my broken heart too. I knew I was boring, but was I also a complete narcissist?

***

My baking had taken a back seat to complaining about Jerry. I hadn't noticed, but Priya brought in a Tupperware box slamming it on the counter. I lifted the lid.

"What are these?"

"Paratha. They're delicious, and I made them."

"Ooh – they're buttery. When are we sharing them?"

"We're not. They're to sell. I'm sick of serving burnt bread," Priya replied, one eyebrow raised.

"We're all entitled to a bad day," I whined.

Priya smiled, stepped around the counter, and touched my shoulder.

"You've been having a bad month. I've served more burnt bread and flat cakes than I can count. You're not a good heartbroken baker."

My cheeks burned.

Had I let things get that bad?

I decided to stop complaining to Priya that I wouldn't call Nat or Mum each night while baking my cakes.

"I promise to make more effort with my baking. I'm sorry."

"No need to apologise to me. I've stopped eating lunch here," Priya said, then stuck out her tongue. It was fun and playful, but a warning, my standards had slipped. I worked hard for the rest of the day, keen not to mention Jerry or look too mopey. But when Priya left, all my mooning around exploded out. I sat beside a customer who seemed friendly and started talking about Jerry. I probably overstepped the mark when I took the napkin from her hand and dabbed my eyes. Or perhaps it was when I accidentally sipped her drink, and my tears dropped into the cup. She made an excuse to leave. I was scaring customers away now with my moaning. That night, I decided to commit to paper what I wanted to say. Then I'd print the letter and post it. I dragged myself upstairs, covered in flour, legs aching, and sat at my laptop:

Hey, Jerry,
I don't often write letters, but here we go...

Only I don't send heart-wrenching emails.

...I'm sorry for how I left things. Upon reflection, I don't think I tried hard enough. At that moment, I was afraid. I don't think we admit often enough that we're afraid, especially such a manly man as myself.
I know we're all scared, and that's a bit of a rubbish excuse, but I was frightened of the depth of my feelings for you.

230

Suddenly it seemed that we were tipping into a different phase of our relationship, and I could see the end before we'd properly begun. I can't take all the credit as you've not spoken to me. I can only assume you feel the same. Ultimately our lives are too different. Many times, we made each other feel uncomfortable, which feels like a deal breaker. Despite what didn't work, I should tell you I did love you. A lot...

Big swing here. We'd not properly said the L word, but what did I have left to lose?

...at least we know I'm capable of love, and you're worth loving. That's given me some comfort over the last few months. I hope it does you too. Have an amazing life, Jerry

I didn't run it past Nat or my mum, or anyone. I printed and posted the letter. It was in the post box and out of my hands. I walked back to the flat in darkness, feeling like Amanda Seyfried at the beginning of *Mamma Mia*. Halfway through my solo of 'Mamma Mia', singing of being broken-hearted, I sprinted back to the café, realising I'd left a bunch of cakes in the oven.

They were in cinders by the time I got back.

14

A Moody Pizza

The weather turned colder, and the trees were bare. I kept up with
my daily ocean swims, but they were increasingly short. Wrapping
myself in a jumper and drinking a hot chocolate on my way home
each morning was the best part of the day. I'd even invested in a
water-resistant watch so I could leave my phone at home. I used to
check my phone fanatically for a reply from Jerry, but three weeks
or so after I sent him the letter, I became obsessed with checking
the post instead. It was nice to stand on the sand, shivering slightly
and sipping from my thermos. I felt thoroughly outdoorsy.

I still thought about Jerry every thirty minutes, but I managed
to stop talking about him all the time. And I still checked his Instagram but stopped expecting to see anything. It was hard not to
feel jealous when schmaltzy Christmas adverts popped up on TV
or Priya, or Nat talked about their plans with their partners.

The night before Christmas Eve, I held a little get-together with
Priya, her husband, Eileen, and her son Trevor. We had mulled
wine, and I made a Yule Log type cake, although it wasn't expertly
rolled as I'd been in a rush. Rather than a nice, neat log, it looked
like a Yule cow pat.

Very festive.

"This is lovely," Eileen said, taking a second slice, which assured me she wasn't just being polite.

"Thanks, it's nice to get everyone together," I said, and helped myself to another slice, wondering if perhaps me and the yule pat wouldn't have preferred being alone together.

I sat down with this motley crew as conversations drifted between Christmas shopping and our collective disdain for cards.

"I hate doing them, they hang over my head, but I do love getting them," said Priya.

"Did you get Jerry a Christmas card?" Eileen asked. I came alive at the mention of Jerry, and even better, I didn't bring him up.

"Oh no, absolutely not. We are not in touch anymore," I sounded more convinced than I felt.

"For now," I heard Priya say under her breath.

It seems everyone wants you to move on when you're mooning over a man. Once you do, they are convinced you're going to end up back together.

"I'm surprised by him." Priya chowed down on some mince pies she'd brought, the crumbs cascading down her front, the filling rolling around her mouth. "Not the man I thought he was."

"You and me both," I said, although I didn't feel it. Jerry was only guilty of letting me walk out of his life – not much of a crime.

As people were getting ready to go home, I gave out my little goody bags and wished them a Merry Christmas. I closed the door and locked up for the last time that year. I cleared and wiped the tables, ensuring everything was perfect for tomorrow. Upstairs I packed my bag and checked the pile of presents I'd stored by the door. I was ready.

I felt strange in that little flat. It was so still. Usually, Christmas was packed with things to do and events to attend, all in a rush before the festive spirit dissipated.

I waved to Priya when I left the next morning; she was too busy singing Christmas music to interrupt with a proper goodbye. I caught the ferry just in time, harrumphing into a seat with my bags, a feeling of relief washing over me. It was properly winter now, and there'd been frost on the windows when I woke up. Sam wasn't running the ferry that day. I read my book but started feeling sick, so I stood where I could see the horizon. I had a choice between facing ahead or looking back at the island that was supposed to be home. I chose to look forward.

Once I arrived back in London, I met Nat, and we caught the train home together. Our parents lived a twenty-minute drive from one another. We met each year on Christmas Eve, ate sweets on the train and had lunch back in Berkshire before going home for Christmas.

"Hello, my love," I said to her as we embraced at the train station. We found the platform and boarded the waiting train. Settling into the flattened padding on the obnoxiously decorated seats, it was a sure sign Christmas was coming. Once we set off, I tore open a bag of Minstrels with my teeth and tipped them directly into our mouths like an overflowing champagne bottle.

"Are you excited for the big day?" I asked.

"What do you mean?"

"Christmas, duh?"

"Of course. It's nice to go home. I'm missing Emmanuel this year."

"When are you seeing him?"

"Well, it's a bit of a departure. We're meeting halfway, between my parents and his, on Boxing Day, with our families."

My face froze, determined not to react with indignity.

"Fff...fun."

It took me a while to land on the right way to end the F sound. Because screaming FUCK YOU on the train was extreme.

"Yeah, it's actually for quite a big reason."

"Oh good."

I was being ditched for a 'big reason'. This had better be good.

I looked expectantly at Nat whilst she wiped her face and covered her mouth with her hand. She scratched her knee with the same hand. It was as though she'd been kidnapped and had written help me on her nails, but she hadn't because I'd checked them. I couldn't remember which side of you loses power when you're having a stroke or a heart attack. Was I being stupid? I didn't get it. Nat wiggled a ring on her fourth finger. Then I got it.

Ffff...fuck.

"You're engaged?" I squealed.

"Yes, he asked me last night."

I launched out of my seat and hugged her.

"And you waited a whole night and three stops before you told me? Where did he ask? How did you say yes?"

Taking a breath, ready to tell the story for the first time, Nat began.

"I was in bed, and he was pacing around getting his stuff sorted. He was being really shifty, but I thought it was because he hadn't wrapped my presents and I could see them in a bag next to his suitcase. He perched on the bed but then stood up and perched again. He was like a bloody Newton's cradle.

"He was nervous," I gushed.

"I asked him what was up, and he said he wasn't sure about anything. I jokingly said, 'That's what all girlfriends want to hear.' His face went deadly serious, and I started hyperventilating, and he started shouting 'NO' at me because he didn't want me to get the wrong idea. I scrambled about on the bed and knocked over a glass of water. Emmanuel dropped something on the floor, and I tried to get up. I landed on him, and we both laid on the floor. He was gonna say something, but I was crying and just telling him, don't say it."

"Why were you crying?"

"I thought he was about to dump me. I was bereft. Then suddenly, he shouted, 'Will you marry me?' I went silent, and he rolled over to show me the ring."

"Very close to Christmas. Are you livid?"

"That's why he did it last night." Nat slapped my forearms in excitement. It hurt.

"He said that a ring had arrived and wanted to ask, but he didn't want to do it at Christmas because he knows I think it's tacky. I blubbed yes, went to kiss him, and he wiped my face with his sleeve before kissing me back. I put the ring on, and it fitted perfectly."

I cried.

"He loves you so much. And you know, the more you tell that story, the easier you'll iron out all the kinks."

"I'm excited. Not about the wedding but just being married to him. And being a hot young married couple. It feels really on brand."

"Who have you told?"

"No one except you. Last night we just celebrated and had sex. It was amazing, by the way. That's why we're meeting halfway with our families, to tell them and celebrate."

"That is lovely," I said, and I wasn't lying.

I was excited for her. It took me a second to get there. It's not as though Nat would get married and wouldn't need me any more. I'd be her maid of honour and then the godfather to her babies. There was still some mileage left in our relationship.

I made us toast our drinks, then I made us toast cookies, and then I made us toast our rubbish before we took it to the bin. Nat was rolling her eyes at me by then. When we reached town, we had lunch at our usual spot before parting ways. Nat was getting picked up by her dad, who was great, but I fancied the walk. I hadn't been home since Mum, and I fell out. I knew things were better than before, but I felt nervous.

About two minutes into my walk, I regretted my decision because I had too many bags, and it was bitterly cold. I walked past the post office where I used to get penny sweets until I became a vegetarian at eleven. I walked past the junk shop I started working in at fifteen. It was the year I experimented with growing a fringe. I remember all summer, grandparents would point to me and tell their grandchildren, 'Give your sweets to the lady'. I was the lady. Then I grew out my fringe.

There was an alley where my childhood bully Matt called me a faggot and threatened to stab my leg with a Biro. My walk from town used to take me past my old school, but it had recently been levelled, and a new school sat in its place. I turned the corner onto my street. Everything was familiar but smaller as if I were seeing it in a dream. I felt the same when I went away to university and came home for the first break. I'd also walked then and regretted it. I hobbled up the path and opened the door. Or I tried to. It was locked. How had she not unlocked the door all day?

"Coming." I could see Mum running toward me. I tried to subdue the bizarre rage that was bubbling inside me. You know that feeling when a stranger could hit you, and you wouldn't be that annoyed because it was a one-off, but when your mum, for the 100th time, doesn't unlock the damn door when you're cold and tired and have travelled miles to see her, you're bloody livid. It was exactly that. The door swung open.

"You're here!"

I smiled and walked inside, dropping my bags. I hugged Mum. 'How was the train?' 'Did you have a nice lunch?' 'Are you hungry?'

Please don't think less of me; the questions are lovely, but I take umbrage with their regularity and timing.

"I have to go to the toilet," I said, although I didn't. More than anything, I needed two minutes to come down from the top of arsehole hill. I was currently the mayor of arsehole town.

At the top of arsehole hill.

In the Provence de Arsehole.

I gathered my bags and jogged upstairs to look more desperate. Bags went into my old room. I went to the toilet. I took ten deep breaths in the mirror and reminded myself that I was being a dick. I chose to come home for Christmas, and there wasn't anywhere else I'd rather be. Then I was fine. I breezed downstairs and joined in the fun.

Mum asked me to bake since I was a professional, so I insisted on showing her how to make some gooey cookies ahead of Christmas day. Mine came out of the oven relatively symmetrical, whereas hers were a bit more avant-garde, but I whipped them straight onto the cooling rack, so the difference was less obvious. We put out a cookie, prosecco, and carrot for Father Christmas. Sherry was the traditional drink, but Mum didn't have any and reasoned Father Christmas would enjoy a glass of what she was already enjoying.

It was a quiet Christmas, just the two of us. We played the PlayStation and ate. Mum has always been weirdly into video games, much more than me. We made a nice lunch, watched a film, played cards, called my grandparents, and played more video games. We played and I tucked into a chocolate shaped like a Christmas tree. At three in the morning, we finally finished the level we were on and went to bed. I looked in the mirror as I brushed my teeth, and my entire face was covered with chocolate – a sure sign of a great day.

We got up late on Boxing Day and headed straight out to walk Willy. When trying to be cutsie, Mum changed Willy to Big Willy, and her nauseating baby voice when she called 'walkies Big Willy' made me cringe and laugh in equal measure.

"Good to get some fresh air," she said before erupting into a coughing fit. I laughed some more, feeling a bit giggly. It struck me I must've been having fun.

"That beautiful commuter town air."

She hit my arm but laughed too. It felt like we were back to our regular selves, which was a relief after not speaking most of the year. Although we'd spoken on the phone since she'd visited London, calls couldn't make up for our time together. I'd have to make more effort to come back. I almost said as much to Mum before navigating a ditch and tripping up – Mum's turn to laugh at me. We'd driven to the field that Nat's house backed onto – our traditional Boxing Day route. I kept checking her bedroom window in case I saw her and could wave. I didn't expect to see her. Knowing Nat, she'd have the whole family on the road two hours early, nervous about being late for her new in-laws.

"So, we haven't spoken much about the café – how's it going?"

"Just ticks along, really. Nothing ever goes wrong. Nothing ever changes. Day in, day out."

"You probably don't appreciate it yet, but consistency is nice. It can make things easier if you're thinking about a family."

I appreciated her for that. She could've said it sounded boring. I thought it sounded boring. I almost wanted to admit I was bored, but I wasn't ready yet to admit my mistake. Not after we'd argued for so long about the exiting of my old life.

"It would be a nice place to have a family. Although I'd need to focus, I've burnt most of the cakes I've made this last month."

Jerry would've made an excellent father to our children. He already was to Dottie. The dog pooed, and I waited while Mum collected it. I felt bad for not helping, but Big Willy's pungent poos, which smelt like dog food but worse, reminded me that he wasn't my dog.

"How's Nat getting on?"

"I don't know. She won't have left yet."

"Of course not. She's over there."

Across the field, I saw Nat storming toward us. I waved, but she didn't return it.

"She seems well," Mum said.

I checked my phone, and I had eight missed calls from Nat. Shit.

"Happy Christmas."

"Merry Christmas, Tina," Nat replied before fixing her glare on me. "Having fun, are we?"

"Yeah, it's a nice walk." I didn't want to look Nat in the eye. I wanted my mum to save me from Nat's mood.

I noticed that Nat's hair was tied up in a wrap, and her make-up was only half done. She was carrying a lot of clothes, a pile of hangers, threatening to break free of her arms. From a distance, it was like she was getting rid of a body.

"Cool. Meanwhile, I've literally got no idea what to wear, and yes, perhaps I am freaking out, but you haven't looked at your phone for thirty goddamn minutes!"

Mum had edged away by this point.

"How am I expected to dress myself? What is the point of you if not for this?"

Nat threw one of her jumpers at me.

"You dress yourself all the time."

"Yes, but how many Boxing Days do I have to meet my future in-laws and announce what I have to announce?"

"You've already met Emmanuel's parents. They love you."

"If you're going to be unhelpful, I'll go back inside, and you won't see me for an incredibly long time. Check your phone."

At Nat's command, I looked through the photos she'd sent me. There were a lot of nude tones and neutrals. She looked tasteful. The pearl necklace, however, was out of character. She reminded me of Michelle Obama. I almost mentioned the comparison but didn't think Nat was in the mood. Nat, of course, is the best person alive, but she's not the First Lady type.

"You look amazing in all of these. I'm just not sure they're very you."

Thankfully, she agreed, and we continued browsing, eventually settling with black jeans, a lavender cotton jumper, and a simple gold necklace. No pearls.

"See, that wasn't so hard, just pick up your phone, and I won't have to run around a field looking for you."

Although there was mirth in her voice, Nat was not joking. I made her hug me, and she called goodbye to Mum before trudging through the mud back home. I stared after her a moment, grinning to myself. I missed being near her. Even at her worst, she made me laugh.

"Nice to see Nat. Is she all dressed now?"

"Yeah, we workshopped some ideas."

We carried on walking.

"It's great that you have managed to stay close despite the distance."

Leaves crumpled under my foot, too wet to crunch.

"We do work hard at it."

I hadn't realised this before, but our closeness made me feel proud.

The week between Christmas and New Year's dragged on in a limbo-like state of eating, watching TV and questioning whether or not I could be bothered to get dressed. Typical of that time of year, 'tis the season. On the day before New Year's Eve, Nat and I travelled back to London. When I said goodbye to Mum, she hugged me tightly.

"Come back soon. Let's not waste any time."

"OK," I said, tears filling my eyes, "love you."

"Love you too," she said.

***

I met Nat at Wokingham station, and we travelled back together. She had a full boxing day of drama to recount. Nat's mum had inadvertently offended Emmanuel's family by suggesting church weddings were boring. Nat managed to smooth things over before dessert. I was excited to get back to London.

Each year for New Year's Eve, we promised one another we would do something witchy and wild before talking ourselves out of it because we wanted to be ready for bed by midnight. We have the *best* time whenever I celebrate New Year's with Nat. We laugh, we cry, we eat delicious food.

This time around was no different. We put on face masks, ate chocolate and watched films, pausing at ten minutes to midnight. I called Mum just after twelve, Nat called her family, and Emmanuel called her. He was a little tipsy and soppy and made her promise to spend New Year's with him next year. I laughed when Nat rolled her eyes at him as though it was fine. But I felt exceptionally single all of a sudden. Nat wandered into the bedroom for a few minutes. I started to write a text to Jerry but then deleted it.

"He'll forget that I promised."

"It's OK. I can timeshare New Year's and other occasions."

I felt a little blue that I didn't have more people to speak with. I got a round robin from Priya, saying, 'Happy New Year. You're a star!' And I replied saying, 'No, you are!' I thought it was cute, but she didn't reply.

"I'm going to have to stop eating soon. I'm so full," I said.

"Where do you think you'll be next year?"

"Emotionally? Probably the same as I am now. Physically where will I be? I don't know yet. Maybe I'll spend it at the café?"

"Hmmm," Nat said, and jumped up to open a window. It was getting a little warm, despite the late hour.

"That feels loaded."

"I don't know how happy you're going to be if you spend another year on that island."

I twisted my neck to look at her, astounded by her frankness.

"I'm supportive, but you've been there six months, you hate the job, and you don't have enough friends. I know you needed a change of scenery, but when will you come back to your life?"

"That is my life."

"George, I have to be honest. You made these huge life changes because you were sad. Trying new things is important, but you've tried this. It's not working."

"I need water."

I stormed to the kitchen, which was hard, considering it was two steps away. I turned on the tap and waited for it to turn cold.

"I love you and want you to be happy, but this isn't it."

"Sorry you're missing me, but I'm building a life. It's slightly different from what I imagined, but it's mine, and I love it."

"Couple of things to unpack there. Of course, I miss you, but that's not what this is about. And do you love your life?"

"I'm hardly living in misery, don't be dramatic."

"I'm not. There's a lot of wiggle room between loving your life and hating it. Can you honestly say the thought of opening the café everyday fills you with joy?"

I stalked back to the living room, wanting the conversation to stop, but I couldn't entirely escape Nat's question.

"The happiest you've been since moving to No'Man, was when you were with Jerry."

My eyes opened wide, enraged.

"And when you did that show for him. You are a stand-up comic. Why are you pretending like you don't miss it?"

I folded my arms.

"Please, can we change the subject?"

"Has he texted you?"

This wasn't the subject I wanted to switch to, but I instinctively checked my phone, nothing.

"Right, anything else?"

We went to bed as soon as the film ended. We weren't arguing, and she made us hug before bed, but things felt strained between us. Nat's words were fresh in my mind when I went home the next day.

15

All Fart and No Poo

The Isle of No'Man loomed ahead, its misshapen outline a familiar sight. The wind was biting, but I preferred to be on the open deck. It was still the best place not to feel so seasick. I looked over the railing, the top of the water was dark, and the fading sun sucked the colour out of the world. Despite the gloomy appearance, the island was a welcome sight after such a long journey. My sofa awaited. It also felt like I was headed toward the end of civilisation.

When I got back to the flat, I stepped over my post and took my things upstairs. I unpacked immediately, like someone without a social life would do. I sat upright on the end of the bed, touching my upper lip to my nose, feeling my facial hair scratch my face. I didn't quite know what to do with myself. I texted Mum and Nat to say I was home. I went to collect the post I'd stepped over when I came through the front door. It was almost exclusively junk mail, besides a little handwritten Christmas card. I opened it:

Hey George,

Merry Christmas. I hope this finds you in time. I want to apologise for the last time we spoke. I'm still sober, and I wanted you to know that. I hope forever, but one day at a time. I'm not sure what I want to say to you after so long. I'm hopeful the words will find me in the moment. Message me when you're back in London. It would be great to catch up.

Jerry.

I held the card to my lips. Fuck.

I'd missed my chance. I took a photo of the card and sent it to Nat. My hand was shaking. She replied with a lot of emojis. If I text Jerry now, it would look like I'd been avoiding him. He only wanted to speak face-to-face. I put the card with the rest of my Christmas cards and switched on the TV. Immediately, Jerry's face popped on screen as one of his *Bad Witches* films was playing. I used to love the franchise, another thing he'd ruined for me.

I watched transfixed and miserable until the adverts and a local news update. Mr Sharp was being asked about his crusade against the seagulls. I was only mildly annoyed that he'd chosen to be interviewed outside the café as though Fifty Shades of Coffee (& Cake) was the only place the seagulls stalked. I messaged Priya, but even my annoyance didn't drive Jerry from my mind for long. I couldn't let the message slip from my mind. I got up and fished around the bureau, looking for a spare Christmas card and wrote:

Hi Jerry,

Sorry to say I only got your card after I came back from London. I'll let you know when I'm next coming back. It'd be great to catch up.

George x

It was a boring card, but I sealed it and placed it under my keys by the door. Taking it to the post box would give me a reason to head out the next day. Only then, finally, could I put it out of my mind. Sweet oblivion filled the rest of my afternoon.

I threw myself into January, determined to push Jerry from my mind. I swam in the freezing sea twice and caught up with Priya as she led me around the island on a litter-picking scavenger hunt. It was an annual event on the Isle of No'Man, with prizes for most litter and weirdest litter picked, on the first Sunday after New Year. Priya won every year, and even with my hindrance, she managed to snag a prize, finding a collection of dolls with distorted crying faces someone had dumped four miles inland. I wasn't convinced she hadn't dumped them herself, only to find them on this occasion.

I'd been back around a week when I called Eileen to invite her to the café.

"What's up?"

"Erm…" I inhaled, ready to pull the plaster off, "I think I need to hand in my notice."

"Oh, OK," she leaned forward to pull her cake closer, "thanks, I guess, for letting me know."

"You're the first person I thought to tell." I smiled, desperate to keep the conversation easy. Eileen took a bite of the cake and grimaced.

"I won't be missing this. This cream is off."

"Is it?" I frowned at her, disbelief written across my face.

"You take a chance on a slice of cake, and it leaves a sour taste in your mouth."

"Cake, right." I moved my chair out slightly for a quicker escape if I needed it.

"Where are you going to? The bloody ice cream shop? Scoop Shoop strikes again."

I didn't reply, distracted by the realisation of why the ice cream shop had added an extra o in its name'.

"I'm going to be leaving the Isle. I think I want to be closer to home."

Eileen took another bite of cake and grimaced again. I'd eaten a slice at lunch, so I knew she was lying.

"Eileen, you seem cross."

"I took a gamble on you. You've not even been here a year. You barely have a GCSE in Food Technology. Did you think I wouldn't check? But I saw something special in you."

I placed my hands on the table, grounding myself.

"I'm sorry I let you down."

"Don't be dramatic." Eileen swigged her drink, emptied it down her throat and stood up.

"A month's notice seems fair."

"Absolutely," I agreed. I put aside my hatred and suggested something I never thought I'd say. "In terms of replacement, do you think Dianne would be worth considering?"

"Bit above your pay grade, deciding who replaces you." She drew her shoulders back. I felt her icy detachment descend between us. "I'll take it under advisement."

Eileen crossed to the door and turned again.

"And George, I wouldn't ask me for a reference. You've not worked here long enough."

"It's been like nine months, but OK." I waved at her, only lowering my hand as the door slammed closed.

I didn't feel the relief I thought I'd feel at handing in my notice. I wanted to return to my old life, but I don't know if I trusted my timing. I didn't text Nat about handing in my notice or my mum. Rare for me since I usually can't wipe my own arse without the approval of a committee. But I wanted to sit with this decision and process how I felt about it for a little while longer. Instead, I locked the door on the empty café.

I'd planned a night of mooning around the flat and looking wistfully out of the window, but I'd forgotten I needed dinner. I marched to the supermarket for a moody oven pizza to match my energy of quiet reflection.

Unfortunately, I'd not left it long enough since Eileen left, and we bumped into one another at the shop. She gave me a curt nod, which I returned with an overly friendly smile. We must've decided to rush, as I next saw her at the till. There was another person ahead of me, so there was no need for small talk, but, of course, Dianne behind the counter. They were talking animatedly until Eileen caught sight of me. I don't think I was imagining things when I saw Eileen doing a shushing action at Dianne. I'd handed in my notice less than an hour ago, and here was Eileen, quicker than wildfire. Dianne looked like the cat that got the cream, and I regretted making her so happy. Eileen left, and it was my turn to pay.

"How's things?" Dianne asked as though she didn't know.

"Good, thanks, you?" I offered, but our conversation was entirely banal.

"Enjoy your dinner," she said as I left. She was so normal that I was convinced she didn't know. Except that the normal and polite from Dianne was out of character.

The next morning, Dianne rushed into the café, cutting ahead of everyone in the queue for their morning coffee. She knew.

"Oh my god, I don't know how to feel," she squealed.

I smiled at her but carried on putting the lid on a cappuccino for Mr Sharp.

"Is this a social club? Or a place of business?" he asked.

"Social clubs are businesses," I said and stuck my tongue out at Mr Grumpy as he turned to leave. Dianne reached for my arm across the café.

"Eileen just told me – you're leaving, and I'm the new manager!"

"Congratulations."

"Why are you leaving? Is it haunted?" She leant in, her eyebrows furrowed in confusion. Why would I leave such a great gig?

"If I'm honest, this whole time has been amazing, but it doesn't feel like a new lease of life. It feels like a holiday from my real life…" I went quiet as the door opened, and Priya appeared. I put my fingers to my lips. I wanted to tell her myself.

"Morning."

Dianne nodded her head at me in greeting as she moved to the door.

"I better get to work." I tried to end the conversation.

"I'll pop back later." Dianne was giddy – a whole new woman.

"You don't need to," I replied coolly, although she paid me no attention. She left and Priya returned from putting her things in the back. She tied her apron around her waist, assessed the café's tidiness, and how the cake fridge looked.

"Your baking is back to normal."

"I put in some extra effort. Are you saying I'm good again?"

"You're back to where you were," she patted me, then pointed to Dianne's back as she crossed the street. "What was that about?"

"She's excited because I've handed in my notice, and I'm headed back to London."

Telling Priya made it real. A thrill worked its way up my spine. I was beginning to feel excited.

"Oh…wow." Priya's mouth turned down, the news slowly registering across her features, before she broke into a smile.

"It's a shame to see you go, but it sounds like you'll be much happier."

"I'm not unhappy here."

"You were exceedingly happy when Jerry was here, but it's been hard to be around you since he left, to be honest. Go to him, like a flower leaning toward the sun." She sang this to the tune of 'I Turn to You' by Mel C.

"I want to be closer to home. I haven't even spoken to Jerry. I'm not going to London for Jerry!"

"My mistake," Priya said before serving a customer. My excitement was replaced with dread.

Was I moving back to London for a man?

What was the point of listening to 'Independent Women' for my entire adolescence if I was going to follow a sexy yet unavailable man around?

I told my mum and Nat about the move back that evening. They were both suitably excited. I shared with Nat my worries about what Priya had said and was comforted by her loyal reply.

"That's bullshit. You're not even talking to Jerry! I'm not being funny. London is a big place, and you'll probably never bump into him. Moving back is a good idea, with or without Jerry. She's gutted because she's not coming with you."

I laughed with her. Nat always knew what to say but secretly worried she knew what I wanted to hear. As though she heard my thoughts.

"You worry about coming home because you're with Jerry, then because you're not. Honestly, you need to stop worrying about what everything means and follow your heart right back to me."

The next day, Dianne came in at closing time. She'd brought a bar of chocolate with her.

"This is for you." She slid it over the countertop.

"Thank you. Is it poisoned?"

"I feel like we got off on the wrong foot. And if I'm taking over the café, I'd love to ask you a few questions, if you don't mind?"

It was tempting to say no and let Dianne feel as overwhelmed as I did when I arrived. But she took a pen and notepad out of her handbag, an action that was so enthusiastic, it melted my heart.

"Sure, what do you want to know?" I agreed, although I was still not thawed out.

Dianne followed me around the café as I tidied and baked for the next day.

"I don't know why I'm helping you. You tried to ruin my life."

Dianne put the pen down for a moment in consideration.

"I am sorry. I don't think I thought what my photo would do. I let jealousy get the better of me."

"Apology accepted," I said, and sort of meant it. Holding a grudge was so tiring. I probably wouldn't be staying in touch with Dianne when I left, but I didn't want to carry around a wish for vengeance either. She insisted on writing down the lemon drizzle recipe as it had become so popular on the island.

"The secret is, I add quite a bit of lime, too," I told her, as if I were revealing the nuclear codes.

"You're so bad," she giggled. God, I wish we'd been friends sooner.

Over the coming weeks, I planned and packed little bits, but I didn't have much to do until the final week. I packed my clothes but left most of my café things there. My baking days were limited whilst I lived at Nat and Emmanuel's flat.

During my final shift at the café, Priya stayed late so we could host a bit of a "going away thing". Eileen and Priya banded together and bought me some souvenirs from the island, so I'd never forget it, as if I ever could. It was sweet that they thought a mug would help me remember the island, not their wonderful friendships. It was strange as I didn't cry. I'm usually a big cry-baby. I didn't feel like I was leaving home; I felt like I was returning there. Leaving the island felt inevitable.

Priya gave me a big hug before she left. Eileen wasn't so warm, but she did pat my upper arm. I returned to the little flat, which felt emptier now that most of my stuff was in a box. I was watching TV, a follow-up to Mr Sharp's tirade against the seagulls and their food stealing. Even Mr Sharp I'd miss.

I got a text from Nat saying she was excited to see me and showed me the bedding she'd washed. I text back a smiling emoji. I looked at my text chain from Jerry, which I'd memorised. I hadn't told him about my return to London. I felt like I'd missed my chance. I'd been pining for him so much it took everything I had not to call. If he'd felt the same, he would've called me. He's the one who gets everything he wants. He had all the power, so I imagined his lack of contact meant he'd moved on. I was sending my thoughts to Nat in a voice note. Sam texted me:

I heard you're going, shall I cum say goodbye ;)

I was a little offended he'd waited so long to text. I'd been talking about leaving for a month by that point. I told him to stop by, and he said he would later. I was fairly certain we wouldn't be having sex. But I showered, just in case. An hour passed, and I messaged, asking if he was coming. He replied:

In a bit

Another hour passed and I messaged again, asking where he was, but he didn't reply. At midnight, I got ready for bed. Sam never replied, and he never turned up at my door.

I lay in bed and I conjured up 100 different things I'd say when I saw him the following day on the ferry:

It's a shame your phone ran out of texts, huh?

I'm a person, just like you. I have feelings and thoughts, and I'm sick of you treating me like I'm nothing.

And the all-time classic:

You're a piece of shit.

However, that moment never came.

I woke and helped Dianne open up. I kept scouting around for things I'd forgotten, putting off the big goodbye.

"Take care of yourself. Don't be a stranger," Dianne said, patting my shoulder.

I turned to Priya.

"My time on No'Man would've been nothing without you. Priya, you helped me become a person again. Thank you. You're incredible."

"I just think the world of you," Priya blubbed, holding my face. I took some napkins and dabbed at my eyes as I walked out of the café for the final time.

Walking toward the dock, I remembered how foreign everything was when I arrived. When did No'Man become so familiar? I couldn't stand the thought that it was my last time on the cobbled streets, with the pastel buildings giving away to the breathtaking sea view. On the ferry, I stood at the back, watching the island shrink into the distance. I took a picture. My time living on No'Man was short, but I didn't want to forget about it for a long time.

I arrived on the island as a husk and was leaving as George.

***

London. Victoria. I disembarked my train and descended underground, sweat dripping down my back within seconds and no seat.

I was back.

When I arrived at her flat, Nat answered the door and hugged me.

"You're home," she said in my ear and I cried.

I unpacked my few belongings in their spare room. Nat said I was free to put things around the rest of the flat, but I didn't want to push my luck. I wasn't moving in properly, just getting on my feet. I cooked them both dinner that night and washed up. I was doing my perfect guest routine. It was good for me, too. It motivated me to get sorted and move out quickly so I could return to being a slob. Nat's flat had the additional disadvantage of being too close to where I used to live with Rob. It hadn't crossed my mind when I was planning to stay with Nat, but I panicked when I arrived at the tube and thought I saw the back of Rob's head. Since I'd become terrified of bumping into him, I was surprised by my wariness each time I left the front door. I'd sneak out with my jacket pulled up around my ears, thinking I looked like a spy, but in reality, I looked like I didn't know how coats worked. I didn't think I still cared what Rob thought. But in a bid to avoid him, I shopped at odd times and was hyper-alert on the streets leading to the tube station. I didn't leave the house unless I looked alright. Not perfect, but good enough for it to be OK if I ever encountered him. It annoyed me that I could accidentally bump into Rob, but I'd never accidentally bump into Jerry.

I returned to work for my first day as a freelancer, working at Wake Up UK with Martha McArthur. It was different. Before I went to No'Man, I was a researcher assigned to a show each week, where I'd research guests and organise getting them into the studios. Now, I was back as a freelancer, doing odd shifts.

I worked on the planning desk, which meant planning ideas for future guests to come on the show. Each guest or thing we wanted to discuss would become an 'item', which makes up a portion of the show. I'd never worked on that desk before; it required a good knowledge of current events, and I hate watching the news. It was strange to be back; everything was the same, but I felt different. People chatted, and I had lunch with Nat and some of our friends, although they weren't really my friends anymore. Not that I was having a pity party; I couldn't keep up with everyone's new aspirations or love interests. Half the group had joined since I'd left, so they were mostly Nat's friends.

At least the sandwich places were the same.

Nat insisted we cut lunch short because there was some breaking news about corrupt government spending that I didn't understand, but following Nat's lead, I knew it was wrong. The office was all the same, except now I had to shove myself onto someone else's desk. Someone called Natalia. Sitting on Natalia's desk was bleak. Natalia was the planning producer. She knew everyone and was fast at everything. All that energy she put into being great at her job left no room to tidy her desk. Every time I looked up, I was confronted with litter, like rubbish, or photographs of her perfect wife and their perfect children.

It was a desk made to make me feel inadequate.

That afternoon, Jerry popped up on my computer as a trending topic on Twitter. He'd been spotted with a model, holding hands. I immediately clicked on the article and sent it to Nat. Jerry and Portabella Belling-Hughes – her name as revoltingly posh as she was heinously beautiful – had been pictured in France, holding hands and chatting. The photos were all papped pictures, but I went onto Portabella's Instagram and dug a little deeper. They were staying in Elton's house. I recognised the whole thing. Oh god, he's moved on. Nat replied, branding the article 'totally fake' and telling me not to worry about it. She then forwarded me the Instagram stories of one of Portabella's model friends. It looked like there were lots of them at the house, for some sort of party. In the background, I could see Patricia, Jerry's publicist.

I bet this was all her engineering – an evil genius.

After work, I'd gotten myself a spot at a comedy show. It was a 'bringer', so I needed to bring a plus one. Thankfully, Nat offered. I would've forced her to come anyway, but I appreciated the enthusiasm. I'd mentioned the spot on my Insta Stories, although I wouldn't have wanted anyone I know to come along. I was grateful Jerry didn't have Instagram. The last time I had performed in London was appalling, so I was extremely nervous. My goodbye gig went much better, but that was a much friendlier crowd, mostly islanders, without many better options most nights. After lunch, I'd plotted some points about things I wanted to chat about, and now I just felt as though I might vomit, waiting to go on.

We arrived at the pub and found the function room upstairs. There was a man in his late twenties with scruffy blonde hair and a Led Zeppelin band T-shirt – very unoriginal. He was fighting with a microphone and its stand, muttering swear words under his breath.

"Hey, I'm here for the show," I told him.

He didn't divert his attention from the microphone.

"We're not starting for about thirty minutes. You can get a drink at the bar. We'll call you when we let the audience in," he dismissed me.

"Oh, I'm a performer."

The man's face illuminated with an 'ah'. He took my name and said he would finish the running order shortly. I could tell Nat was bored because I wasn't speaking with her, but I was horrifically nervous. I didn't have a repeat of the diarrhoea incident, but I did have tremendous burps, which didn't feel great. Nat looked at her phone, going through emails and unsubscribing from sales messages. I was torn between feeling guilty for being boring and rage from her inability even to pretend to be entertained.

"I'm sorry it's boring," I said.

"It's fine, you're never very fun before you perform. Keeping it for the set, I guess." Nat smiled at her comment. "You can make it up to me with chips on the way home."

The room filled, and the sound was deafening. I kept trying to remember my talking points, but then I'd be interrupted, listening to someone else's conversation. I was grateful when the MC, the scruffy guy from earlier, came over and gave me the third spot. I was glad to get my set over with. I was a little pissed off that I'd been off the stand-up scene for less than a year, but everyone acted like it was my first time on stage. As a person who contains multitudes, I was simultaneously nervous about failing and looking forward to proving to this smug MC that I was hilarious.

The show began with the MC talking to the audience, warming them up and ready to laugh. He launched into a story about his 'crazy ex'. It was lazy material, and I was annoyed to hear it get a smatter of laughs. The first guy was up, clearly a pal of the MC. They seemed to spend ages chatting on stage to one another, almost forgetting the audience keen to get in on the jokes. The first guy did a breakdown of how he would become a serial killer. It was less obnoxious than the emcee guy, but that wasn't hard. The next guy also got laughs, which I found annoying. If they found this guy funny, they'd never find me funny. Also, if I did badly, it's not because the audience were crap, it would be my fault. I was spiralling a little, trapped in my mind, when the guy bounced off stage to applause.

My name was called, and I stumbled through the chairs and onto the stage.

"Hey," I said with a curtsey. It got a few little laughs, which was nice. I repeated it, and the laughter built a little. The bright light in my eyes made the audience almost entirely silhouetted. I went into some material about being bad at being gay because I hated going to the gym and giving hand-jobs. I moved on to some newer material about being dumped.

"I'm currently single, not to brag, but I'm doing very well on my own. I was dumped, which was hard. It was so hard, in fact, that I went on to dump someone who was basically a movie star. Don't repeat that!"

A smatter of laughter.

"The original dumping was tough because I was painfully unhappy, but do you know what happens when you're dumped? You forget that. Everything bad about that person disappears. All you're left with is wanting to impress them. That's why I spent night after night outside my ex-boyfriend's window, trying to juggle. As you can imagine, that didn't end well. My juggling act wasn't enough to convince him I wasn't unbalanced anymore."

More laughter. I was killing it.

"I went through the process of being broken up with. You have to grieve and go through all the stages. These are different to when someone is dead, though. Death grief is denial, anger, bargaining, depression, and acceptance. Being dumped is trying not to cry all the time, remembering that you hated them, hiding your phone so that you don't get in touch, having sex with anyone who'll have you, and then…stand-up comedy."

Occasionally, I do stand up, and it's like you can't say anything wrong. This was one of those times. I forgot how funny I could be.

"I'm jesting, of course. I'm very much over my ex. What really helped was falling in love with, and then having my heart crushed again, by an Oscar winner. Distracting, yes, but ultimately good."

I was sure Jerry was an Oscar winner, but it wasn't for a film I'd seen.

I got the laugh. That's the main thing.

"For a little while, something that helped were the violent fantasies about murder – those I enjoyed. And before you act as though that's really bad, remember all my exes are men, and actually, it's OK to murder men. If I were straight and saying this, then I should be cancelled. Men are awful, and it would be my dream that we keep them all in cages, including gay men. It's a sacrifice I'd be willing to make to make the world a better place. Please don't call me a hero. Or, well, do if you want."

I returned to my seat and relaxed totally. It was over, and I didn't embarrass myself. Was it the best I've ever been? No. I was rusty, but there was some good material there. I looked at Nat, who smiled and whispered, 'well done'. She even grabbed my forearm and squeezed it. The squeezing didn't stop, so I looked at her. She was staring at someone a few rows ahead. I followed her eye-line.

There, third row, unmistakably, was Rob's back.

My ex-boyfriend.

The one I'd just spoken about for five whole minutes. He was with the man he'd brought to No'Man. I gasped. It was audible. I squeezed Nat's hand back. She leaned in and whispered, "Do you want to leave?" I shook my head.

The next act made their way to the stage. I had to sit through this entire show because I was an act and I couldn't leave early. More than that, Rob couldn't push me around anymore. I wondered briefly if I passed out or wet myself, whether I'd be allowed to leave, but I wanted to stick to my guns. It was uncomfortable because I knew Rob was there, and he knew I was there, but did he know that I knew that he was there? Needless to say, I paid no attention to any of the acts.

At the break, I told Nat I'd stay in our seats, and she went to get us a drink. I felt like if I stayed frozen, then maybe I'd escape notice. However, the break was running out, and I needed the toilet.

Traitorous bastard bladder.

I checked to see where Rob was – still in his seat, thank god. I hurried up and sprinted across the room as best as I could. In reality, I was moving slowly, avoiding people and accidentally spilling their drinks. In the toilet, I did what I needed to do and washed my hands.

"Good job, mate," a handsome man said to me, and I mumbled thanks, relieved it wasn't Rob in there with me.

In the antechamber, the door opened, and Rob stepped in.

"Sorry," he said and stopped. "Hi."

Neither of us spoke.

I had to squeeze past him to get out. "Hey," I did that no-teeth smile and tried to switch spaces.

"It's been a while, how are you?"

"I'm fine, thanks, I'll let you get to the toilet."

I pushed past Rob and got back to my seat, thank god. We watched the rest of the show, it was miserable. The lights came on and I saw Rob looking around.

"We need to go," I whispered to her.

"I need a wee." She looked at me apologetically. How could I hate that face? In that very moment – easily.

"No worries, I'm going to run outside and hide in the street. Text me when you leave."

I rushed past her and out into the cool evening air. I crossed the road and stood behind a van. I stopped to put my coat on and hesitated. I couldn't imagine speaking to Rob and feeling better about what happened between us. But I didn't want to run away anymore. I went back to the pub. I was going to wait for my friend outside the toilets. I wasn't afraid anymore. As I reached the pub door, Rob appeared with his boyfriend. I stepped back into the street, allowing them to pass.

"You're rushing off before we have a chance to chat?" Rob said, crossing his arms.

"I'm not going anywhere. I'm waiting for Nat."

The perfect amount of breezy.

"That set was a lot."

He smiled, but there was no mirth in it. I shrugged. Rob turned to the guy and asked him to walk ahead. The man smiled, but I could see how angry he was. Rob fixed me with a stare.

"Violent fantasies?"

"You know what it's like. Mostly all bollocks, really. I'll say anything for a laugh."

We went quiet. I looked along the street behind me.

"So, how have you been? I haven't seen you in ages."

"I moved. That's probably why."

"Where to?"

"I'm back now, living with Nat, it's cool. She's engaged."

"Wow, that is cool."

"What are you doing here?" I asked him, remembering all the shows I did when we were together that he didn't come to.

"I was surprised to see you were back in London…and I was curious about your act, whether you'd mention me."

Neither of us said anything. He'd basically admitted that he still thought about me, which felt like a win. And he'd seen my Insta Story. My mind cast back to the many nights I laid in bed, imagining what I'd say to him when we met again. But now he was here, and there was nothing left.

"What's new with you?" I asked to escape the awkwardness.

"Not much. Work is the same old. The only new thing, I guess, is that Adam is moving in."

"Fun."

I looked at my feet, considering how I could spin and jump and kick him in the head before deciding not to.

"Are…you…seeing anyone?" he asked. His tone was well-practised and nonchalant. He's wondering if I'm with Jerry. I felt a moment of smugness, but it left quickly when I remembered Jerry, and I didn't speak anymore.

"Not much to report here. Just doing a lot more stand-up."

"Oh, OK. You'll find someone," he said.

I put my hands in my pockets and then took them out again. I wasn't going to have his pity.

"I know. I did for a while, as you know." I looked at him, not afraid. "It takes time to process things. It's not good to run from one relationship to another."

"I don't want you to hate me," he said.

"I suppose that's not really up to you."

"It's a shame we can't be friendlier." His arms fell to his sides. He seemed sincere.

"I think I'm making a mammoth effort to be friendly with you. You hurt me. Time has passed, and I'm all better now, but that's not the same as you making amends. I have amazing friendships, and you don't cut the custard. I'm not being snarky, but you know Nat, do you think you can compete?"

Rob smiled.

Again, it was quiet. I was debating whether I wanted to shout at him. I opened my mouth a few times.

"Good to see you." I decided it was best to leave the conversation there. He was about to say 'you too', but then Nat appeared in the street.

"Hi Nat," Rob called out. She narrowed her eyes at him and walked past. Rob seemed unfazed and walked back toward the other side of the van, presumably to Adam.

"Do you want me to go back in and hit his head?" Nat asked.

"You know, I think I'm alright."

Nat joined arms with me, and we walked toward the tube.

"So – what did he say?"

Telling Nat, I realised I didn't feel that much at all. It was like bumping into a bully from school. You don't have an incredible moment of 'look at me now.' But you also don't run away crying. The feelings you had of being hurt and humiliated, you remember them, but it's not the same as feeling them freshly in the moment.

"I can't believe how calm you're being. He broke your heart. That's a well-used phrase, but it applies here – you were a broken person."

"You're right. If I think about how often I tried to avoid seeing him, it's all fart and no poo."

"That's disgusting," Nat said, pulling me toward her and linking with my arm. She tugged again and kissed my cheek. We descended underground and headed home together.

16

Hot Crotch

I was in bliss, halfway through my second bar of chocolate, when Mum came home, determined to ruin my evening.

"Yes, please." She reached out and took a couple of cubes. I grimaced but said nothing.

"How was your night?" I asked her.

"Lovely, thank you. They have paneer in the Indian now. I tried it like you suggested. It's to die for."

"I knew you'd love it."

"How's your night been?" she asked.

I shrugged. Mum took her earrings out. I missed being home and seeing her do day-to-day things like this.

"You know, it's lovely to have you home. But don't feel like you have to hang around with me. If you want to spend more time at Nat's, I'm alright on my own."

"I know. I'm happy being home for a bit."

"You don't seem happy."

I huffed air out of my nose and rolled my eyes. In a film, I'd look off into a mirror and see my teenage self angsting back. But this wasn't angst; Mum was being annoying. Concerned but annoying.

"What do you mean? I'm honestly happy to be home. I'm back in London. I'm doing stand-up again. What do I have to do to appease you?"

"It's not about appeasing me. I can tell when something is up with you."

"You're losing your touch because I'm fine," I replied through a thin-lipped smile.

"OK..."

"For god's sake, I'm fine."

"So, you don't wonder what is missing from your life?"

We held eye contact, and I felt tears building in the corners of mine. I closed my mouth, which Mum noticed as she turned away and fluffed a sofa cushion.

"Just something to think about," she muttered on her way out of the room.

I ran through a list in my head, first of expletives because she'd irritated me, then later in bed, I thought of another list. I wanted somewhere to live. I wanted to make people laugh. Doing a stand-up tour would be amazing, of course. Just getting paid would be incredible.

Further down the list, I wanted a boyfriend and to travel. I wanted a baby – that was a big one. But those were long-term things. What was missing now? I needed to solve this equation to stop arguing with my mother.

***

The next day, I caught the train to Nat and Emmanuel's as I'd been booked for shifts back at Wake Up. I dished up the enchiladas I'd made for everyone, still doing my perfect guest routine. Our elbows knocked as we crammed around the little table in their kitchen, designed for two.

"This is good," Emmanuel was already chewing and speaking at the same time, which is fine because I live in his flat for free.

"My pleasure."

"I've never seen you in such a good mood," said Emmanuel. Nat smacked his arm.

"Don't say that."

"No, he's right. I'm usually really miserable. I don't know what's come over me."

"It's probably all the stand-up you've been doing. Laughter is infectious," said Emmanuel. I agreed.

"Go on, George, tell us a joke," he replied.

I shook my head and smiled, hoping to god he'd drop it.

"What's up, scared we won't laugh?"

"Does anyone else want more sour cream?" I asked and stood up.

"Well, that wasn't very funny. I want my money back," Emmanuel laughed at his own joke loudly – the entire time it took me to collect more sour cream. I glanced at Nat, expecting her to look back with a look that said 'Do you believe this guy?' But she was laughing along. Genuine laughter. She must love him. And that was beautiful to see. I let myself laugh along. Things were looking up.

My happiness bubble promptly burst the following day at work when I looked in our script and saw Jerry on the show. I was confused by my feelings.

"Is Jerry Hilk pre-recorded?" I asked the producer, Thandi.

Thandi read a newspaper with laser focus, and I almost asked again. She tipped her head to face me before answering.

"No, he's in the studio. Zack's looking after him." She returned to her paper. "Is that alright?"

Did she know about me and Jerry? Why was I so unsubtle?

"Sounds like a good item for Zack."

Zack was the irritatingly keen new researcher we were working with. He'd always been a bit of a blank space in my mind, this posh, muscular gay guy who was now working with my ex-boyfriend. I asked where Zack was; apparently, he'd gone to another part of the office to do his research chat with Jerry. My cheeks felt hot. No one at work had mentioned the photos of Jerry and me, but Nat said they'd all seen them. How long was I supposed to go along with this façade?

I distracted myself with my guests. I had a human-interest guest talking about bowel cancer awareness month. Her name was Leanne, and she'd raised loads of money hiking the entire coast of Scotland, Wales and England. I read the brief as it was. The trouble with joining a team the day before the show is that a lot of things have already been done. It's not always clear how much attention something needs. I spellchecked the brief and fact-checked a few things. It all seemed correct and in order, although I wasn't giving it my all as I was so distracted by thoughts of Jerry.

I raised an SOS to Nat via instant messenger and filled her in on the Jerry situation. She replied almost instantly:

That's intense.

On WhatsApp, she sent me a photo of a centrepiece she liked. It was a nice distraction having two conversations going on at once. I was advising her on her choice of wedding décor whilst she stopped me from having a violent panic attack.

Tit for tat.

Zack returned and sat between Thandi and me. I listened to their conversation, but Zack gave nothing away. I'd say he was being careful, but with Zack, it seemed more like he genuinely didn't know about my connection to Jerry. "Did you ask if he was single?" Thandi asked, and I was giddy that she'd asked what I wanted to know.

"He said he was but also said, 'Nothing to talk about there, I'm really boring' and laughed," Zack replied.

Despite being such an obvious media-trained answer, it hurt that he'd not told Zack it was complicated or that he'd just ended something serious. I suppose our fling last year wasn't long-term, but it felt serious to me.

The whole day passed with little hints and snippets of Jerry's name being mentioned. He'd asked for some lemon and honey in the morning for his dressing room. When we were together, he liked cake and hot chocolate. I felt like I didn't know him anymore.

I returned to my desk after crying in the stairwell for a moment; Zack was still talking about Jerry. He needed two parking spaces for his team, and the trailer for his new film was too sweary for TV. Nat headed over to my desk.

"Will you be here late?"

"I've just got a few things to do, and then I'm headed to Greenwich for my show," I pouted.

Stand-up after a day's work. What an effort.

I decided to walk Nat out of the building to talk more about Jerry. Once we were outside, I let loose.

"I can't believe he's on this show." I was flabbergasted.

The wind blew in a mini tundra down the side of the building, blowing leaves against our legs.

"It's kind of good, though. When else can you guarantee you'll see Jerry and have enough time to look cool and in control?"

"That's what I mean. I'm going to get closure. I'm not going to hide away from him."

"Before you go tonight, print Jerry's brief and see what it mentions about you."

"You're a genius."

I hugged Nat and ran back inside. As I was winding down, I had a look at the brief. There was no mention of me, except a scribbled note at the bottom that read:

*** *Minefield: Jerry will not answer questions about his love life and rumours surrounding his sexuality* ***

That note probably came from Patricia, the PR guru, but I was glad I had dodged a bullet.

Before we were allowed to leave for the night, Thandi made us gather at her desk, where she listed out the notes she'd made ahead of tomorrow. They were highlighted and calligraphed.

"Looking good for tomorrow. Can you make sure you're watching the news tonight and keep an eye on social media – see what's happening in the world," Thandi asked.

I resented being asked to do something I would do anyway, but I didn't want to be a dick about it, so I agreed. Thandi's pretty nice as bosses go. She was quietly in command, and I wanted her to like me. Not as much as Zack, who was taking notes and doing meaningful hums.

I made a hasty exit, took the DLR to Greenwich and went to be funny for five minutes. I talked about some work things that I found annoying, got a few laughs, and then went into more break-up material, which got more laughs. People enjoy it when I'm humiliated, it seems. After the halfway point, I spoke to the MC about leaving.

"I have an early start tomorrow," I explained.

"We all have to get up early for our day jobs," he said, without looking up from his setlist.

"Totally. It's just that I have to be in the office at 4 am, so my day job is almost like a late-night shift." I continued explaining until he relented.

When I got home, Nat and I brainstormed what I'd wear the following day.

"I think you should wear that silky PJ top thing with jeans. It's low-cut and shows off a bit of chest hair."

"It's not really 'work appropriate', but I don't think that's stopped me before. Maybe I should wear something he hasn't seen, like my Ivy Park boiler suit."

"I love that for you, but the office is hot in the morning. You can't see him sweaty."

Nat chewed the inside of her cheek, mentally knee-deep in my wardrobe.

"I might not even see him. You know what it's like. I can't just go knock on his dressing room."

"Why not?"

"His agent will answer the door and be like 'Who are you?' and I'll be like 'an old friend,' and then the door will slam in my beautiful face before Jerry even sees me."

"Wow, then what happens?" Emmanuel asked from the doorway, freshly arrived from football practice and fascinated.

"The way I see it, I'm laughed out of the building, and then probably I wet myself or something. I don't know, there's many embarrassments to be had."

"I thought you wanted to see him?" Nat added, standing to kiss Emmanuel.

"I do, desperately. I need to plan it just right. I'm going to wait until after the show, walk past and casually devastate him. I'm going to win the break-up because I'm totally fine."

Nat and Emmanuel looked on at my wide-eyed, unblinking stare.

"Totally fine," they said in unison.

***

At 4 am, when that buzzing noise cuts through my sleep, only one thought gets me out of bed. I get dressed, get in my taxi and get to work to tell them I quit. Typically, by the time I get to the office, I decide to finish the morning, and usually, by the end of the show, I'm euphorically happy that it's over and I no longer want to quit. I'd scrapped my thoughtfully planned outfit for a floral floaty jumpsuit.

I looked like a sad clown, as I sat miserably in the taxi as it drove across London whilst a drizzle fell on my window. I felt like the most unhappy person alive. Until we stopped at a red light and I saw people waiting for a bus in the middle of the night in the rain. I shouldn't complain, I thought, here in the taxi I'm *not* paying for. I ran through my conversation with Jerry in my mind. I was going to tell him that he looked good. I thought a compliment would give me some power. My only goal for our meeting was to leave with the upper hand. I still had so far to go to get over Jerry. I couldn't risk seeing him and moving backwards.

I get into the office and set to work. As well as dealing with our guests, there was also a cooking demo and an entertainment news item to prepare for. There's very little chatter at that time of the morning; we're all heads down, working. And, in my case, trying not to fall asleep. Thandi and some of the more senior team went to talk to the presenters, and I rolled my chair over to Zack for a ten-minute gossip break. Although Zack didn't look up from his computer, and his forehead was screwed up in concentration.

"It's my first cooking demo. Do you know when they're going to dress the set?"

"Yeah, it all happens pretty organically. There's a meeting at the moment. You don't have to worry about the set for a little while yet."

Zack laid his head on the desk.

"I'm just freaking out. If I'm in the studio, can you brief Jerry Hilk?"

It was disconcerting that Zack said Jerry's full name. He was just Jerry to me.

"Why don't I go in the studio, and you brief Jerry?" I said, then panicked I was being too familiar. "Hilk. You want to meet him, right?"

"Not really," Zack grimaced.

What a dick. I was lost for words, luckily, as Zack wasn't finished.

"I want to impress Thandi with this demo."

"We'll see. You should have time for both, but sure, I'll help out where I can."

I rolled back to my desk and carried on with my script. Zack was in no mood to gossip, and I needed to make sure my work was done to help him and avoid Jerry before the show. Thandi and the team returned to the office and piled on the changes they'd made. I took on more jobs as they were called out in a bid to keep Zack free. Time evaporates on the morning of a show, and before I knew it, I had to brief my own guest, Leanne. I took a headset and went to find her in the green room. Leanne smiled when I introduced myself, but she kept wringing her hands with nerves as we sat.

"Are you looking forward to it?" I asked.

"I'm shitting it, to be honest." She smiled, then covered her mouth. "Sorry for swearing."

"It's totally fine; just don't do it on air," I laughed. "If you stick to the stuff we talked about, people are going to love you."

I was impressed with myself because I was calm and friendly despite having quite a long to-do list waiting for me back at the production office. Usually, I'd speak to the guests for about four minutes.

"Is she nice?" Leanne asked, pointing at a picture on the wall of the show's presenter and national treasure, Martha McArthur.

"She's the best, honestly. It's a conversation with Martha and some guys in shorts hiding behind big cameras. You're going to have so much fun."

Leanne seemed happy and relaxed, so I left her and returned to the production office. I crossed off things I'd already done. I'd edited everything that needed editing, spoken to Leanne, briefed the entertainment news presenter, and things were running smoothly. I dug some brioche out of my bag for breakfast and Zack radioed through on my headset.

"George, can you please go and brief Jerry?"

Involuntarily, I squeezed my brioche bun into a tight ball.

"Absolutely," I replied, knowing everyone in the gallery could hear our conversation, and therefore, I couldn't say no.

This was not the plan. I wanted to face Jerry, but not in his dressing room. I'd expected to walk past him and pretend not to notice him. I'd be casual, and our meeting would have merely been in passing, but it would, hopefully, inspire a text. Going into the lion's den, or dressing room, was too much. I counted to ten and stood up. I had a quick check of my outfit – not too crumpled. I also took a swig of my water and dribbled half down my shirt.

I trotted up the stairs to our slightly fancier dressing rooms and knocked on Jerry's door. I realised I was breathing heavily from a combination of stairs and horrifying anticipation. I thought about ducking around a corner and catching my breath, but knock knock, Ginger wasn't very professional. The door opened a crack, and Patricia's face popped into view.

"Yes," she said to the space around me until her eyes settled on my face. "Hello."

"Hi, long time, how are you? I'm just here to brief Jerry."

"You work here?"

"Yeah, I used to work here, and now I'm back, freelancing. I need to run through some things for the interview."

"Do you want to tell me, and I'll pass it on?"

Agents and publicists often insist we talk to them instead of the guests. I always insist on speaking to everyone so there's no crossed wires. However, I was relieved to chat with Patricia and not Jerry on this occasion. I could stick to my plan.

"Come in. We can do the brief thing, no problem," Jerry's voice called out.

Fucking idiot.

Fucking idiot, who I loved.

Patricia opened the door the whole way. I saw Jerry's face through the mirror as I stepped into the room. He turned around in his chair.

"George, what are you…?"

I repeated the thing about working there. No one said anything. There was a man with an apron doing hair and make-up, someone attending the clothes rail holding a portable steamer, a woman with a phone, another woman on her laptop on the sofas, and Patricia guarding the door.

"Good to see you," he said.

"I didn't volunteer to brief you. I mean, nice to see you, and I would've come to say hi, but this isn't the best time for a surprise visit." I waffled on before remembering my plan and added, "You look healthy."

I shrugged, out of things to say. Jerry didn't get up to hug me. I felt very embarrassed to be there and launched into my briefing.

"We don't write questions for Martha, but she won't ask anything outside the research chat. We'll play a film clip ahead of the item, and then Martha will introduce you. Please, no swearing and that's basically it. Any questions?"

"Will Martha say that the film is in cinemas this Friday?" Patricia asked me.

"Yes, it's in the script. It's also written on-screen when the clip plays. Anything else?"

"No…sorry. I'm just surprised to see you here," bumbled Jerry, who hadn't blinked.

"Well, I'll let you finish getting ready," I said and bowed out, by which I mean I literally bent at the waist like an Elizabethan court jester.

Patricia opened the door for me, which, on the surface, seemed kind but probably motivated by her desire to get rid of me. I thanked her and escaped. I was halfway down the hall when I heard Jerry call my name.

"Wait up," he said, and I turned around. I could see Patricia's head sticking out the door.

"A question?" I said.

"I wanted to say that I meant to text. I haven't yet, but I was planning on texting."

"No worries, I meant to text you. I was going to say thanks for the card, but then I moved. Then I would text to say I moved back, but it's been busy. It's a busy time for us both, and the new film looks great, by the way.

"I've missed you."

"That would've worked in a text," I replied before I could stop myself. I wanted to follow up to apologise for being a dick, but the words wouldn't come out.

"Not texting, who would do a thing like that," he joked.

He had me there.

"I've missed you too," was my much better reply.

"Great, we're the same. What are you doing after the show?"

"We're headed to Radio 1!" Patricia called out.

"Ah, no worries. Another time. You'll have to come back here and talk about the sequel or something." I went to turn away.

"Hopefully, I'll see you sooner than that."

Thandi buzzed in my ear to ask if Jerry had been briefed.

"Just with him now," I said into my headset, "you're right, now is bad timing."

I walked off into the stairwell, but I heard Jerry follow me.

"So, we'll talk, catch up, see what's happening?"

"Nothing is happening, though. I loved spending time with you, but we've done the hard bit; we stopped speaking. Our situation hasn't changed. It's not just you. You're all I thought about for months, but I couldn't tell you. And you obviously couldn't tell me. We don't want to look stupid in front of the two of us, let alone the world. I want you in my life, but I don't want to duck whenever someone takes your photo."

"I know, I agree, but this is so new, I'm just asking for time."

"And you make me laugh, and you're incredibly kind and insanely talented, and I'd love to give you as much time as you want. But I'm not a perfect person with enough security to give you what you need. I need someone who isn't ashamed of me or themselves or whatever. Text me, don't text me, it doesn't matter. I can't be patient with you, and you can't be open about me."

My bottom lip trembled.

Thandi shouted something in my ear.

"I have to go, I'm sorry."

I turned and ran down the stairs. This time, Jerry didn't follow me. I got into the production office and rested against the door.

"Where have you been? Your item is going out. You should be in the studio," Zack explained.

"I was talking to your guest." I emphasised the 'your' and felt bad for being a big bitch. Thandi came through on my headset and insisted I get into the studio. I turned my phone on silent and then ran down the corridor. I entered the studio in time for Leanne to say her goodbyes to Martha. They went to an advert break, and Leanne stepped off set and came to stand with me.

"That was amazing," I lied, having not seen a frame, although I'm sure someone would've mentioned if she was terrible.

"Was it OK? I really enjoyed it."

"Honestly, the best."

The studio filled up with Jerry and his 'people'.

"Is that Jerry Hilk?" Leanne whispered to me, and I nodded. She rushed forward before I could stop her and asked him for a photo. There was a flurry of activity where Jerry stood with Leanne, and she gave me her phone to take the picture. I took the phone with a fake smile plastered all over my face, mentally deciding I wouldn't give Leanne a goody bag for appearing on the show. No Martha McArthur tote for Leanne. Then, Jerry was ushered behind the set, and Leanne was back by my side.

"Can I stay and watch the interview?" she asked me. I smiled and gave a thumbs-up. The break ended and I whispered something about needing to leave. I figured I could sneak out and maybe even leave the building undetected. Someone would always take Leanne to her car, I'm sure. I snuck around the set, avoiding Patricia and heard them play the trailer for Jerry's new film. Behind the set, I saw Jerry standing in the wings, waiting to walk on. He was in his head, serious face, preparing for live TV. I didn't think he'd notice me. But he looked up and smiled. I mouthed 'good luck' just in time for Martha to bring him out. Jerry walked into the studio lights, and I managed to finish creeping around the set. I watched the interview on the TV screens outside, and the sound continued playing in my ear through the headset. Martha asked about Jerry's character and when the film would be out.

"It's out Friday. I can't wait for people to see it."

Jerry was dazzling. I couldn't stand to watch the whole interview, plus I didn't want to look like I'd waited to see him, so I returned to the production office.

"And are you taking a certain model to the premiere?" Martha continued in my headset. I lifted my hands to take the headphones off my ears, then hesitated.

"I won't be. I'm not dating at the moment. I've been struggling with sobriety, so I'm taking a break from dating," Jerry said.

"Was that in the brief?" I heard Thandi shout at Zack through our headsets.

"He didn't say that in the research chat," Zack screamed. I moved a little faster, hoping to help calm Zack down.

"Yeah, I was in rehab because I'd been struggling with alcohol use, which is where I met a guy. He wasn't in rehab but lived nearby, and I liked him. But I think I messed things up." I heard Jerry explaining through my headphones.

What the fuck was he doing?

I turned around and sprinted back to the studio. At the door, Patricia was catatonic; her lit-up phone held in one hand and the other slightly outstretched as though she could've stopped Jerry. She saw me, and her face flipped to anger. The floor manager manoeuvred between us, allowing me to move further into the studio to watch Jerry.

"Anyway, this guy isn't coming to the premiere with me, and there's no one else I'd want to date."

"So, are you coming out?" Martha followed up.

"Er...yes, I am. I'm pansexual if it helps to put a label on it. But I'm single now, so maybe I don't need to come out." Jerry paused, inhaling and exhaling for what seemed like years before he carried on. "But I miss that man I was seeing. We were only going out for a short while, but I'm sure now that I loved him."

Jerry leant forward in his chair.

"It sometimes seems like we live in an accepting world, like being LGBTQ is no big deal, but the moment the photographs of us were released, the reaction...freaked me out. That made our relationship hard, and keeping this secret might've ruined things."

"Is he talking about you?" Thandi was asking in my headset.

"Yes," I replied.

"I think I made him feel like my dirty little secret, like I was ashamed of him, and I wish I hadn't done that. I want him to know George is his name. I want George to know that I'm not ashamed of him." Jerry looked off camera, directly at me. "George, I'm not ashamed of you. And, if you're interested, I'd like to be together after this interview. Or go for a bit of cake, whatever you want."

It felt like nothing else was happening, just us two looking at each other. Jerry's chest was rising and falling, slower and slower, as a smile spread across his face. I realised I was holding my breath.

"That's sweet, and I think George has joined us, so maybe he'd like to reply?" Martha said, and hearing her say my name brought me back to the studio. Patricia was waving frantically, trying to get Jerry's attention. She silently screamed 'cut' and made a cutting motion over her neck with her hand. I was taken aback at the vacuum of sound in the studio. A room full of people and equipment, and only Jerry and Martha dared to speak.

One of the cameras swivelled around and was on me. I could see the red light and my face on the screens around the studio. My mouth was open, and my head was shaking. Jerry still stared at me, smiling.

"SAY SOMETHING," Thandi screamed through my headset. I jumped in place, having forgotten the headset was there. I tore it off my head.

"I'm not meant to be on camera," I told no one in particular, as though I was clearing up some misunderstanding.

The camera panned past me to Zack, who'd just run in, the more obvious choice. I would've laughed, but Jerry was out of his seat, walking toward me, and the cameras followed him. Patricia moved forward, but Zack stepped in her way. He was wearing a headset, probably on orders from the gallery.

"Do you have something to say, George?" I heard Martha ask as Jerry stopped in front of me. I looked blankly at him as though I'd just arrived.

"What are you doing?" I asked.

"Did you hear any of that?" he said.

I smiled at him. His full-beam grin was infectious.

"I'm actually really busy," I said with a laugh, looking off to the side of the studio as though this were a normal day at work.

"I'll paraphrase. I've been so frightened about people knowing my secrets, but keeping secrets means losing you. I'm still scared I could never work again. But worse than anything, what if you're not in my life? You make it so I can be myself. You make the most banal things better. I'd rather go to the dentist with you than sky-dive with Rhianna. I'm not trying to be brave or even romantic. I'm probably just embarrassed. But I couldn't let you go without telling you what you mean to me. I'd be bloody proud to be with you. I love you."

He stepped forward and took me in his arms. I felt shy, hiding my head in his neck. I inhaled Jerry, and he smelt clean. All celebrities smell good, but they don't all smell like my Jerry.

"It was a bit of an overshare. I hope you don't mind," he added.

I faced him. Since we'd broken up, I'd told myself a million stories about Jerry and me. How we were unsuited or being together would only lead to my heartbreak. But I looked at his beautiful face and how happy he was, looking at me. Something inside me came undone. I didn't want to run away. I couldn't resist my feelings anymore.

"You didn't have to do this."

"I needed to tell you that I love you. And everyone else, of course, two birds, one stone."

"I love you too, but this is a bit much," I grinned.

"You definitely might not enjoy this next bit, then," he said, leaning in and kissing me. And, as the clip clearly shows, I kissed him right back. And I did enjoy it – a lot.

It was awkward when we finished kissing, and Jerry had to return to the sofa and fill another two minutes. Thandi instructed Zack to tell me to stay in the studio, and they kept cutting back to me, looking goofy. I love him.

After my little TV debut, Priya sent me a voice note, where she just sang 'I Told You So' for a minute. We came back on the show the next day, where Jerry proposed, Elton John sang at our wedding, and we started our own reality show.

I'm kidding, although I got invited to Elton John's house for dinner with Jerry. I wasn't allowed to take a selfie, though. We were finally free to be in a relationship.

Three months later...

I stepped out onto the stage to rapturous applause. The lights were much brighter than at the rehearsal earlier that day. I was worried that the applause would stop before I reached the microphone. The Apollo stage was a bit too big, if I'm honest. Flashy.

"Thank you, gosh, don't I feel welcomed. Hey everyone," I said with a curtsey, and a little laugh began. I gestured my hand out and flicked my wrist back, an invitation to 'say it back.'

The room erupted in saying 'hey'.

"That was gorgeous. What a sexy audience. So, I'm George Elizabeth Barnes. Some of you will recognise me from ignoring my messages on Grindr." I glared off stage, although I couldn't tell who to, but I'd pretended well enough so that got a laugh.

"Some of you might recognise me because my movie star boyfriend professed his love for me on national TV."

Applause.

I was booked because Jerry made us go viral, but I didn't care. Opening a show for Katherine Ryan was a dream come true. And she'd always made it seem like I was talented. After I'd performed, I paused to watch her from the wings. Katherine thanked me, and the audience applauded again. My breath caught in my throat. What a moment. I felt hands circling me, then warmth in my ear.

"God, you're so talented."

Jerry had snuck backstage to watch me. We kissed, but only briefly, as I dragged him through the tunnels of the auditorium to our seats. We were right in the gods, but I'd insisted we sat out of the way so that we wouldn't make any interruption. I wanted them to see my first time at The Apollo. I settled between my mum and Nat, who squeezed my arm and whispered 'brilliant' at me. Mum leant toward me and whispered 'I'm so proud.' I blushed and whispered thank you.

The show ended, and we stayed in our seats so I could go backstage to thank Katherine again and introduce my mum, Nat, Emmanuel and Jerry. We were a fun little crew. A couple of people stopped as they passed and asked for a photo of Jerry and then one of mine when they noticed me next to him. I felt shy, having my whole gang with me, but it was the biggest night of my career, and I couldn't be there without any of them. We didn't linger long.

"I'm so proud of you. I know you'll say I'm cringe, but I'm your mum, and tonight I got to see, you're a star," she said, squeezing my face just before getting in a taxi to go home. Nat and Emmanuel jumped on the tube back to the flat where I was still staying with them.

"I'll see you tomorrow?" Nat asked me at the backstage doors, between the bins and various taxis.

"Yeah, I'll come home soon as Jerry leaves for the airport. I've never been wedding dress shopping. I might try some on."

"Please don't embarrass me," she laughed. We hugged and they left.

Jerry and I got into a taxi and headed to his house. The memory of my stage time played on a loop in my mind:

"I describe Jerry as a movie star because he is one, but also, it's good to clarify which of my lovers I mean. I'm also having sex with one of the guys from One Direction, but not the one you're thinking of. And a couple of world leaders – shout out to Justin Trudeau."

I was getting great laughs in all the right spaces. There's a thing that happens when you're doing stand-up, and it's going well. It feels like flying or typing without looking at the words. You could make a mistake, but you know you won't. It's precarious. It's better than heroin. I wouldn't know really, but I knew I was addicted:

"Finding love wasn't easy. I had to go to the Isle of No'Man to find a man. Before that, I'd just been dumped savagely. I hate it when some-one says 'gay men love me' because it's stereotypical and wrong. I know one gay man who is incapable of love. He has herpes now – whoops. I

was heartbroken, hence No'Man. And I hate puns. We're better than that, but I had to go. I tried being celibate for a little while. Surprisingly hard, I guess not surprisingly, I'm gorgeous. I considered being one of those incels, you know, involuntary celibate. But the gay version, so it wasn't that I couldn't find someone who wanted to have sex with me, just that I had IBS and ate too many beans. Also, I couldn't be an incel, I like women. They're a lot like people."

It wasn't clever comedy, but it kept them laughing.

We went back to Jerry's house, but there was no time to relax. I was too awake from being on stage, and Jerry had to pack for a trip to LA.

"I wish I could pack you," he said as I lounged on the bed, watching him.

"I don't have to be packed. You could offer me a seat on the plane?"

"You can come," Jerry was exasperated.

"I'm working," I replied. Was that a hint of resentment in my voice?

He lifted his T-shirt a little and scratched his tummy before turning back to his bag. I leafed through a script that Jerry was considering. He'd scheduled a meeting whilst he was in LA. It was his first film offer since coming out, starring as the love interest in a gay romcom.

"This is funny, at least," I said, trying to convince him gently that it would be a good idea.

"It's funny, but is it romantic? I need to re-read it."

"Of course, it's romantic." I sat up, incredulous.

"It ends on a sixty-nine. That's not happy-ever-after."

288

"Are you kidding me? Sixty-nine is the happiest. I don't wanna hear about a couple getting married. I wanna see their bums. I'm the audience for this film."

"I love your enthusiasm."

He disappeared into the bathroom. I didn't want to be pushy, so I squared the script up and put it in his bag before returning to my position on his bed. Jerry returned with a washbag, seemingly ready to go. I scooted to the end of the bed, remembering I'd bought a going-away gift.

"I have something for you," I said, more breathless than I meant to be after some gentle scooting. I fished around my overnight back and took out a crumpled gift bag. Jerry eyed the parcel in my hands with a shine in his eyes.

"For me?" he mocked and opened the bag ferociously.

His head tilted to the side, and he breathed out of his nose, a suppressed laugh.

"My very own copy," he said, bringing my framed nude photo to his mouth and kissing roughly where my bottom appeared.

"Do you love it?"

"It's the best. Now, I don't have to use my imagination." He smiled and placed the frame in his bag.

"Aren't you loaded? Couldn't you pay someone to pack for you?"

"Other than the fact that would be a bit gross," he scolded, as though I had staff. "My stylist will be packing most of my clothes."

"So then, technically, someone has packed for you."

"I like to pack a separate bag of things I need, and no one knows what that is except me."

He took a small crystal from his underwear drawer and tucked it into the bag.

"You're taking a crystal but not underwear," I said.

"The crystal has healing properties, and I don't wear underwear in LA," he said without a hint of a smile.

"What? Why? For easy access?"

"It's hot. I don't want the extra layer."

"Gosh, my thighs would rub so much, they'd start a fire."

"You do have a hot crotch if I say so myself," said Jerry.

"Hot crotch sounds like an STI. Underwear keeps everything where it needs to be."

"Stop thinking about my underwear, please." He was laughing as he zipped up his bag and put it on the floor. I'd half expected him to be cross with me after talking about him so much on stage:

"So, you all want to know how I, an incredibly good-looking fat gay man with a shit personality, managed to bag film and TV's most eligible bachelor. And by eligible, I mean fuckable, and by fuckable I mean, let's wrap this up, he doesn't like to be kept waiting."

I mimed looking at a watch and got another great laugh.

Jerry stood over me, pausing as if to say, 'What now?' My head was at the end of the bed, and he was in reaching distance, so I stretched out to touch his body. He bent over to kiss me. He went to straighten up, but I pulled him onto the bed instead. I loved how unselfconscious we could be with one another. We took our time to enjoy one another's bodies. Jerry moved away, assessing me.

"Move that way," he ordered me into place before whipping my jeans off. He stumbled as they came loose, and I grinned. The rest of our clothes became a bundle on the floor as we indulged in the happiest ever after I could think of.

"George," Jerry moaned. I loved hearing him say my name. We moved in unison, and the pleasure began to build. I arched my back

290

and thrust forward again, Jerry responding in body and sound. I closed my eyes and saw god, basically. The universe was reborn, and our love was the catalyst. It was just he and I, together, in eruptions of pleasure. I leaned forward, and we kissed for a while. When our hearts returned to a normal rate, I lay in his arms:

"I met the love of my life, I made some nice cakes, things were going well. It didn't feel right. I wasn't used to being adored. It doesn't make sense because I'm adorable. I should only be adored. I used to joke with people that I needed to become a famous comedian so that people would revere me the way they were supposed to. Does that sound arrogant? I'm easily one of the best people in the world and should be treated like a god, but people behaved like I was a loser. Look at us now; I'm kinda funny, and you're all falling in love with me. It feels right."

I was laughing at their laughter. It was intoxicating. There were the usual people walking in halfway through my set, a bit of chatter, but mostly, I held their attention.

"I feel like we're so good at that." Jerry rubbed my forearm.
"I certainly enjoyed myself."
I breathed into his neck.
"When I get back from LA, I'd love it if you were here."
"I'm sure I can arrange that."
"Permanently."
"Are you planning on locking me in the basement?"
"Seriously, why don't you move in?" Jerry asked me.
I looked up at the ceiling. What could I say? 'Do you mind if I go and call Nat before I decide?'
"That does sound good," I said, not technically agreeing.
"Is that a yes?" Jerry asked, seeing through my vagueness.

I rumpled around the bed, turning to face him.

"I need to think about it."

"Look, George, I love you. I'm done with dating. I want to have a life with you, and I want that to start straight away."

"I love you too, that's important." I spoke slowly and stared into his eyes. "But celebrity relationships famously don't last long, isn't that because they rush things?"

"You make us sound like reality TV stars."

"Even Oscar winners have short relationships. I don't want to fuck this up."

"I don't want to force your hand. I appreciate you need to think about it. But I didn't think this on a whim. I've been dreaming of us living together for months now."

I bit the corner of my mouth. I wanted to move in. I wanted to make that decision. The house was incredible, but it was more than that. It was almost a drawback. The house was so Jerry I worried whether I could make it mine too. Other than that 'not real' problem, the idea of living with Jerry was perfect. I loved it when we shared anything: chores, dinner, feelings. It felt too good to be true. This fun, smart hunk of a man wanted me to move in. No one gets everything they ever wanted without some compromise.

Who would I become without any adversity?

"You've been a terrific audience. What a way to break my cherry on the Apollo stage. I've loved being here. I usually like to do material about body positivity because I love myself. Usually when I touch myself, I'm looking into a mirror. And we don't always cum at the same time. But tonight, you've all been so wonderful, when I touch myself, I'm gonna close my eyes and think about all of you."

More laughter.

"That's all from me. Please welcome, to the stage, the main event herself, Katherine Ryan."

The audience lost it, and I shuffled off stage. I turned around and watched the smoke and light show that welcomed Katherine. Not for the first time on her tour did I think *I'd take a bullet for this woman.*

Back at home, lying with Jerry, hearing his heart beating and feeling the warmth of his skin, I managed to stop my mind whirring. I didn't listen to my head, just to my gut.

"Let's do it," I said.

He kissed my neck and pulled me closer. And that was the decision made. What was the worst that could happen?

DON'T answer that.

Acknowledgements

I want to give a huge thank you to Troy for commissioning this book. You've literally made my dreams come true. You spoke about my writing like it was good and I'd considered things, and it was so weird and so wonderful. And a huge thank you to Mark for taking this book over the finish line. Your insights have made this book something I'm really proud of. And I think your jokes are very good!

Huge thank you to everyone at Vulpine press for making me an author. This is the best thing that's ever happened to me really, so I can't say thank you enough.

Thank you to Ruby too! Your cover is wonderful and exactly what I wanted. Everyone should check out Ruby immediately! @fugitiverabbit

To my beloved and wonderful friends and family, what a bizarre mix of people who love and support me. Mum, Dad, Charlotte, Vernon, extended family, Gemma, Amy, Jess, Laura, Grace, Kate and all my other sweet baby friends – thank you. This book is all of ours, you all heard about it enough!

Through proximity and force, I do owe a special thanks to Rose, for letting me read this bedtime story to you, again and again. This book wouldn't exist without you, even though it sent you to sleep for about 2 years.

Thanks to Harry Styles – this book started as fan fiction. And thanks to Jude Law, my first love, I changed this story to be about us. If you are ever, ever, ever interested, I'm yours. And thanks to Beyonce – everything I do that is good, is in your holy name. Thanks to Lorraine Kelly for your lovely and generous quote.

A huge thank you to anyone who reads this book, reviews this book, or shares it, or buys it and doesn't read it, or puts it on the shelf in a library or any other contribution. You are just wonderful. All of this writing and editing, it was for you. Seriously, thank you.

Martin J Dixon lives in Croydon and works in TV. He is also a stand-up comedian and has been doing that for over a decade. He has taken several shows to Edinburgh, Brighton and Camden fringes. A lot of his comedy looks at fat liberation, and fat acceptance. He also makes chocolate from scratch and enjoys outdoor swimming. *Isle of No'Man* is his first novel.

Twitter: @martinjdixon
Instagram: @_martinjdixon